ZODIAC CHAOS

BOOK 2

R.C. LUNA

ZODIAC CHAOS
Warrior Shifter Series – Book Two

© 2022 by R.C. Luna
First Edition: 2022
Second Edition: September 2025

Published by Lucid Publishing, LLC
Cover Design: Miblart
Editing: Shavonne Clark

ISBN: 978-1-967364-01-5

OTHER WORK BY R.C. LUNA

Welcome to Book Two of the Warrior Shifter Series. If you've been enjoying the ride so far, it would mean a lot to me if you left a review—your words help new readers discover this series. Scan the QR code below to get updates, lore, and exclusive content delivered straight to your inbox.

The *Warrior Shifter* series:

Zodiac Shadows (prequel)
Zodiac Fate (Book 1)
Zodiac Chaos (Book 2)
Zodiac Prison (Book 3)
Zodiac Throne (Book 4)

I dedicate this to all the powerful people out there—those of us who are still discovering exactly how powerful we are.

Letter from the Author

Welcome to the second book in the *Warrior Shifter* series. This is a dark fantasy romance, a work of fiction that delves into intense and themes that could be sensitive to some readers.

This book contains a range of triggers, including steamy, open-door romance, betrayal, despair, explicit sexual content, and violence—physical, mental, and psychological. Please take this warning seriously and proceed with care.

You may find yourself walking through hell alongside these characters, feeling their pain, their passion, and their struggles. But on the other side, there is strength—perhaps even your own, reflected back at you.

To reach that strength, you must endure the journey. Please read responsibly.
—R.C. Luna

Chapter 1

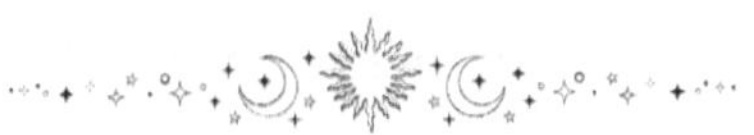

Sasha

Now in the body of a huge and deadly black jaguar, I tried to glance behind me, but I couldn't make the thing move its head. A few seconds later, the creature slowly looked back at the large iron gate adorned with battle scenes. We had just entered the massive enclosure and a whole new realm. The gate clanked shut. Two soldiers dressed in all-black tactical gear, each with two swords strapped to his back, stood on either side.

The ruggedly handsome shaman who abandoned me my entire life, Damian, and my jaguar walked along a stone path surrounded by a lush landscape of mountains, hills, and valleys. Everything looked and seemed a lot like the places I was familiar with. Some of the mountains had snow on their peaks, and large, magnificent homes dotted the various mountainsides. The sun was just as bright as it'd been on the other side of the Aries Gate, and the shape and forms of the clouds were entirely the same, too. Yet, something was off. We were walking where the ocean was. And when the jaguar glanced back at the gate, I saw ocean where the land was. *Are land and ocean reversed here?*

The path led us through a village, and Damian expertly navigated the passageways as if he'd done it a million times. People went about their day all around us, and several of them stole glances our way. They were looking not at me, as I knew myself, but instead at an oversized feline prowling next to a tall man with a square jaw, a short brown beard and brown hair with golden streaks. From what I gathered, the people here were into fashion and trends. They had on chic, modern clothing, which felt familiar, but there was something distinctly unearthly about the entire place. People dined at cafés, and a group of teenagers laughed by a fountain. All of this appeared normal, but the energy here was strange in a euphoric kind of way.

Is everyone glowing?

My jaguar took a deep breath, and when the fresh air filled her lungs, at once I felt positive, powerful, and my mind was clear.

"This is a border town," Damian said with a quick look over his shoulder. It was beautiful. Cabrón. Everything was so fucking beautiful. "Because we're so close to the Gates, these towns tend to be the most like Earth." He pulled a key from his pocket, opened a garden gate, and gestured me inside. "The Planetary Transit will close tonight, and it takes me a while to work up the transformation spells. Just settle in, and we'll get to it."

I followed him into a large garden just inside the doorway. The center had no roof, reminiscent of ancient ceremonial compounds that were open to the sky, where the divine met the earth, stone and nature. An arrangement of ceiba trees, orchids, bromeliads and cacao thrived within the square-shaped center. The garden was surrounded by a covered walkway, and Damian moved at a fast pace under covered halls until he reached an expansive room. Inside was a large wooden table lined with glasses, bowls, tools, and various bottles filled with herbs along with some modern technology and appliances.

He shut the door behind us, and I felt my jaguar tense, and then what felt like claws raked against her insides. My jaguar snarled sharply. *He better not be setting me up.* I was trusting this scumbag who had a shitty record of owning up to his responsibilities, who had avoided me for almost two decades, and who had kept important details of my life a secret until the very last moment. *Why am I trusting him again?* Oh, right. Because I had no other choice.

The process to prepare the herbs took well over two hours. After pacing about for a while, my jaguar sat down in the far corner of the room where she could watch the door and his every move as he shuffled about at the wooden worktable. There was a large stone mortar and pestle in the center of the table where he placed the seeds he'd fetched from bottles on the shelves, and then he began to grind them.

He worked meticulously, his back straight and his eyes focused, while his hands expressed the art of this spell-making craft. They glided in the air to a methodical rhythm and swept in sequence as they reached for fresh water from the faucet. He filled a carved wooden mixing bowl with the water and added the ground seeds. Those masterful hands pulled dried flowers from the windowsill and ground them as well, adding them with measured precision to the fresh water.

I heard him curse as he looked in every drawer for something he couldn't find, until he found it and chuckled to himself. He whispered incantations and selected more bottles from shelves, adding them to a separate glass jar he had brought to a boil with the wave of his hand. My jaguar's eyes felt heavy, and she laid her chin on the cool stone floor. I heard water running from the sink again, and her eyes opened into slits. He was washing his hands in the sink, then he patted them dry on a towel and turned to face me.

"I've got to go and get some tools we're missing." His thick Spanish accent snapped me into the moment, and I moved to stand up. He raised his palm toward me as if he was telling me to stay, like a dog. My jaguar hated that; she lifted her head and snarled at him. "I'll be right back. Please, don't leave this room." His lips curled upward awkwardly.

He better come back. My jaguar snarled one more time before he closed the door behind him. It was infuriating being here, unable to rush back to help Trent. Powerless to save him from the fangs of a vampire.

Well now what? Aromatic herbal smells filled my senses. My stomach growled, and it was as if it growled in both bodies. It seemed my human mind and my jaguar body were hungry at the same time. I pushed the thought of eating aside. How could I think of food when Trent was in such danger?

My jaguar seemed to have her own agenda here. Her heartbeat was slower than it had been when we'd shifted, but she still paced the room that really wasn't designed for a wild animal her size. Using her teeth, she opened the door to the garden and set out to prowl the grounds. There were several rooms and stations set up just like the one we'd been in.

In one room, two men who looked like twins, both with hair like a silver fox and round glasses, bent over astrological charts on a large table. They glanced up briefly, then went back to whatever they were doing without a word. In another room, there was a person in a floor-length white robe with the zodiac wheel embroidered beautifully in gold on the back. The white-robed person was speaking to a tall, blond woman in a form-fitting, floor-length blue dress. A jaguar like mine was curled up and napping in the corner. My jaguar turned away and padded along the corridor.

If I were to take a guess at what this place was, I'd say it was the shaman version of one of those shared office spaces like WeWork. My jaguar found another doorway that led out to another green garden, though this one seemed to go on for a few acres and was surrounded by colorful plants and a canopy of trees. After stepping out onto the grass, she retreated quickly under the covered walkway; I sensed she wasn't fond of the bright sun and preferred the veil of night.

She continued to peruse the campus and found a massive three-story library stacked with books. I immediately wanted to jump out of the jaguar's body and get my hands on some of them. What kind of books did they read here?

It felt like a long time had passed by now, and I became anxious about going back to see if Damian had returned. My jaguar must've felt it because a low growl rumbled in her chest.

Interesting.

We were definitely able to communicate with each other through our emotions. She turned and padded quickly back to the room where the shaman had left us. As soon as we saw Damian already in there, we quickened our pace to stand at his side and watch what he was doing. My jaguar's body was so large her head met the level of the table and she could watch his every movement. His hands worked quickly, and when he was done mixing and blending, he grabbed a drink from the fridge and took a seat in a large leather chair.

"Carly, my apprentice, will be here with some food for us soon," he said. "I need to retrieve the final ingredients from the botanist, so I'll be going out again." He seemed distant as he stared out of the large window behind the table.

His gaze turned back to my jaguar for the first time since I'd returned. It seemed a hint of fear of this beast still lingered in his eyes. Or maybe it was just respect for the wild, massive beast seated at his side.

Whatever it was, my jaguar had sensed it. Again, I wondered what powers she held. I could feel them charge through her blood. It was a constant rush surging through her veins, and I was beginning to understand that there was much more to being a nagual. It wasn't just about being a strong animal. It was about what she was capable of.

I have so much to learn.

"At precisely eleven twenty-one tonight, we will go outside on the grassy field, and you'll take the herbs that will complete the transformation." Damian arched a brow. "Once we complete the ritual, you'll be able to shift between the jaguar and human forms more freely. You'll still need to learn the process, of course, but I'll teach you. For now, just rest and relax. You're safe here."

Of course, my mind couldn't relax. What had happened to Trent? But my jaguar tuned me out completely. She had a mind of her own. When food and water was delivered, she ate. When she was done, she slept, and when it was time for the ritual, she would go.

Chapter 2

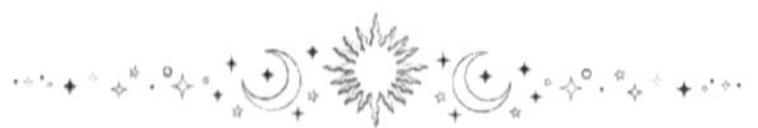

Damian

Here I was again, stocking up on supplies for yet another transformation ritual. How many of these had I done over the centuries? Felt like a thousand. But who was keeping track? *Twenty-one.* This was my twenty-first ritual.

These humans had it all wrong. They gave up their simple, mortal lives to become supernatural beasts. Immortality was overrated. After Lily had died, I'd made a vow over her dead body never to do this again. I never wanted to look at the face of another jaguar shifter. I thought I was done with this. It worked for one of my colleagues. He'd abandoned his last case before the ritual and dropped off the grid. I saw him every once in a while, socializing at the clubs in Aquarius Gate, and no one even blinked an eye at him. There was always another younger, naïve shaman wanting to climb up the ranks and impress the great Zodiac Houses with the metahumans they found as they scoured the Celestial Database for potential matches.

The only reason I'd come out of retirement was because Sasha had found me, not the other way around. And the second I sent her to Aries Academy, I was going to disappear again. She didn't need me. She'd come this far on her own. Besides, her presence unsettled me. She reminded me of Lily, and I didn't want any more reminders. The only thing I wanted was to find whoever was responsible for killing Lily and make them pay, over and over. If they weren't immortal, I would use arcane magic to make them immortal just so I could torture them longer.

My feet carried me along cobblestone streets downtown; after centuries of these walks, they knew exactly how to get home. Colonial Spanish-style buildings that never changed guided my way. The walk brought me to the end of the street, where I made a right. This was the way to Ixia's, the Zol botanist who'd once been my mentor centuries ago during my initiation to the world of shamanism.

When I arrived, I could tell she was there because the vines lining the ornate metal gate at the entrance of her grotto were alive with blooming purple, gold, and white flowers. The vines detected my familiar presence and opened the gate.

"Ixia," I grunted her name from the entrance.

She appeared before me after a several heartbeats, leaving the dryads to toil away at the vast herb garden. The dryads dressed in off-white and brown dresses with plunging necklines and knee-high beige boots. Every time I walked in here, I felt the beginnings of an erection climb to the surface. *Down boy! Focus on the one thing you came here for.*

"You look well. Stars write the path," she said, cascading her eyes up and down my body. "I heard you brought the nagual back with you. I thought you left her to choose."

"Stars write the path," I grumbled out. As far as I knew, she wasn't aware of Lily or Lily's connection to the nagual or the people I was hunting. I wasn't about to explain now. She was a vicar and alchemy advisor to the Zol Council. Her loyalty was to the path, and I still hadn't ruled out that the Council was somehow involved in Lily's death.

"I assume she's here for the transformation ritual tonight?" She turned and walked over to a shelf lined with small wooden crates, each identical and filled with several bottles of herbs and liquids.

"Yes. She'll make a fierce nagual, I'm sure." I took in her rich, deep-brown skin that was a sharp contrast to the lightness of her golden eyes. Despite being centuries old, she still looked like she was in her mid-twenties. Her curly hair was soft and brushed gently down at her sides. Her arms and neck were lined with delicate gold jewelry. The jewelry was far more than just decorative; it served to ward off the energy and spells that would do her harm. Behind her gentle, plant-loving demeanor, she was a master of protection and had developed much of the botanist program at the twelve Academies ruled by the Zodiac Houses.

Ixia removed one of the small crates from the shelf and handed it to me. "We packed these just this morning. Everything is fresh."

I counted five other crates on the shelf. "So, there are six shifters at tonight's ritual?"

"Now that you're back, there are seven. Even though they all told me only six nagual would be at the ceremony, I knew there would be seven, so I prepared an extra crate." She placed her hands at her sides, and a hint of mirth glimmered in her eyes. "My count has never been off. The extra crate is under the shelf." She loved to be right.

"Thanks, I'll see you there tonight then," I grumbled back at her.

"Was it my fault that you left?" Her eyes lost their bright glimmer, and her face deadpanned.

She should know better than to ask me that.

"No, Ixia. It wasn't your fault. But you did make it easier to decide," I huffed and walked out of there, carrying my box. I didn't owe her any explanations. And she didn't owe me any.

CHAPTER 3

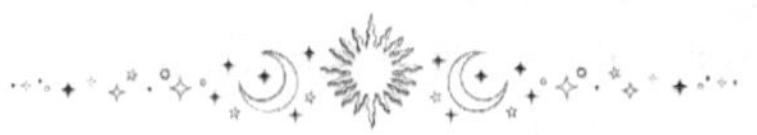

SASHA

My jaguar form was surprisingly docile, as though she had some deeper knowing that she belonged here in the shaman's atrium. When I first shifted just a few hours ago, I'd felt her wild power overtake me. Yet now, her intelligence and ability to comprehend the situation was impressive. I mean, she could just go savage on anyone that stands in her way and take off running. Instead, she made the wise choice of not listening to me. She just sat by and waited for the shaman to finish preparing the herbs for the transformation ritual.

He was so slow, too. It was driving me crazy. Every time I watched him at his worktable, he was grinding an unfamiliar herb and mixing it with an unfamiliar liquid. Then he would let the bowls sit and simmer, one under heat, another at room temperature, while he ground herbs and mixed other concoctions. I could have sworn I saw him chop up a human eye and fire it up. Gross. But of course, I couldn't ask him anything about it because I was inside this massive black jaguar that couldn't speak.

Yet inside this beast, the sounds were different. I still heard the harrowing whispers and screeches of the shadows that had tormented me over the past year. But this time, the screeches came through clearer, less menacing, and more natural. It was like I was hearing another aspect of nature that I couldn't understand. It didn't make me crazy with fear like when I'd first heard it, and it wasn't as annoying as it was after I'd begun to accept it. Now, it was more like a cadence to life that I merely needed to know how to interpret.

The jaguar would scratch, lick herself, go outside and relieve herself, and I was just along for the ride. I was just a bystander inside this beast as we waited for the ritual, and I wondered for the billionth time what had happened to Trent. Had he survived that crazy vampire bitch? Was he alive? Was he out there worried about me? How could I let him know I was safe?

Am I safe? I'm inside a jaguar! And what if the shaman can't turn me back into a human? What if something goes terribly wrong? What if Damian is setting me up? These questions got me all worked up, and my jaguar snarled. It felt like she was telling me to shut up. I couldn't believe it. We were *so* not connecting on this.

As the jaguar sat patiently on the wooden floor, I soaked in the décor of the room. Much like the rest of the building, the walls were made of beige stone, and they were lined with wooden shelves that held tools, instruments, books, and plants. The furniture was simple but more ornate than I was used to.

Yet even beyond the architecture and design, there was something different here. I could feel it in my bones. I was sure it was more than just being inside the form of a jaguar. There was magic here. I felt it tingle against her fur and smelled it in the richness of the air. The jaguar took another nap, drawing me into sleep, too. I guess our brain function was connected in this one aspect. When we slept, I had the wildest dream...

⁕

I was back in my human form and running wildly back across the Aries Gate. "Trent!" I called out over the expansive Plaza de Armas inside Castillo San Felipe del Morro where I now found myself.

"Trent!" I screamed in desperation. I fell to my knees and cried fiercely for him. I couldn't teleport and I had no idea how to get back to him. That was when I remembered my meditation. I moved into a seated position in the middle of the limestone plaza, surrounded by ocean and worked to calm my mind and focus.

I opened my eyes and gazed upon my familiar human limbs, seated on the massive pillow in Villalba, Puerto Rico. I wasn't sure how the magic worked exactly, but I knew if I shifted into my jaguar form and looked at my reflection in the lake, I could find Trent. I ran down the soft mulch-covered path under the moonlit sky and peered over the edge at my reflection. Then I focused on Trent's energy. Was he alive? Would I be able to find him? My heart thudded in my chest as I fought to calm the rising panic.

As much as I tried to find his energy, I couldn't. I tried again. And again, and nothing came through. Finally, I decided to seek out the dark energy of the vampire, Grange, even though he was dead. Maybe I still could? It was like searching for a single strand of hope in a massive tapestry of darkness. Then I felt a familiar darkness, one I had experienced before. It wasn't Grange; I couldn't find him. I assumed it was because he was dead. *Because I ripped him apart.* But I was on the dark magic trail left by the female vampire with the flowing dark-red hair who had accompanied him. Solana.

She was still in Colombia, still in the house where I'd left Trent and five of my captured squad mates. That bitch! *Did she drain them all?* Blood dripped from her mouth as she sat on the bed with their bodies lying motionless all around her. She seemed to have had quite the time with them. Her pick of any to feast on. *Are they even alive?*

Then I spotted Trent, sprawled on a couch across from where Solana sat on the bed. I focused on him; his energy was very low, but that was normal when people slept. Their auras weren't nearly as bright. I let out a shallow breath when I saw he had a dim aura.

He's alive!

I watched for a while, soaking in as much as I could of his face, not sure when I would see him again.

After a couple minutes, Solana sat up, and that vampire bitch pulled a cell phone from her pocket. "Yes, the stars have taken Grange." She let out an exasperated breath. "I know. I know. But listen, I need you to get over here. Now. There is some garbage to take out."

She fixed her hair in the mirror, mussed after she'd killed and drained my team, my fellow soldiers. They appeared to be resting, their naked bodies unmoving and covered with blood. *She's the fucking garbage. Not them.* My throat constricted, and my rage fought to come to the surface. I shifted my attention to Trent.

Trent stirred and opened his hooded eyes. He made an attempt to sit upright. Solana eyed him thoughtfully. She was practically glowing from all of that fresh blood she had taken.

"You're that little black cat's boyfriend, aren't you?" she hissed as her eyes landed on him.

Trent just stared back at her. He knew better than to give up any intel.

"I think I'll keep you all for myself."

She walked over to him. He reached his hands up and encircled her waist as though he knew her. She lowered herself onto his lap in a slow, snakelike movement. His broad arms and shoulders encased her slim frame. She moved her head to the side and swept her long hair across her back, lightly gracing his defined biceps as his hands reached slowly up her shirt. He seemed to be enjoying the caress and feel of her body against his.

I clenched my teeth as I saw desire for her in his eyes. Those eyes that only hours before had sought me to satisfy him. She had him under her spell. My nails dug into my palms as I watched them. It must be the same kind of spell that had had me lusting after Grange.

A fire began to burn deep in my root chakra, spiraling up into my core. I felt the heat of it, spinning and swirling inside me with no form of release. I wanted to scream out, to yell, to make her stop and tear the flesh from her neck just like I done had to Grange. I couldn't do any of it, though; I was a formless nothing peering into an imaginary lake somewhere in the back of a jaguar's mind. Fuck my life.

Chapter 4

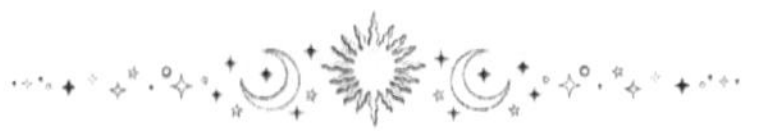

Damian

"It's time," I said to the three-hundred-pound beast stretched out on the mediterranean tile floor. She didn't move. The sun was beginning to set, and there were seven zodiac beasts to convert. The sooner this was over, the better.

"Wake up, come on," I said again, resisting the urge to kick her. The last time I'd done that, the nagual had nearly ripped my head completely off. I didn't even want to be back in Zol Stria dealing with this. But here I was, against my better judgment, doing the right thing. Now the creature wouldn't wake. Her front paw started to twitch slightly. She was probably running back to her boyfriend in her dream. This kid was crazier than most, and I was still trying to understand how she'd gotten this far in her transformation without any help from me, or her soul guide, Lily. Just the thought of Lily brought an ache the size of a mountain to my chest. *No time for that.* I shook it off.

These beasts were always reluctant to give way to the human form. There was something about being set free after years of being enclosed, like the genies of the House of Pisces. They never wanted to go back in their bottles once they'd granted their keeper the three wishes.

I prepared a cup of water from the sink and poured it over her big, black, furry head. She immediately jerked her eyes open and leaped up off the ground. I stepped backward, stumbling over the chair behind me. She surged on top of me, throwing me to the ground and pinning me down. Her breath was hot on my face as her teeth came within an inch of my eyes. *Fuck. She's going to rip my face off.*

"The ceremony, it's starting now. We have to go," I said in the calmest voice I could muster, although I could hear it crack.

That water thing had probably not been a good idea, I just now remembered. Sasha had been tortured to death with waterboarding during her military training. She'd come back to life a full ten minutes later. *This is exactly why I hate being a nagual-sitter.* I didn't care about her personal life, and I wasn't about to start.

The jaguar's huge emerald eyes flashed with understanding, and then she backed up off of me. She still snarled like she wanted to take a bite out of my leg, but at least now I was free of her massive weight. She could have broken my bones when she'd knocked me over. These creatures were unbelievably strong. The second strongest in Zol Stria, right on par with the minotaurs of the House of Taurus, second only to the dragons of Scorpio.

Standing up, I tried to brush the dirt off from the huge paw marks that had imprinted on my shirt. I didn't even want to be here, which meant I had to look my best. I walked over to the closet where I always kept extra clean, pressed Italian shirts in the wardrobe for moments like this. I slipped the other one off, my muscles tensing when I felt the cool air wick against my skin. Glancing back over my shoulder at the fierce black jaguar, she glared at me intensely but had stopped snarling. I slid the clean shirt back over my head.

"Ok, time to go." I drew out that last word, hoping if I slowed my speech, she would think I was being friendly and wouldn't assault me again. I grabbed one of the three jars I'd prepared for the ritual and brought them over to her. "You've got to drink this now, so the herbs settle before we're under the stars. At the ritual, I'll give you the second one."

She stared at me, less intensely now, as if she was trying to understand. This was when I had to grab her feral face and pour the dosage into that massive mouth. I approached her, and she took a step back, not ready to let me do it.

"Hey... I'm sorry." I hated those words, but we were running out of time. "I didn't mean to pour the water on your face. My bad." I gave her doe eyes. The jaguar looked away for a second, as though letting that sink in. She turned her head back to me and shifted her eyes to the two potions left on the table. "Oh, yeah. The third one is for me. We drink them at the same time out there. Among other things, the potion helps me merge my magic with yours so you can shift back into human form. Your essence needs a little help remembering how to be human. It also gives you access to my magic for traveling between the Gates."

The jaguar seemed to relax a little when I said this and took a step forward. I reached for her huge jaw and held it in my hand. The bristly black fur prickled against my skin as I poured the yellow liquid down her throat. She drank it in one gulp.

"Ahora vamos. It's time to go." We turned to the door, and I stopped in surprise.

"Sorry! I didn't expect you back here, Damian. I came as soon as I learned of your return." Carly stood at the door, taking us in. I loved the way she spoke English with a heavy Mexican accent, even though she knew both our native tongues were Spanish.

I began to wonder how long she'd been there, hoping she hadn't seen me stumble under the nagual's fierce grip.

"Your deflector spells are quite strong. I didn't even feel you approach," I chuckled with pride. "You used to have so much trouble raising the deflector spell. I see you've come a long way in my absence."

Carly used to be my apprentice. She would be a shaman soon. She had thick, straight black hair, brown, creamy skin, and she was wearing an apprentice's traditional purple shroud for today's ceremony. She'd been about twelve years old when I'd found her, homeless, parentless and starving. Her magic was faint but I could tell she had the ancient bloodline of the shaman. So I'd brought her here, from the streets of Mexico City, so she could study the craft of shamanism. Now, she was probably about forty but only looked sixteen. The magic of Zol Stria slowed our aging.

"Yes, well, let's make haste. Thank you for helping me tonight." I patted her on the shoulder and gave her a quick kiss on the cheek in greeting. I hadn't seen her in about twenty years. She was the only person I trusted under the stars. "How have your studies been under the illustrious teachings of the Zol Shaman?"

The Zol Shaman was the head professor of magic and mysticism at the Scorpio Academy. I'd made arrangements for her to become his protege when I left.

"The Zol Shaman has been an exceptional mentor. He said I am ready to ascend to shaman by the next ritual." A smile graced her face.

"Wonderful news. Well-deserved. Well, let's head off then." Seems she was better off without me.

We approached the garden clearing, and six other nagual were already there with their shaman. Twelve were always called, one to protect the different Fae forms of each of the twelve different Zodiac Houses. But they never all made it. Some refused to go with the shaman, some were never found in the system and a few died during the shift to their jaguar form. Sometimes their bodies never completed the shift, and they would die a horrible, painful death in that grotesque in-between state. There were some things our alchemy still couldn't control, some level of Fae existence that was left entirely up to the stars. For as much as we shamans cast spells, yielded elemental magic and concocted potions to bend circumstance to our will, the stars inevitably wrote the path.

Even still, up until now, only one or two ever fell before the transformation was complete. Never five.

Each nagual was in a designated place marked with a glowing orb which held a sun sign. They formed a circle in precise alignment with their respective constellation. The nagual and their shamans took their positions under the orb aligned with their assigned Gate. The fierce black creatures were so enormous and deadly that it had taken me about ten rituals before I could relax in the presence of so many of them. I shifted my feet as we settled into our positions.

Nagual were always black. Spotted jaguars were the mortal creatures, and they were revered as a novelty here. Everything human was a novelty on this side of the Gates. The Fae of Zol Stria did enjoy their people-watching, or people-plotting, I should say.

They made games of tracking and toying with the star alignments and transits of those who interested them, for whatever reason that was most convenient at the moment. Power, control, political gain and sport were some of the motivators. Such games were a jumbled mess I preferred to avoid, especially since they were forbidden by the Houses. Yet, the great Houses of Zol Stria were the biggest culprits. Always predicting and wagering on mortal politics, celebrities, sports and whatever else they could come up with. Everything was a game to them, all you had to do was place a bet and let fate do the rest. After all my years of service, all the nagual I'd brought to their forces, they still hadn't prevented the death of my Lily. In fact, they may have been behind it. Fuck them and their fate games.

I rubbed the back of my neck and glanced at Sasha's nagual. The feral creature's face was large, wise and intimidating. I sent a prayer to the stars for this to all be over quickly. I would never come back here again.

Chapter 5

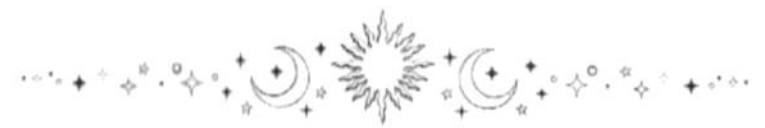

Sasha

I couldn't believe it. There were other nagual just feet away. I counted six other huge, burly black jaguars standing in this circle under glowing lights I couldn't comprehend. Were they floating there? How did they do that? Were those drones or something? This was all so confusing. And that potion he'd given me had tasted like shit. I'd wanted to cough it up as soon as I drank it, but the nagual, well, she hadn't seemed to mind as much. How was it she knew to listen to him?

My jaguar was curious, and I felt her getting anxious. She bolted from Damian's side and ran up to one of the other nagual. She sniffed around it, and they walked in a circle. Then she ran off to meet the others. I guess this was some sort of nagual greeting. She seemed to be absorbing information about each one: where they were from, how they felt, what their scent was like. When she got to the nagual under the Leo orb, her hackles raised instantly. Heat stirred through her body. She snarled at the male jaguar that had intrigued her and turned away very slowly, looking back as she walked away. A sort of feral mating greeting?

Ugh, this is awkward.

My jaguar walked back to where Damian was standing and took her place next to him. She laid down and began licking her paws as if this situation was boring her. I, however, was curious about the orbs. Somehow, she either decided to humor me, or was curious herself, and looked up at it. Underneath was the zodiac symbol for Aries.

Damian stole a glance at her as he was chatting with the shaman next to us. "You've been assigned to the Aries Gate. Nagual get assigned to defend the Gates of their birth signs. You're lucky you weren't born a Scorpio. Everyone hates that assignment." He sighed and shook his head, grumbling more to himself than to me. "The Scorpio Gate is notorious for its crime syndicate and arcane antics." Damian's voice was hushed, his posture stiff.

There were seven jaguars, seven shamans and seven apprentices standing idly in the circle when I saw two insanely gorgeous men walk into the center. And I mean male perfection. Holy hell they were hot! One wore a white suit, and the other was deep navy. The suits were elegantly tapered over their muscular frames, and their necks were adorned with gold chains that seemed both ancient and royal. Their presence was magnetic and compelled all attention to focus only on them as they walked into the center. They towered over the entire circle; they were certainly tall, but they seemed to dominate the space entirely.

Entranced by their presence, I couldn't shake the feeling that I had known and adored them my entire life. The mist that curled around and created my jaguar's form pushed to the surface, as if it was being called to them. My shadows were theirs to command.

Their skin was a deep, dark caramel, hair shoulder-length and straight. The two men seemed cut from the same stone.

"The one with the gray eyes and silver hair, that's Hun-Cane. The other, with black hair and eyes, is Vucub-Cane. They are the twin Mayan gods of the Underworld. They created the nagual, so they are the only gods that can conduct the ritual of transformation." Damian spoke softly, never taking his eyes off the twins.

"My friends. Good to see you all again. It's been too long," said Hun-Cane, his voice rippling across the garden in a soft thunder.

"Let's have a look at the new recruits," said Vucub-Cane immediately after in a calming, resonant tone.

A current threaded through me, and all thoughts ceased within my mind. I felt both a stillness of emotions and yet a powerful reverence wash over me. This was what it was like to be in the presence of the gods.

They walked the circle and took us in, one by one. As they approached Damian and me, the shadow mist within me froze in place, and the jaguar stood as still as a statue. I wasn't even sure if she was breathing. It was as though time had stopped. The twins seemed to spend a little extra time looking at my jaguar.

"She's already wielded her fire element," Hun-Cane said to Damian. It was a fact, not a question. How could he tell? The jaguar would not turn her head or move a single inch, so I couldn't see how he'd reacted. Yet out of the corner of her eye, I could see Damian nod without speaking a word.

"Yes, she will make an excellent Warrior," Vucub-Cane agreed.

"Excellent work, Damian. She will be fit for Xibalba when she graduates," Hun-Cane met Damian's eyes and nodded, his eyes seemingly grateful.

Damian whispered out the side of his mouth, while keeping his eyes forward, "The twin gods rule over Xibalba."

I knew what Xibalba was, at least the version they told us about in the history books. The place of fright. A vast Underworld where the twelve death lords lived, including these two.

The twins walked away to the center, their strides entirely in sync with each other. Strange as it was, I understood my jaguar's need to stay completely still. Their presence was divinely overwhelming.

More people came to the garden to watch, standing just outside the circle. They seemed like celebrities by the way they were dressed: their clothing modern and impeccable, their hair styled and skin glowing. Any other time it would've made me uncomfortable to be watched by people who seemed so blatantly wealthy, but I was too mesmerized by the twin gods to pay them any mind.

"Bring forward your offerings," the twin gods commanded in unison. One of their assistants came forward with an ornate gold tray with several partitions. Each shaman brought forward a large jade stone and set it within the tray. Then the assistant placed the tray on a table between the twins and stepped away. They began to chant incantations in the same tongue that Damian had taught me in the weeks before we crossed the Aries Gate. As they did, the familiar Zodiac Shadows came slithering out toward them from every imaginable crevice. There was not a single place from which the darkness did not come. That familiar, deathly mist that had filled my days and nights with horror. My own shadows pulled at me, aching to join the others as they crept toward their twin masters.

As the shadows joined in the center, they swirled around the gods. Electric sparks flared within the mist, accompanied by thunderous hums and thrums. Hues of deep indigo, blue and gray circled them from within while the black mist coiled around their bodies. An ancient wind swept through the circle, blowing the hoods of the robes off the assistants' heads and causing the celebrity-like onlookers to murmur amongst themselves at the sudden blast. I felt movement from behind my jaguar and had the urge to look back, but she wouldn't move from her frozen position. I heard the final incantation, *"Xit la kue pali."* That was when Damian drank one of the potions he was holding.

"Culo arriba," he mumbled with a smirk and quickly finished drinking it down. He picked up the other bottle from the tray Carly was holding. He grabbed my jaguar by the jaw and poured that potion down our throat. I felt her gulp down the bitter-tasting liquid without objection.

"You're Fae now," he whispered to us.

My jaguar returned to her frozen position. Her insides were quiet. It was as though she instinctively knew the steps of the ritual and some part of her wildness was being suppressed. There was an energetic connection with the glowing zodiac orb above that kept her locked in place. She was facing the crowd, and I could hear them murmur amongst themselves as servers brought them trays of fresh champagne.

The gods in the center of the circle raised their gaze from the jade pieces before them. Their chins and eyebrows were slightly lifted as they looked proudly at the seven new recruits. They swept their hands in the air, then swung them ceremoniously around the circle. As they did, the mist crackled something fierce. Electric pulses, surrounded by the black misty cloud, shot out to each of us—and when it reached me, an excruciating pain reverberated through my bones.

It wasn't pain I could describe. It was unimaginable.

CHAPTER 6

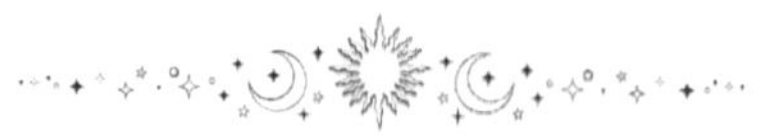

DAMIAN

This was the worst part. Watching these massive, strong beasts—that were people, after all—squirm in pain on the ground like that. Several of the nagual I'd guided through previous rituals had confessed to me at some point during the transformation that they'd wished to die or live the rest of their lives as jaguars running through the forest, rather than endure that kind of suffering ever again.

It should be me. I should be tortured like that, for leaving Sasha when she needed me. Lily would have wanted me to stay with her. She could have been lost to the darkness for hundreds of years.

"It will be over soon," I tried to reassure her, unsure if she could hear me. I had already stepped back about six feet to give her plenty of space. The feral creature cried out in agony. A high-pitched wail, mixed with snarls and screeches, left her throat as she squirmed and twisted on the ground. All of them were like that. You could hear the sounds of bones snapping, crunching and wrenching coming from all of them.

My eyes darted to the orb next to ours where the nagual assigned to Libra was having some sort of convulsion. Her body trembled viciously. It appeared to me like a seizure, and white foam spilled from her sharp, pointed fangs. Then my eyes shot to Capricorn's nagual, who was having a spasm. He fell to the floor and slowly rose again. With trembling legs, he lunged back weakly then shot forward, as if to run, only to collapse after taking just four steps. On it went with each of them, pain and agony, whines and roars, as the transformation back to their human forms continued.

Staggered "Aaaahhhhs" and "Ohhhhs" came from the crowd as they sighed in unison. Their faces contorted as they watched the spectacle of jaguars writhe under glowing yellow orbs. Although I knew the council members and royal guests in attendance, I hadn't missed being around them. Humans have a saying: Evolve or die. Humans could say this because they would certainly die if they never evolved and had a chance to try again at their next incarnation. Eternals had a different choice: Evolve or don't. Most of them didn't.

At this point, all of the champagne flutes had been collected, and the crowd began to form an alternating double line. They raised their palms flat out in front of them and sent a cresting wave of source energy to the writhing jaguars. I pulled from their energy and held my hands out on top of Sasha, channeling the healing energy into her. I let out a deep breath as the energy curled around her, and she stopped whining and twisting on the ground. The elegant women and finely dressed gentlemen lowered their hands to their sides and relaxed. They smiled at each other and chanted in unison,

"Darkness reborn, serve the Zol as one."

I caught sight of the twin gods, who had been watching all the while from the side with the cosmic priests and priestesses. They were the Zol Sen, dressed in long, hooded golden cloaks embroidered with the zodiac glyphs. The Zol Sen were sacred to Zol Stria and meticulously aligned the ceremonial traditions with the alignment of our planets and stars. The gods engaged them as sacred entities and respected them above all other Fae.

Light exchanges filled the air. I shifted my eyes down. I hoped they'd forget they saw me. The crowd followed the Zol Sen as they walked toward the ethereal music that played from the greenhouse. Sasha would at least enjoy this part.

The food here was exceptional, and judging by the way she liked to eat, she would be ravenous.

CHAPTER 7

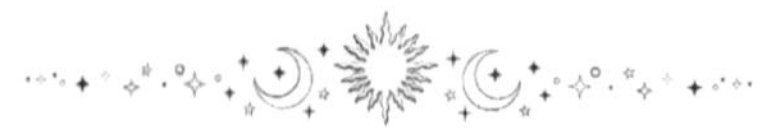

SASHA

I had to think.

My brain. It wouldn't stop spinning.

Breathe.

I took a deep breath.

I rubbed my palms against a smooth floor. My eyes were squeezed shut. I relaxed them. I brought my hands up to my legs and felt my skin again. No fur. I heard chatter around me. There were others. I felt a draft. I was naked. My eyes were swollen shut. I struggled to open them.

"Here you are." Damian's assistant, Carly, held a robe out.

I came up on my knees and stood. She draped the dark gossamer material over my shoulders. I was starting to feel better. Fresh, alive, and human. My headache was only a lingering tremor in the back of my head, fading to nothing. A rush of energy pulsed through my chest, pushing, moving and then it stilled. It was my jaguar. She was settling back in. I glanced around the garden; each nagual was standing, putting their robes on and walking away. I exhaled. It was over.

I shot a glance at Damian. He had a drink in his hand and was chatting it up with the Libra shaman.

I walked over to him and came within his personal space. The Libra shaman stopped talking mid-sentence because of my proximity, and I imagined she could also see the fire in my eyes. I hated Damian. He'd hidden from me for years, not owning up to his responsibility as a shaman. He was probably the reason my aunt was killed, and he'd never once explained the insane level of excruciating pain I would experience in that ritual. I pulled my arm back and clocked him with a stiff jab to his left cheek.

"You're an asshole." I spat on the floor next to him. He deserved that punch and so much more. I glanced over at Carly, who was gaping at us. The Libra shaman raised her eyebrows and turned to attend to her nagual.

"Take me back. Take me back right now!" I wasn't going to wait. Not one more second.

"Take you back? You're not ready."

I was so sick of everyone always telling me I wasn't ready. "I don't care if I'm ready. I need to know Trent is safe." My voice cracked. My knees buckled and I slumped to the side.

Damian grabbed my arm and held me straight. "You need to recover. Then you will begin your orientation. There is no time to go back."

My throat felt scratchy and as dry as sandpaper. "I don't care about any of that. Trent isn't safe with her. Don't I have a choice in any of this? I don't want to be here." I was drained of all energy, completely depleted. My head started to spin.

"If you go back right now, you won't be of any use to anyone. You've got to restore your energy. Plus, you have no idea where he is. They'll be long gone by now."

I didn't like what he was saying, but I knew it was the truth. My head felt heavy at that realization.

"Go back to the room with Carly. Rest. Get dressed, then join us at the reception." His eyes shifted between me and her, and for the first time, I saw the centuries of experience in his face. He was thinking of something. "Tomorrow, after you've rested, we can track him."

"How? How can we track him?" I eyed him suspiciously. I didn't believe he would help me track Trent. This guy was all about doing the bare minimum. He was probably lying to shut me up.

"Just like the other times you've tracked him. You already know how to track. It's one of your unique abilities. And now that you've shifted, those abilities will be amplified. Tomorrow we'll go to the Wall of Mirrors where this is done with precision."

"He might be dead tomorrow. I need to go tonight."

"You can barely walk tonight. You need power to do it, and right now you don't have any."

My head was spinning something vicious, and I hadn't even noticed when Carly came to my side. She was holding me up with her body. I draped my arm around her shoulders.

"Fine. Tomorrow." I knew he was right. My voice quivered from exhaustion. "You better keep your word." I felt a draft wisp beneath my robe and was reminded that I had nothing at all on underneath it. "Where can I get dressed?"

Carly glanced at Damian for approval. He rubbed his jaw and nodded his head.

"Follow me." Carly walked ahead, and I followed her.

We entered a small villa, the front door facing the garden. I could smell the cedar. The walls were dark, similar to the wood I saw in the atrium. There was a modern couch facing a chimney and a bookshelf with a variety of books. I was curious about what they read on this side of the Gates. The small kitchen had oak cabinets, marble counters and stainless-steel appliances. There was a fine balance of modern living with ancient design.

"This is your villa," Carly said. "In the bedroom, you'll find everything you need. Drink this elixir, it will speed your recovery, along with your bath soak, which has been already drawn. I'll come for you in about an hour, and we'll go to the soirée for dinner." She turned to leave.

"Carly." My voice was soft.

"Yes?" She turned to face me.

"Is it always...this painful?"

She dropped her gaze to the ground, her black hair falling forward. Her skin glimmered in the dim light. She lifted her eyes to meet mine. "This is the first ceremony I've attended. But I've learned that it can be worse. Some nagual don't make it through the pain. It rips at their soul to the death. And sometimes the vicars take even longer to cast the amending energy."

"Why? Who are those people, anyway? And why did they wait to heal us?"

That pissed me off. They held back the healing when they could have spared us so much pain. Her eyes opened wide and she lifted her chin. My hands were on my chest, pulling my robe closed at the seam.

"You earned that pain. The pain of transformation is holy, and it marks the first of the Trials of the Houses. You must pass twelve trials to graduate from the Academy and step fully into your role as Protector. This is the path." She nodded.

She was much older than I'd originally thought. Not because her skin or her features revealed her age, but because of the way she stood. The certainty in her eyes. The knowing.

Her eyes narrowed slightly before she spoke again. "Pain is a right, not a privilege. There is knowledge in the pain. The deeper the pain, the deeper the lesson. After today, you are wiser because you overcame it. You are better prepared for the trials you must still face." She looked at me with her head cocked and a directness in her tone. "Now, you must get dressed." She turned and opened the door before I could ask any more questions. "I will return." She slipped out.

I stepped in the drawn milk bath and felt warm water envelop me. Petals floated at the surface, and earthy aromas filled my lungs. The memory of the hellish pain still lingered beneath my skin and I wanted to be free of it. The bathroom was equipped with rosemary-and-mint shampoo, natural cleansers and the most delicious-feeling sponges that had ever graced my skin. I soaked in the bath for as long as I could until the dizziness finally left me. The steam in the air had gone, and the water was no longer warm. Yet my limbs felt firm and my back and shoulders stronger. Even still, as I eased up out of the bath, my muscles felt sore and my stomach growled in complaint.

After applying the natural lotions and creams, I realized I should be getting dressed by now. *How will I do my hair and makeup?* I opened another drawer in the massive vanity, and there were all the products I'd ever need to glam-up. Was this some kind of reward for making it? I had never had access to so much luxury. Ever.

The closet had three dresses to choose from. I assumed it would be semi-formal from how the twins and vicars were dressed. I settled on the deep-green, floor-length dress. It had an interesting, embroidered edge and a plunging neckline. There was no fabric on the sides, revealing the skin at my waist. As I laced up deep beige heels—a perfect complement to the dress—I wondered more about the vicars and this bizarre place. About Carly and her anti-social mannerisms. The coldness I felt at not knowing anyone, and how familiar that feeling was to when I first left my parents' house.

As always, my mind guided me back to him. The only time I had felt truly loved, truly not alone was when I was with Trent. What was happening to him? Was he ok? Where was he right now? A cold stone dropped into my stomach at the thought of him in the clutches of the vampires that had attacked us. Would I be able to find him? How would I get to him?

But there was a deeper feeling. It was underneath all of the thoughts swirling in my mind and the memory of the pain from my shift back to being a human. There was always this void inside of me, and inside that void, in the dark corners of my mind, the Zodiac Shadows tormented me. There were days I felt so empty I filled the void with just about anything. Like the things I stole, or the bad boyfriends I attracted.

But right now, I couldn't find that void inside of me. Instead, I felt a kind of fullness. An energy that surged from within. It felt as though the darkness that had been calling me had brought me here to Zol Stria. It was always just bringing me home.

As I finished lacing up my heels, I heard a tap at the door.

I stole a glance at myself in the mirror. My makeup was on point. My jaw was set, and my hair was flowing.

It was time to go.

CHAPTER 8

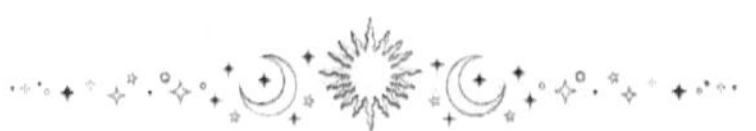

DAMIAN

I was never much for gatherings. Having to socialize with the twin gods, the vicars who thought themselves celebrities—reeking of privilege—and the fresh new recruits was sure to drain my energy like vultures emptying a carcass.

I held a glass of whiskey as I stood alone under a fig tree, surrounded by orchids, ferns and lilacs. The greenhouse was the size of a large ballroom with winding passages of flora from around the world. In the center was a fountain of carved marble, Poseidon holding his staff amidst the stone sirens lounging on the shore. Ushers passed out champagne flutes and hors d'oeuvres. Several bars were serving drinks and a DJ was playing remixes. The buffet would open soon. The plan was to get my food, shake a few hands and get back to my villa.

"How long do you plan on staying this time?" Her voice crept up from beside me. She laced her hand into mine.

I turned my head to meet her eyes and the scent of lavender and rosewater filled my lungs. "I'm leaving tomorrow," I grunted roughly, but I didn't release her hand. I let it warm me.

Her beige gown held tight to her waist, and her full lips were polished, tempting. Our history was long; it spanned centuries. There was love once, long ago. We lived so long that we lived past the love. Now, there was only lust. She began to lace her energy with mine. I considered rejecting it, but instead let my deflectors down for her and allowed her magic to waft over me. She wanted to share a vision with me, and I could easily guess as to what kind of vision it was.

I may have had my differences with Ixia, but sex wasn't one of them. When her magic charged through me, the memories of us flooded back in. I had been alone for a while. There were many nights that I missed a woman's warmth in my bed. A shared memory played in our minds.

Rays of sun crept in through the cracks in the curtains. A faint and distant sound pulled me away from a dream, but I wasn't yet awake. There was movement on my bed. Careful, soft movement. I didn't stir. I only opened my eyes slightly, still in the haze of sleep before fully waking.

There she was, kneeling on my bed in a white nightgown, open at the front, revealing her full breasts. Ixia leaned in toward me and I felt her body creep up mine until she straddled me. She wrapped her thighs around mine as her hair brushed against my face, rich with the smell of her. My hands reached for her, landing on her hips and squeezing. My mouth watered for her taste, and I licked my lips. She thrust her hips forward, and I responded by rocking into her, again and again.

"Tonight?" Her chest rose and fell quickly with small, panting breaths from our shared vision. I could feel her heart beating fast from the contact of our hands.

"You're sure?" I didn't want to lead her on. My heart had nothing left. I'd told her the last time I'd been with her that lust was all I had left to give. "I haven't changed."

"I know. And yes, I'm sure." Her look was determined.

"Ok." I kissed her hand.

Chapter 9

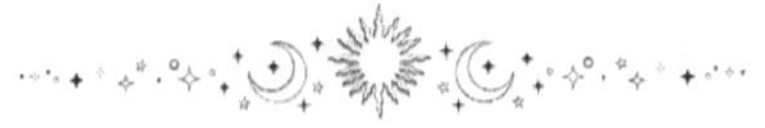

Sasha

"It is time." Carly looked absolutely stunning in a sequined, deep-blue dress that hugged her curves. Shiny clear gems that reflected the light decorated the seams. Her black hair was slicked back into a midway ponytail, revealing her heart-shaped face. This was the first time I was ever going to a formal event. My stomach fluttered in excitement.

"You look gorgeous," I couldn't help but tell her.

Her cheeks turned pink for a hint of a moment, and her aura fluttered out from her restraints. Everyone on this side of the Gates kept control of their auras. They weren't on display for me to read like they were back home. Damian had explained that it was part of the protective spells Fae cast for our bodies and minds. He called it deflection. Everything is energy, he would say. Therefore, when the energy of a shaman or a Fae tried to enter the energy of another, whether in their mind or with their magic, we could deflect it away from us. This was how we could prevent them from coming in, reading our energy, and influencing our behavior. Stronger deflection spells could deflect sound and even contain sound so that others couldn't overhear conversations.

We could also deflect elemental magic and glamor. A deflection spell would've protected me from Grange, the vampire military training instructor that had bitten me in Texas and attacked my rescue unit in Colombia. But because of Damian's incompetence as a shaman, I didn't know how to perform one, and five soldiers may have died because of it.

As soon as I entered the expansive double doors to the greenhouse, I soaked in the scents and smells of the fresh greenery and flowers. I was still reeling at how quickly I'd recovered from the torture of the shift. The pain was now a memory, forever ingrained in my mind. Yet after the bath and the rejuvenation elixir that Carly left for me, my body wasn't as sore as it had been. I thought I would never recover from such pain. Glad I was wrong about that.

I scanned the room. These people, this place, was a whole other level of unbelievable perfection. It was as though everything shone and glowed. And the craziest part about all of this was that I didn't even feel insecure. For once, I felt like I deserved to be here. Like I was worthy of it all, and more. So, this was what it felt like to be confident. Well, I could get used to this.

I was positively starving. I grabbed several bites of the free food being passed around, but that was just a tease. I needed the buffet to open already.

Carly gave me the details on who was who. Then she pointed out the nagual that shifted with me and their shamans, and the nagual of prior transits. There were a few them from the last transit, which was fifty years ago. Funny how they all looked my age, even though they must be about seventy years old by now.

"I can't promise I'll remember all of this, Carly." I studied her face, unsure if I could be myself around her; I couldn't get a read off her or anyone else. It was beginning to frustrate me. "So, are you showing me around as a friend? Or as part of your job?" I had to know where I stood with her, and everyone I met from this point on.

"This is my role, as an apprentice. But yeah, I'm a friend. We're on the same team. Your success is my success." She then gave me a faint smile and a slight, reassuring nod.

She was ambitious. At least I could tell that without having to read her aura. She had her own story, her own motivations for being here. I wasn't picking up on any of that fake women-supporting-women bullshit from her like I had in others. I made a mental note to keep my eyes open and my emotional guard up until I could be sure.

"Who is that? Who is Damian talking to?" I asked Carly.

"Oh, that's Ixia Cantress, Dean of the School of Botany and advisor to the Council." She lowered her voice, and I could feel her put up a deflector spell before she said, "And Damian's ex."

"They don't look like exes, considering how close they're standing." He looked a little too happy right now. He didn't deserve to be happy. It unnerved me how he could just go on with his life like he'd never done anything wrong. Like he didn't abandon his responsibilities when he was the very definition of "loser." I began to imagine the kind of pain I could inflict on him in my jaguar form.

Carly's eyes shifted to the right as she looked past me. I followed her gaze and turned around. Ripples. Tiny ripples of energy fluttered underneath my skin and goosebumps lined my arms when I saw the man that was approaching me. *I know him. How do I know him?*

He had some sort of cocktail in his hand. A lemony looking drink with a basil stem and juniper berries in a crystal tumbler. His hair was a thick, wavy light brown. His shoulders were broad, and his suit fit his muscular frame snugly. Smooth stubble lined his square jawline. He strode over to us from across the room.

I didn't know his face. This was the first time I had ever seen it. But I felt his energy course through me as though I knew him quite well. He reciprocated the energetic connection, and allowed our magic to flow between us.

"Do you see that?" I nudged Carly's shoulder; it seemed to catch her off guard. Nudging maybe wasn't something they did around here.

"See what?" Her eyes searched the area where I was looking. So, she didn't see it.

Black coils shot out from him and wrapped around me. It was the dark mist I'd seen in the bathroom when I'd learned to count the drips of the faucet to keep myself from going mad. The shadow mist that had covered me and filled me before I'd known anything about Zol Stria or becoming a nagual.

As he closed the space between us, my mouth gaped open, and I had nothing to say. No way to be sure yet that he was who I suspected. He caught me off guard, and I remembered just then to deflect his energy.

"Hi, Carly."

"Hey," she returned, glancing between us.

"I'm Zayne," he said, staring at me intently.

I met his gaze. His eyes were a light brown flecked with gold.

"Oh…" I couldn't find words yet. My eyes focused in on him and raked up and down his body. His suit was double-breasted, navy blue with a white shirt and tie underneath, and it had a sheen to it that made the fabric look very expensive.

This time, Carly nudged me. "Zayne, like you, is a nagual, only from the last transit."

"You know who I am." The words tumbled out of my mouth.

"Yes. I know. And you know who I am." His gaze was penetrating.

"I do."

Carly glanced back and forth between us as though she didn't understand.

My mind was whirling. I took a step back as memories crashed in my mind like an avalanche. The emptiness in my stomach. I needed to eat. After all my body had been through in the last few hours, I didn't think I could handle having this conversation with him until I had something solid in my stomach.

"I need to sit down. Join us?" I said softly. I knew he would. He had to.

We walked toward one of the high-top tables and took a seat. I picked up a freshly poured glass of water and took a long drink. So many incredible things had happened in the past twenty-four hours. I shouldn't be surprised that I was meeting him, but I was. I thought he was just part of my madness back then. I never thought he would walk up to me and introduce himself.

"Look, the buffet is open. Let's get some food and then we can talk?" I made a move to stand, but before I did Carly explained how the food situation worked.

"Oh, you don't serve yourself. We just lift the orb up and they'll bring you a plate."

In the middle of the table was a miniature version of the zodiac orbs that had been outside during the ritual. She made a sweeping gesture with her hands and made it levitate. Within minutes a plate of roasted sweet peppers was placed in front of me by a young man in a tuxedo, along with scallops in a lemon sauce. He then served the three of us a Cortese wine. Zayne and Carly made small talk about the beauty of the greenhouse and the freshness of the food as I stuffed my face and raised the orb again for my second course. I dabbed my mouth with the napkin and finished the wine in my glass. My strength was starting to return.

"So, Zayne. The whole time, inside my dreams. It was you?" I already knew. I just needed to hear him say it.

For two whole years he'd tormented me. Stalked me. Bringing shadow beasts within inches of consuming me through the dark, penetrating mists that had howled in my ears and basically scared the living shit out of me over and over again. At one point, I'd thought I belonged in a mental institution.

"Yes." His eyes darkened.

"Why? How?" I shook my head. I wanted to ask more, to say more, but the words stayed stuck in my throat.

CHAPTER 10

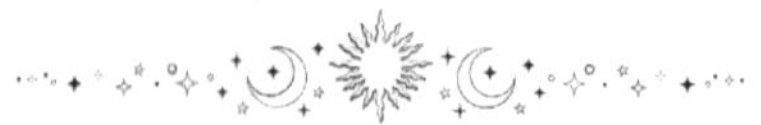

SASHA

My palms were sweating. My heartbeat raced. Would I finally get answers?

"Should I go? You guys seem like you need to talk in private." Carly glanced between us awkwardly.

"I don't know, should she go?" I shrugged my shoulders. I had no idea what he was about to tell me.

"Yes, Carly. Give us a minute please." He had the pretentious British accent I recognized from my dreams. It was the same exact voice.

Carly left us.

I straightened my back and smoothed out my dress, preparing myself for whatever he was about to say. "How could you? How could you do that to me? For a long time you made me believe I was crazy."

I didn't know whether to be angry at him or thankful for him. He was there when I was utterly lost and confused. And he was my only connection to Zol Stria. If it wasn't for him and his cryptic messages, I wouldn't have sought out Damian. He was the one who had kept telling me to find the shaman. He was the reason I knew anything at all about crossing the Gates. But his approach was horrible.

He leaned in and spoke in a lowered voice. "I can't say much. I have a deflector up now, but the twins..." He tilted his head slightly in the direction where the twin gods were sitting. "They have ways around deflector spells, and we can't trust anyone. But you should know, it was the only way I could reach you. If you didn't get through Aries Gate, you would have been lost. Our numbers decrease every year. There is a greater danger…" His voice trailed off.

He sounded like James Bond. I think. I mean, I hadn't watched that many James Bond movies, but the resolute stare, the intellectual demeanor, well, it reminded me of him.

"When can we talk then? I need to know." I glared back at him.

If anything, I was the resolute one here. I was the one who'd been ripped from the arms of the man I loved—maybe forever. I'd gone through a hellish transformation, I was about to start at an Academy, and one of the twin gods told me I would be assigned to Xibalba. There was just too much happening.

"I'll come for you tomorrow morning before your orientation. We can go to a nearby cafe for breakfast." Cool air brushed upon my skin as he released the deflector spell that had covered us both.

I was tracking Trent tomorrow, and if he wasn't safe, I would be leaving Zol Stria to save him. "No, that won't work. We need to talk tonight." My brows cinched.

Several heartbeats passed before he spoke again. Finally, his lips turned up in a slight grin. "Fine, then I'll drop by tonight after these…festivities." He dipped his head before standing from the table and walking away.

I finished my second course alone, and while I enjoyed the mushroom risotto, I couldn't help but wonder where Damian was. Many were standing, drinking refreshments while others ate. When I'd had my fill, I began to look around, taking in the unfamiliar extravagance of it all.

"So, how are you holding up?" a slim woman asked me. My ears perked up at her Jamaican accent and I returned the smile, but smaller. She was about my age and height, with curly hair and coffee-colored skin. Her green eyes were mesmerizing against her dark skin, and I believed they were the same shade as mine.

"I'm ok, I guess. As good as could be expected." I'd seen her at the ritual. She was the Libra nagual. "How about you?"

"I'm fine. I heard you only found your shaman just before crossing over. That must have been crazy. I've been guided by mine since I was a kid. He's family to me."

I smiled dryly at her. If only we could all be so lucky. "It's fine. I made it. That's more than I can say for five others."

"This is true." She took a sip from her wine glass. "I'm Jenna." Her friendly smile was so wide, I almost released my aura.

"I'm Sasha, nice to meet you."

She had glammed-up for this event, just like me. Her nails were manicured. Her dress was perfection. The crimson, silky material hung just above her waistline, sheer balloon sleeves were cuffed at the ends and a matching long skirt had a slit right up her leg.

"Maybe you can help me understand something." I cocked my head to the side. "Do you know anything about what it will be like at the Academy? Or even where it is?" My expression was flat and dull. I didn't want her to see any of the anxiety snaking just beneath the surface.

"Yes, it's here. In Aries. There are many Academies within the different Zodiac Houses, but the strongest warriors in all of Zol Stria are trained right here. I've been to the Aries Academy once. My shaman brought me to watch one of the gladiator qualifiers. It's one of our senior trials. And it was brutal. The Zol Wolves fought this massive three-headed fish-like beast to the death."

I let out a deep, long breath.

"It was fun! Very inspirational to watch what we will become as warriors. And have you seen your Zol account? It's more money than I could ever spend in a human lifetime."

"No, what Zol account?"

"Oh, that's right. You haven't met with the Zol Ministry yet. Well, they'll fill you in on our compensation. It's the very definition of abundance."

Damian told me about the money before, but honestly everything happened so fast I didn't even think about it until now. I could see myself making a life here, especially if there was compensation. As long as Trent could be here with me.

Just then the DJ lowered the music briefly and switched it up to a thumping hip-hop beat. My eyes shifted to the crowd as they started to dance. Memories of carefree days washed over me as I took another sip of the bubbly drink. Jenna took a sip herself and started moving her hips right on the beat.

I matched her sway as the familiar cadence thrummed through me, pulsing with the drum of my heart. I let the music drip into my soul, edging me closer to releasing myself. My hips moved without my permission; my arms played right along. Then I shot Jenna a glance. She smiled mischievously and reached for my hand, tugging me toward the dance floor.

"One more sip before I go." I drank down the rest of that delicious fizz and followed her.

"How many of those have you had?" She laughed as she asked, keeping pace with the rhythm thumping from the speakers.

"That was my third." I giggled happily.

"Ok." She laughed again. Her smile was intoxicating. "Time to slow down, especially if it's your first time drinking them. Those are infused with a happy potion."

I didn't care what she was talking about, but happy sounded good to me. I smiled widely and raised my hands over my head. I moved my hips and felt the bass vibrate all over. Jenna smiled and laughed with me on the now-crowded dance floor. The music pumped while my body swayed, and I let go of all the stress from earlier that evening.

How long has it been since I've danced like this?

I could do anything. Be anything I wanted. My whole life was in front of me. A new life, one with superpowers. This girl was on fire. I was going to be amazing. I just knew it. I smiled again, and my eyes locked with Jenna's. I reached my arms around her and hugged her close with my cheek pressed against hers.

"I'm so glad I met you," I told her, still smiling.

I could tell she was smiling too. Then she said, "Yeah, me too."

We danced to the pulsing sounds for a while longer. Is that DJ playing merengue beats just for us? When he switched it up to EDM, the dance floor got even more crowded. My body ached to move like this. The music filled my ears, threatening to bring me even closer to the cadence of that carefree happiness I'd felt once. Was that an eternity ago? My eyes were closed. My shoulders rocked me instinctively, knowing where the next chord would hit.

Then briefly, my mind brought me back to yesterday. I didn't want to remember the heartache of losing Trent. I didn't want it to be real. My eyes burned as tears welled up behind them. Not now. Not here.

I walked off the dance floor.

"Hey. Well, ok. Let's go back and get a drink I guess," Jenna joked as she followed behind me. We returned to our table where the server brought us some fresh water. "You know, I could get used to this treatment. People bringing you drinks. Rent-free luxury villa. Beautiful dresses in the closet." Her eyes swept across the room, and she smiled, not realizing the agony that had washed over me.

I pulled myself together and slapped a fake smile on my face by the time she met my gaze. "Yeah, me too. Don't forget the massive library. And can we talk about the battle gear?" I saw the strappy black leather outfit hanging in the closet. The seams were invisible, as if it was thought into existence and not created. I could tell that it was designed for flexibility, comfort, speed, and ass-kicking.

"Girl, it just slides right on and you feel like a total badass."

"I can't wait to try mine on." I was definitely looking forward to becoming a trained warrior. Even if that meant fighting some of the darkest, deadliest Fae and beasts ever to have existed. A chill coursed down my spine at the thought. *What in the world did the stars have in store for me?*

Luckily, Jenna changed the subject and made me laugh about some of the amazing creatures we'd already seen in this place. Like the three-eyed troll that managed the library, the goblins perched on the columns around the atrium and the fire pixies flying about in the garden. Unlike her, I wasn't prepared at all to see them and was still in complete awe. Then I remembered a question I had for her, from before we'd started dancing.

"I have to know. Where are the unicorns?" I imagined a purple unicorn with white wings and a golden, glittery horn.

"Those are a mystery, even here." Her brows pinched together and her mouth was soft, but her eyes were still smiling.

"Well, then I guess we'll have to search for them. Have you been to any of the other Houses? Maybe they're in one in particular."

"I've only ever been to one." Her eyes were full of wonder as she explained what she'd seen. "My shaman brought me through the Libra Gate. It's different there, but equally beautiful. Art is big there. And it's luxurious and grand. I'm told each of the Houses are different, as are the Fae from each of them."

I was beginning to think I could trust this girl. In Miami I had friends from all over the Caribbean, and as I spoke to her, it felt like a little bit of home was here. She kept most of her aura retracted, like the others, but I could see the faintest golden glimmer emit from each chakra, and it warmed me to her.

"I must tell you, I'm impressed you made it in. The other nagual and I, we were all being prepared by our shaman for years before we crossed. With the exception of Virgo, who was born into a deeply mystic family and raised in the path of the Zol since the start. We said goodbye to our families a month ago and began to acclimate in preparation for tonight. You just showed up and went for it. Kind of wild when you think about it." Her lips curled up into a smile, and I caught a bright admiration in her eye.

"Thanks, I guess. I had no choice, though." I shrugged. The joyful buzz I was feeling began to simmer down. Although I was curious about what she'd meant by "the path of the Zol," I had a more pressing question to ask. "So what do you mean you said goodbye to your family? Until when?"

Her eyes darkened briefly, her smile turning into a sharp line. "Never. That's it. You can't see them again. In that ceremony, we were reborn into this new life. There is no going back."

Heat rose in my chest and spread straight to my hands. The heat surged as my palms ignited, and the wine glass I was holding shattered to pieces. The sound of glass crashing against the ground startled several of the guests nearby. That's when I spotted Damian across the room. The absolute *fuckhead*. When I bent to down to clean the glass, a few servers rushed over and got to it before I could.

"I'm guessing fire is your element?" Jenna asked lightly. My head was dizzy. "Hey you, ok?" She placed her hand on my arm to steady me, concern in her eyes.

"No. I'm not." I could still feel heat simmering beneath the surface. "What do you mean there's no going back?" I bit out. I probably said that a bit more intensely than I'd meant to.

"As Zol Warriors we can travel between the Houses and back to the mortal world, but we can't have any contact with our prior life. This is your path."

Why the fuck didn't Damian tell me this? I swear, he was the worst shaman ever. He knew I wanted to find Trent. I wanted to see and talk to Nikki again. See my mom. I didn't realize my life in the mortal world was entirely over.

The deep beating of drums came from the center of the room, and a group of dancers dressed in black bodysuits began choreographed moves to what sounded like a modern Reggae or Bomba beat.

"Excuse me." I couldn't sit through a show right now. I turned away from Jenna and felt her eyes on me as I left the room.

She must think I'm a completely unprepared disaster.

I just hoped there weren't any more surprises. But I couldn't have been more wrong.

Chapter 11

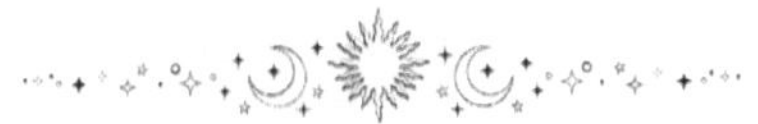

Damian

I heard a glass shatter and turned. Sasha bent over to clean it up, but a server interrupted her. *I wonder what that's about?* She looked over at me, and her eyes darkened. I felt a sting through our bond. Something else I must've done to piss her off. The nagual were never warm, bubbly or sweet. They were these fiery beasts that would tear out your eyes if you crossed them.

I took a long sip of my Fernet Branca on ice. Once in their Fae form, they were immune to magic. No spell, incantation, glamor or ward could stop them. The only thing that stopped them was the code to protect the zodiac that they learned at the Academy, and the call of the twin gods who had created them.

The Houses saw them as both an asset and a liability. They were an asset in as much as the enemies we defended against couldn't take them down. They were a liability because in their beast form, even I couldn't stop her from coming after me if she wanted to, and I knew she hated me. She had every reason to.

I shook it off. I sauntered back to the bar, and the mixologist topped me off.

"Remember when your nagual had cholera and I made you that recipe?"

I turned around to look at her. Ixia smirked. Her almond-shaped eyes and smooth skin drew me in.

"Yes, and then you gave the recipe to the nagual's father, Fernet Branca himself, and it made him famous." I lifted my glass. "Cheers, to changing the world one spirit at a time."

Ixia clinked her glass to mine and released a sultry laugh. I kicked the bitter-tasting drink back and set my glass on the table beside me. "I saw you chatting it up with the vicar of House Scorpio earlier. What are they up to at Xibalba lately? The twin gods want Sasha assigned there upon graduation."

She glanced around the room with her usual bored expression. Loose curls framed her face while the rest of her long curly hair was pulled up into a twist. I preferred her hair down. I downed the refill the mixologist poured for me and motioned for another.

"Xibalba remains the only division of the Underworld undamaged after the Twelfth War. Their security is still as tight as ever," she said.

"Honestly, don't look at me like that." She twirled a lock of hair as she considered me. She licked her lips, and my dick twitched.

"Tell me what you really think," I whispered in her ear with heated breath. I made sure a strong deflector spell was in place around us so no one could hear.

"Because the gods like novelties and your little kitty is a novelty. She shouldn't even be here." Her alluring eyes didn't match the all-business words.

Her hands ran along the crease of my jacket and then right into it so that I could feel her hand against my side. I wanted to watch her moan under the sweet pain I would give her. That kind of pain was the one thing she and I connected on, and it had been long enough since I'd felt hers.

"Let's go," I said and grabbed her hand. We walked out the back way through the garden unseen. She kept pace with me, not missing a single beat. When we reached the night air outside, I tugged her to the right. "This way. Let's go to my place." I led her down the long walkway to my villa and entered from the back.

I had the fireplace lit within seconds of us entering. She turned to face me. Her hands reached for my jacket, and she pulled me in for a kiss. In the instant my lips met hers, my erection grew thick under the fabric of my pants. She didn't hesitate and playfully squeezed my bottom lip between her teeth as she fisted my shirt in her hands.

I eased back and looked at her. She was always so beautiful. Her light-brown curls fell softly over her shoulders, no longer pulled up and styled. "Are you sure you're ok with this?"

She let herself fall back on my couch with a laugh. She nodded her head yes and curled her fingers in, beckoning me over. I fumbled with taking off my jacket, finding it a bit more challenging than usual. With enough fernet in my blood, my head got to that nice faraway place where my thoughts and emotions became nice and fuzzy. I managed to shake it off and pulled off my shirt as I gazed down at her hungrily.

"Do you want a drink first?" Her eyes were innocent, like she wasn't over five hundred years old.

"No." I considered it. "Maybe...later."

Enough years had gone by for Ixia to realize I was no longer in love with her. That this was a mutually beneficial, no-strings-attached arrangement between us. I was long past being the man she wanted me to be. I could only be the man I was now, and this man had no more love in his heart. But I did have lust. A lust that overpowered thoughts of putting things right as a shaman for Sasha. My desire for Ixia distracted me from the pain of my past and the longing for a life with Lily, one I would never have. Those were exactly the kind of thoughts that needed to stay fuzzy.

I slipped one hand along her body. Another moved up her thigh as I tugged her closer. I could feel her back arch and her chest rise in desire. I pressed my erection against her thigh, wanting her to feel how ready I was for her. I placed my mouth near her ear and breathed in her scent as lavender filled my lungs. My tongue flicked her earlobe and down her neck as a low moan escaped her lips. I felt her hard nipple in my palm and moved my hand to cup her breast, caressing it and exposing them both out of the material of her dress. I took her breast into my mouth as I pushed her hem up to her hip. Then I slid my hand between her legs.

At the apex, she was warm and wet. I moved my hand around her moist center, and her body responded with even more desire. Another moan. Another heated breath and I began nibbling on the curve of her neck.

"You can still back out now, Ixia," I whispered teasingly in her ear. She snapped her head to look at me as I moved lower down her body with kisses.

"Stop fucking around, Damian." Her words came out in a heated, breathy moan.

I slid off her panties and placed my hands on her knees, spreading her legs. I lined her thighs with kisses until I reached her center. My lips met her warm inner folds. My tongue caressed her in circular motions while my fingers entered her hot center. Her legs quivered. I moved my tongue faster and slid another finger in until she started moaning louder. She seized my hair and yelled, "Yes, yessss..."

Her legs trembled in satisfaction, and her fingers in my hair went slack.

I sat back and smiled for a few heartbeats as I watched her move sensually with the pleasure she had just experienced. My eyes soaked in her curves, and my dick got even harder for her.

I stood up, and she looked at me with a half-smile. She shifted off the couch and reached for my hand, leading me upstairs to the bedroom. With each step up I watched her sway her thick ass. She pulled off her dress as I shucked my pants. She laid back on the bed; her smooth skin and the contours of her body were a tempting invitation.

I brought my lips to meet hers, igniting a fire within. I pushed myself into her as my muscles contracted, pulsing and pounding into her flesh as I filled her with my erection at last. She moaned deeply and clawed at my back, bringing me closer and closer to finishing. *I don't want to finish yet.* I turned her around so I could soak in the look of her from behind. She took me in over and over, harder and harder. Until I was ready to release. A growl escaped me as I finished.

After a short nap, she rubbed my stomach and said softly, "Let's go again."

Chapter 12

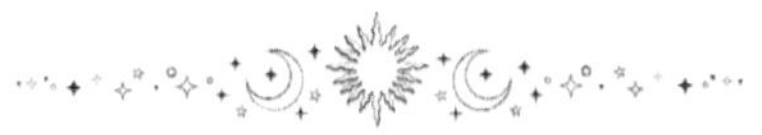

Sasha

Under the light of the full moon, I entered the open courtyard en route to my villa. Crickets chirped in the distance, and the night was cool and welcoming, so much like the mortal world I'd left behind. My hands were still singed from the heat, and I cursed under my breath as I stomped through the garden home.

Was Trent even thinking about me? Did he ever wonder what had happened to the huge, ferocious jaguar that had almost mauled him to death? Or was he too busy trying to escape and survive? I absolutely hated that I had to wait until tomorrow to track him, and hated even more that there was some kind of rule that said I couldn't go home. I had to go home, and I would find a way.

"Sasha…"

I barely heard my name being called from a short distance away. I didn't want to be bothered. I just wanted this day over already so I could track down Trent.

"Sasha… wait up." I recognized that voice. The voice that had kept me up many sleepless nights.

"Zayne," I whispered and stopped. I took a deep breath before turning around. He sauntered up to me, and I realized how incredibly handsome he was. Definitely not the monster I'd imagined in my head.

"You know, you're missing all the fun. Soon everyone will be drunk, the twin gods will surely seek you out for a dance and if not them, at least one or two of the highest-ranking vicars will invite you into their beds."

"So actually what you're saying is I didn't miss out on anything," I scoffed.

"Yes, well. That depends on what you're into," he said. "Let's talk, shall we?"

"Yes, let's. Where?"

"Come with me."

Trees lined the path as we circled the villas. The path was lit by the same small glowing orbs that had been in the center of the tables in the greenhouse. We entered a gazebo at the edge of a coastal canal, and the smell of salt water reminded me of home.

"I'm fairly certain no one will hear us in here." He glanced around the edges of the gazebo; for what, I didn't know. I felt the warmth of the deflector spell once again. He was taking every precaution. He turned to me, and the intensity in his eyes was unsettling.

I started to feel like a dumbass for being alone with a guy I had just met, in the dark of night, in a place where no one could hear me scream. I still couldn't do shit. I couldn't shift on demand, I didn't know yet how to make more than a flicker happen with my fire element, and I couldn't read energy because everyone in this place retracted their auras. I was way better off in the mortal world.

I took a few steps back and positioned myself next to the entrance so I could run if I needed to. "Is it my lucky day? Am I going to hear all about this danger you told me about and why you were in my head all that time before I shifted?" As uncertain of him as I felt right now, a huge part of me was relieved. It was so refreshing to know I didn't make him up.

"I sought you out, just like I sought out the five others who didn't cross the Gate. I couldn't save them, but I'm glad to see you made it. I hope my messages helped in some way. Did they?"

My eyes opened wide, and I shifted on my feet uncomfortably from the serious tone of his voice. His glare remained fixed on me, but he relaxed a little. "Well, yeah. It was a confusing time and when you hear something in a dream, you don't know if it's real or not. But I wouldn't have believed in any of this if it wasn't for those messages." A breeze swept through the gazebo, and the trees swished around us. "But why were they so dark? Did you send those shadow beasts after me?" That'd been the worst part.

"Any time a Fae contacts the mortal world, the veil gets thinner at our point of entry. And you didn't know it then, but you were pulling them through the veil whenever I spoke to you." He searched my eyes for something. Maybe he was trying to see if I believed him? "I'm sure you noticed that you feed off the energy of that kind of darkness. Did you know you also feed off the dark thoughts of mortals and the souls and spirits of the damned? That's what makes the nagual unique. This is how you channel your elemental power of fire and shift into a jaguar."

I nodded. I understood all that by now, especially after everything that had happened.

"This is what makes the nagual a liability in the mortal world, and an asset to the Zodiac Houses."

But there was so much I still didn't know. I turned away from him and made my way over to the far side of the gazebo. I stared out over the lake and into the starry night. The light breeze brought a chill to my shoulders as I was reminded I would never live my life as a human again.

I turned around to face him. "Fine. Ok. I'll take your word for it. Why is it that there are fewer nagual? Why would they need saving? And who exactly are you?"

"It's the Dark Zodiac. I became a nagual over fifty years ago at the last transit—"

"Wait, you're what, seventy? You look like you're in your early twenties!"

"We age slowly."

"How long do we live?"

"The oldest of us is over three hundred years old, still alive and looks like he's sixty. But most of us return to the stars around two hundred and twenty years."

"And why does the Dark Zodiac want to kill us?"

"The short answer, they want to take over the mortal world and make humans into their puppets and slaves." He walked over and leaned on the column in front of me, running his hand through his thick, light-brown hair that fell just over his shoulders. Something about his serious expression told me I could believe him.

"Let me see your aura. I need to know you're telling me the truth." I peered at him. Instantly his aura was released from his seven chakras. His colors were gold and blue, and there was no hint of the dark-gray colors that indicated he was being malicious or deceptive.

"Thank you. Go on." My voice softened now that I knew he was being honest.

"As I was saying…" A tiny smile tugged at his lips, then disappeared. "They want to control the Zodiac Houses. They've been ruled by the royal zodiac families for centuries, and these families are governed by the Zol Decree sanctioned by the stars themselves. The decree declares that humans remain protected and untouched by Fae. Of course, there is some level of coexistence, such as the creation of the nagual. Most of what Fae do in the mortal world is good, and some is not so good." His brow creased. "But if our kind had free rein, life in the mortal world would be completely different. It would throw off the equilibrium of balance, power, equity and natural order." He looked out over the water as though searching for something, then turned back to me. "Do you remember when the Mayan calendar ended and everyone thought the world would end?"

I nodded. "Yes, that was in 2012. I remember my Titi telling me stories about that. She told me Pluto and Uranus squared seven times that year, and that combination called for destruction, transformation and unforeseen revolution. It felt like the astrological world braced for an apocalypse, but nothing like that happened."

"Right, nothing major happened in the mortal world. But here in Zol Stria, it was all of that. Four of the five factions of the Underworld were compromised."

My throat dried up like I had just swallowed a cup of flour. Now there was a collapsed Underworld I had to worry about? For the love of fuck!

"What do you mean, compromised?"

"The Underworld is divided into five factions, ruled over by the gods of the Underworld. You met the twins Hun-Cane and Vucub-Cane, they rule over Xibalba, the third faction."

"And I'm guessing Hades rules over the first?"

"Yes, of course."

He was dead serious, but I didn't care. I laughed until my sides ached. I wrapped my hands around my waist and kept the "you're fucking with me" smile on my face when I met his gaze again. But he wasn't budging. He still looked as serious as ever, and if anything, he looked offended.

"Fallen angels, gods, demigods and all manner of demonic beasts escaped and attacked the villages, towns and royal houses. It was what we called the Faellen War. They killed thousands of Fae, including countless children. After five years of massive destruction, we were able to round up many of them. Xibalba was the only faction that wasn't compromised. There are several masterminds that have managed to remain at large. We believe they're getting help from the inside, from someone in our Zodiac Houses." He paused for a moment and stood up straight.

"The Dark Zodiac have been growing in number. Building up their forces in the mortal world and recruiting Fae from this side of the Gates. They killed the five nagual before they could make it to the ceremony. They killed your aunt Lily to stop you from making it this far. And they will keep killing until they get what they want." His words stung a little less than the first time Damian had mentioned that Lily was murdered, but they stung nevertheless.

"How do you know all this?" I asked him as his aura turned black and red, streaking from his chest like lightning bolts. I kept my face expressionless, but I knew he had to be coping with a lot of emotional suffering.

"I lost my family in one of their attacks. My wife, my two children." He looked away. He gripped the railing so hard his knuckles turned white. "I've been tracking them ever since."

The red bolts that shot from his center were exactly the same as the ones that had shot out of Trent when he'd lost his mother. I recognized the rage in his grief. The desperation. I was curious how he'd come to have a family at all in this life, but I didn't dare ask.

"I'm sorry." I lowered my eyes and looked away. "But I have to ask. Why is it such a secret? Shouldn't everyone be after them?" My eyes met his again.

"Because we still don't know who is helping the Dark Zodiac. They have ties to all of the Houses in one form or another. We have our leads, but nothing is certain. The Houses tell us they're doing everything in their power to track them down and stop them. But none of them even tried to save the five nagual that died. They didn't try to save you. They still don't believe the Dark Zodiac is sophisticated enough to take down the nagual before they shift, but I know they are." He paced up and down the gazebo.

I fought the urge to roll my eyes and walk away. Annoyed as I was, I began to draw in the dark, and he could see it. I mean really, couldn't I just go and get Trent, join this magic school and be on my way? Why did I have to be part of some elaborate plan to take down a criminal organization in a world I'd just come to yesterday? FML.

"So, what do you want from me?" I said through clenched teeth.

"First of all, I wanted you to live, and that you did. Congratulations." He dipped his head slightly. He seemed genuinely pleased. "Second, I'm going to be your combat professor and I didn't want you to be shocked the first day in the Academy. And third…" He straightened his jacket and pulled his shoulders back. "I'm hoping you'll be motivated to join me in finding out who is running the Dark Zodiac and how we can take them down."

I took in a deep, stilling breath. Zayne was the second person to suspect my aunt was murdered, and finding her killer was motivation enough. Add to that the fact that I was behind in my training because she'd been killed, which put me at a huge disadvantage. Damian had told me the Academy was cutthroat and highly competitive. The Academy was hard even for the most well-prepared nagual, and even for them, completing it without a few scars was impossible.

But what about Trent? If I had joined the Aries Academy back when I was supposed to, I never would have met him and left him to the mercy of evil vampires. That whole ordeal was entirely my fault.

No, I wasn't just motivated to help Zayne. I was downright determined to burn the Dark Zodiac to ash for what they had done to me. I turned to him and unclenched my jaw. "Fuck yeah I am."

CHAPTER 13

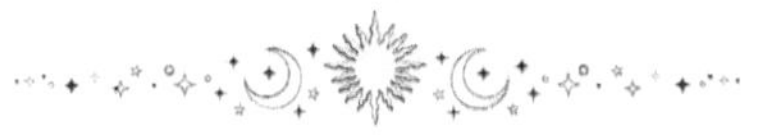

SASHA

The next morning, I dressed in the black leather battle gear. It was the only clothing in the closet besides the dresses, and it was badass. The pants were black and form-fitting, tapered at the bottom but not too tight. There were creases that ran diagonal across the thighs and a double buckle at the high waist. The short-sleeve black shirt was an even thinner leather, with two buckles on the mock-neck collar and an intricate design of the Aries glyph embroidered on the arm. But my favorite thing of all was the blade that hung from my side. I slid the knife out of the thick leather sheath. It caught the light as I turned it by the handle. The blade was thin and pointy, and I dared to bring my finger close to it. When I did, it brought a tiny bead of blood to my finger at the slightest touch.

I put my finger in my mouth, then returned the blade to its sheath. I went to the bathroom, and after cleaning up my finger, I pulled my hair up into a high ponytail and applied some warrior-esque eyeshadow and eyeliner. As I did, I noticed the green in my eyes shone brighter than ever before. Was that because I was over here, in Zol Stria?

I stole a look at the clock: half past six in the morning. I'd barely slept last night in anticipation of tracking Trent today. Damian said he would be at my door at six a.m. sharp. He was missing again. No surprise there. Orientation was at eight thirty, so I wanted time to track Trent and then convince Damian to get me to wherever he was before anyone noticed we were gone.

The sun hadn't yet risen, but the birds knew it would be soon. A flock of them pecked the grass in the garden right outside my door. Their colors were spectacular. Golden feathers shone in the faint light of the moon, still high in the sky. Their deep burgundy bodies had a satin sheen, and a few curved feathers bounced on the top of their heads. They sure looked otherworldly to me.

I continued on to the end of the row of villas where I knew Damian was staying. I knocked on the door. Then knocked again, and again. Nothing. I didn't want to wake up anyone around us, but he wouldn't answer.

"Are you even home?" I mumbled and peeked in the long window adjacent to the door. I didn't see anything.

He was going to throw my whole plan off schedule. I banged one more time and waited. Now I had to break in. I tried to open the door, but it was locked. I inspected the lock; it was unlike anything from the mortal world. I bet I could still pick it, but it might be easier to go through the window. I checked the window for any openings; they seemed sealed shut. If his villa was like mine, it had a second entry point from the inner corridor, through the kitchen. I made my way around back. In fact, it was like mine, and lucky for me, he'd left the door unlocked.

I didn't even knock. I walked right in and looked around.

He dressed impeccably and always smelled divine, and his office in Colombia was immaculate. So, it surprised me to find his villa in such a state. There were dirty plates in the kitchen; empty bottles of liquor on the table and counter; clothes thrown about messily. Including very lacy female lingerie. I was getting a hint that something sexual went down last night.

"Damian," I yelled loudly, more than a little annoyed. I heard a shuffle and grunt from upstairs. "Damian, you up there?"

More shuffling, more grunting.

I headed toward the stairs. "You are the biggest good-for-nothing, irresponsible, inconsiderate, worthless, hijo de puta shaman asshole I have ever had the misfortune of being paired with," I said to myself as I went step by step up the stairs. There were just not enough deprecating words in the world to describe the level of pendejo this guy was.

"Sasha?" he grumbled from behind the door at the top of the stairs. The same place the master suite was in my villa.

I thought I heard a women's voice in there, too. The door creaked open, and I slammed into it, hoping it would bang him in the head. I heard a thud and felt it hit him.

"Ouch, Sasha. What the fuck?" He sounded pissed.

A small smile played on my lips. "Sorry," I said insincerely. "Are you ready? We need to go."

"What? Where?"

He'd completely forgotten! My hands began burning from the building heat all over my body. The door opened wider, and I could tell from the crease of the blanket imprinted on his cheek that he had just woken up. I could smell the alcohol oozing off him. My gaze drifted past him to the woman on the bed. I recognized her. I'd met her at the reception.

"Oh no. You're not getting out of this because you had a night full of hot sex with the herb goddess of the stars. Get dressed. We are going to the Wall of Mirrors and tracking Trent, right now." I didn't scream or blast him with the heat gathered in my hands like I wanted to. I still needed him intact, but by the stars, it was hard controlling myself. He infuriated me to my core.

"Oh, yeah." He rubbed his head softly. "I'll be down in ten. Make coffee."

I rolled my eyes, and he slammed the door in my face.

"Five," I yelled back.

Chapter 14

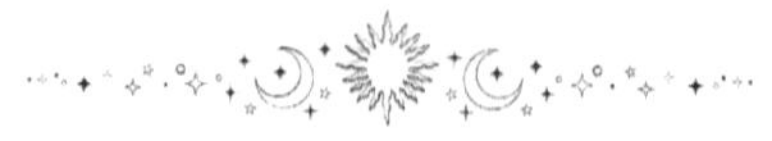

Damian

My head pounded with each step, as though nails were drilling in on four sides. The coffee only helped remotely. But Sasha seemed to ease up a little after she'd had a cup herself. As we approached the large wooden door to the Wall of Mirrors, I remembered the elixir Ixia had given me and drank it down. Alcoholic beverages on this side of the Gates were twice as potent as the ones on Earth, and I was no longer used to them. *That explains this major hangover.*

I felt Sasha's hateful stare on my back, and honestly, I didn't care. I had zero intention of sticking around Aries Gate after today. It was time to head back to Sierra Nevada in Colombia, where I believed Lily's killer was hiding. This was just one last favor for Lily's niece. One last thing to rid myself of the lingering guilt of almost leaving her to a fate worse than death.

"I can feel you staring daggers at my back. Strong emotions can be sensed by us all." My voice was as steady as the tide.

"Great. So now you know I think you're a self-centered fucktard. How could you not tell me that I'd never be able to go home again? That I would have zero contact with my old life? That I would never be able to make contact with Trent? How dare you!"

I stopped walking. No one had ever called me a fucktard. I shook my head and sighed. I turned to face her, waving my hand to conjure air magic and slam her half as hard as I wanted to against the wall next to the door. I stood directly in front of her as she writhed in place against the wall.

"Watch your mouth, young lady," I spat out.

"Only if you promise to watch yours." She winced as though something smelled terrible to her.

She was such a pain in the ass. I kept her there, grunting and resisting the air pressure that locked her in place. If she only knew a fraction of the magic she was supposed to know, she would be free right now.

"There are rules, and then there are rules. And I guess I'm going to have to spell it out for you. I am not known for following rules." I stepped back and breathed into my hand, taking a sniff. I grimaced and released her from my hold.

"I told you. I could smell every drink you had last night." She glared at me, defiance gleaming in her eyes. "Anyone ever tell you that you have a drinking problem?"

"The only problem I have is you," I growled. My head pounded even harder from the use of my powers while recovering from a hangover.

"So, you're telling me I can contact them?"

"No, I'm telling you I don't care what you do."

I stepped toward the door, and it creaked open on its own before us, by way of magical recognition. I entered, Sasha directly at my side. This space was only accessible by the Zol Sen and shamans of my rank because of the powerful magical properties of the mirrors themselves. Finally, her attention shifted away from me and onto the dimly lit expanse before us.

The room was cool and dark, rich with the smell of aged wood and bricks. You could feel your skin prickle as you entered; the air was thick with the ancient spells that had settled into the physical properties of the mirrors and had made them come alive.

It had been a while since I had been here. The Capricorn shaman was standing at one of the seventy-seven mirrors along the sixteen-foot wall at the far end of the room. Each of the mirrors had been created by the original seventy-seventh shaman over five thousand years ago, before the beginning of recorded history. The mirrors created a channel between Zol Stria and Earth. Some were hanging on the wall; others were suspended in the air with magic.

"There are so many, how do I know which one to use?" Sasha prodded me impatiently.

I scratched my beard, the elixir finally doing its part to soothe the banging in my head. "That one." I pointed to the center of the room, to one of the six Aries mirrors. "See the mirrors that have the Aries glyph? You'll have more clarity using the mirror of your same birth sign."

She began to walk toward it, and I grabbed her arm. Her face turned to me sharply.

"You ready? You might not like what you see."

Her face softened and her jaw unclenched. She nodded slowly and approached the mirror cautiously this time.

"What do I do now?" She stood in front of an oval mirror about four feet tall and three feet wide. Two winged dragons made up the silver frame, their faces touching at the top and their wings cascading down the sides to join at the tails.

"Same thing you did when you sought him out back home. Just use your mind to search for him in the mirror. He will appear."

Her eyebrows pinched and she hesitated. "Back home I did a whole meditation thing in my mind. I didn't use a mirror. I dove into a lake that I visualized and when I left the lake..." Her voice trailed off. "When I left the lake, I looked at my reflection in it. But I was in the form of the nagual." Her eyes opened wide with tempered excitement. "So, this is just like the mirror of my visualizations? I can just skip ahead to that part?"

"Yes, exactly," I said.

I watched her chest rise as she filled her lungs with air. She took one step closer to the Aries dragon mirror. She closed her eyes for a few stilling heartbeats, and I watched the shadows curl around her arms and face. She was getting better at commanding them. The moment she opened her eyes, they were glowing green. I grunted and shifted on my feet. Truth be told, I hadn't expect her to get it right the first time, especially considering her lack of training. Which was more than a little my fault. I pushed that out of my mind. No use feeling guilty about any of that now.

I followed her gaze into the mirror and watched as Trent had quite the night with the red-headed vampire. They seemed to be having a good time until she decided it was time to cleave into his neck in a fit of monstrous rage. The veins around her eyes turned a dark red, her pupils dilated and her teeth were sharp and beastly. She was a Dark Vampire. Those nonconformists believed they were owed dominion over humans: because human blood gave them extraordinary powers, heightened senses and longer life spans, they believed they should have the right to feast on human blood as much as they wanted. They were who the Zol Houses believed to be most closely affiliated with the Dark Zodiac. They were the reason I'd been in Colombia in the first place.

Sasha's face was expressionless, save the sadness in her eyes. When looking in the mirror, she had to remain focused on drawing in the power of the shadows while channeling Trent's aura. It was like walking on a high beam. One thought or movement in the wrong direction and you would lose alignment with the vision. She seemed to instinctively know this because she stood as still as a statue.

I turned back to the mirror and watched as Solana offered her wrist to him, explaining that he could either become a Dark Vampire or remain human and take his chances at dying. After a short heartbeat, he drank the blood thirstily from her wrist, and we watched as he writhed and screamed in pain as his body contorted on the floor. She seemed bored with him and left the room. Several men and women came in a few moments after. They picked him up and placed him in restraints as his muscles contracted and his face strained in agony. They hauled him out and into a large black trailer just outside the building.

"That was last night. Search for him now, Sasha," I offered her, but I knew what came next wouldn't be anything good.

Her hands were balled into fists at her side, and I could see her pulling in many more shadows than she needed. The vision shifted to right now, and the mirror turned black. Sasha blinked several times. Nothing changed.

"What? What happened?" she asked desperately.

"He's locked in a lead chamber. He could be in there for some time. We can't get readings through lead." Thankfully the elixir had kicked in because she went to punch the mirror, and because of our bond, I anticipated her move and blocked her. No longer retracting her aura, a whirlwind of colors and crackling energy erupted from her center as she unraveled into one big emotional wreck.

"All your guards are down and you're spiraling. It's more dangerous to do that here in Zol Stria than anywhere else in the universe," I said roughly. The Cancer shaman was looking over at us right now, a bit too judgmentally, if you asked me.

Sasha quickly retracted her aura and replaced the deflector spell, pulling her spirit together. Yet, her eyes gave away her desperation.

"How. Do. I. Find. Him?" she bit out through gritted teeth, tears swelling in her eyes.

"You don't, Sasha. Not now. It will take several full moons for him to transform into a Dark Vampire. You understand, right?" I stepped back and raised my palms in case she decided to punch me. I wasn't sure how much she knew about the vampire change cycle. "She has to feed him as he changes. Even if—by some miracle—you find him right now, you would kill him if you removed him from the chamber and separated him from his maker. He will be completely and forever changed, and he will be immortal. You may not even want to find him if you do. She will become his mentor, and he will be a completely different creature by the time you find him."

She shook her head quickly. Her eyes darted to the ground, and she raised her hands to the sides of her head, pressing them against her temples while she took a stilling breath. The shadow tornados that once spun fervently at her sides subsided and dissipated in the air.

She fell to her knees and sobbed, staring at her hands that lay open on her thighs. I didn't know what to say. I was the absolute worst motivational speech giver in the thirteen realms.

"You'll be late for orientation," I managed to grunt out after she wiped her nose on her sleeve and sniffled. She looked up at me with an all-too-familiar sadness. The same festering sadness that had ripped my soul to a thousand pieces when Lily died. I felt the pull of our bond, and my aura released as if on reflex. I reached out to comfort her with my white energy.

"I, uh, I'm sorry..." Stupid thing to say.

"I know." She stood up, smoothed out her leathers and narrowed her eyes. In a blink of an eye, she transformed. No longer a broken woman crying on the floor, now she looked like a fierce warrior. "Now I want to see Nikki. My friend from back home. I want to see my mother. I need to know they're ok." Her gaze was unwavering.

"Have a look, then. One by one, take your time and call them into your mind. As you do, they will appear. But do this later. Trust me, you don't want to be late on your first day," I growled at her. It was time she started to listen.

She stepped toward me in a challenge, then hesitated and stepped back. "Let's go to orientation, then. Lead the way."

Chapter 15

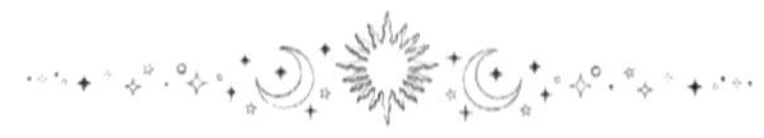

Sasha

Trent had chosen life as a Dark Vampire over death, and in some twisted romantic fantasy in my mind, that meant he'd chosen me. I told myself he'd done it just so he could see me again. So that there could be a chance for us to make our way to one another. I had to believe that, especially now. It was all my fault. Trent was alive, and that meant I wasn't alone. He might be a dark and scary vampire, but what the fuck, I was kind of scary myself. We could be broken together after his transformation. I would be counting the days.

But for right now, I had to sit in this auditorium of glass and sky. The modern design seemed a direct contrast to the old-world design of the rest of the buildings, save for the artifacts placed at the end of the rows of seats. I sat in the section with the Scorpio glyph, as I was instructed. At my desk was an electronic device that reminded me of the smartphones back home, only it had my Aries sign lit as the lock screen. I gazed around and took in the other attendees. The auditorium was full; there must have been about three hundred Fae seated around the rotunda in the elevated seating arrangement.

I saw everything from different hair colors and pointed ears to winged centaurs. I caught sight of a few of the other nagual. They weren't hard to miss, as they were all wearing the same black battle gear and held the most rigid postures of everyone in attendance. We were the only Fae in this gear. They were laser-focused on the podium and not chitchatting, looking around the room or engrossed by what appeared to be cell phones, like the majority of the group.

What an intimidating bunch. Capricorn's arms were massive, and he must have been well over six feet tall, his ebony skin a striking contrast to his short, immaculately trimmed, platinum-blond hair. The Virgo nagual straight up looked like a hot Viking with a thick blond beard. The Scorpio nagual must have been an athlete considering how the black leather material clung to her defined arms and legs. Of course, there was my new friend, beautiful and strong Jenna, in the Libra section. Before I could study the others there was a loud crack of thunder inside the auditorium.

"Great, now that I have your attention, welcome to your first day at Aries Academy. I'm Professor Zendtra and as you may have noticed, I am a Thunder Mage." Bolts of purple-and-white lightning coiled around her arms and concentrated at her palms. When it subsided, she began speaking. "The semester begins today, on the first day of the Lunar New Year. This happens to be the year of the Tiger and wouldn't you know, we have the feline Fae in attendance this semester. This is very special indeed, because the nagual only attend the Academy every fifty years when they are reborn."

Everyone's eyes turned to the seven of us. The girl next to me had big, round purple eyes that looked at me in wonder. She gave me a shy smile when I returned her gaze. It felt strange to have so many eyes on me.

"You'll have plenty of time to get to know them later. Today we're going over everything you need to know to excel at Aries. First, let's review the curriculum. It's designed around the secondary progression and solar arc directions of your individual natal chart. You'll be matched in classes with students within the same predictive influences to optimize your learning potential."

"What are these devices for?" I whispered to the girl with the purple eyes, gesturing to the cell-phone-like device. The professor went on talking about specialized programs and a lunar school system.

"That's your oracle." She pulled hers toward her and opened to an interface much like the cell phones we used back home. She clicked on an app that opened up her curriculum, and I could see all her classes listed on it.

I lifted my device and started flicking at the icons. Technology. Finally, something I understood.

Professor Zendtra went on for a while longer, and to me, this school system made much more sense than the ones back home. She ended the session and the Fae students spilled out of the large glass doors. According to my oracle, I wasn't due to go to another class for about an hour.

Jenna bounced up next to me. "Hey girl, how are you?"

I returned her smile and relaxed my shoulders a bit. "Oh hey. I'm good. Just feeling a bit stiff in this uniform. Is it really necessary for our classes?" I turned my head from side to side. It wasn't that the suit was uncomfortable, but it drew a lot of looks and singled us out from the others.

"Nah. This was just for today so everyone would know we were nagual. I think they like to show us off. You can wear regular clothes tomorrow. See." She pulled out her oracle and opened up a calendar. "Here, it shows you the schedule and the clothing needed each day, depending on the curriculum."

"Oh good. Thanks. I'm feeling kind of lost here." I gave Jenna an uneasy smile.

Suddenly a strong canine scent filled my nostrils. When I looked over at Jenna, I could tell she'd noticed it, too. I turned my gaze to the source of the scent. It was coming from a group of guys and girls hanging and joking over by an ornate water fountain, about a hundred feet away from us.

"What's that smell?" I asked her. It didn't exactly stink, but it did put me on high alert.

"Those are the Zol Wolves. They're one of the most common Fae of all of us. There are packs everywhere. Each of Zol Stria's twelve Houses can have up to ten packs."

One of the largest among the rowdy group of Zol Wolves stood up. He stopped laughing with his friends and glared at us.

I held my stance and glared right back at him. "Do I have to worry about them?" From this distance it was hard to tell if the tall, meaty, hard-looking guy was staring me down because he wanted to get in my pants or because he was threatened by me.

Just then a few of the other nagual walked up to us on the veranda. "You don't have to worry about them, or anyone." The Capricorn nagual addressed me but didn't take his eyes off the Zol Wolf.

"Good to know." I shifted my eyes to the wall—I mean man—standing before me.

"You're a nagual, and the only Fae that can take you in your jaguar form are the twin gods who created you." His eyes met mine for a heartbeat, then he laughed heartily. I felt that. He seemed at ease with it all. "I'm Lex, that's Eliana, Andres, Bjorn, Leo, and I believe you met Jenna last night."

I looked around at them, and suddenly I was hit with déjà vu. This was just like the dream I'd had before all of this started. Back when I was dating Omar, I'd dreamt of a group of jaguars together. I remembered thinking how strange it was because cats were generally solitary creatures. Yet unlike my dream, I wasn't running away from them. I was one of them, and I had a hundred questions.

"Great to meet you guys. I'm Sasha. Now can someone please tell me, where is the cafeteria?"

That's when Eliana, a dark-haired, tan-skinned and full-lipped young woman looped her arm in mine. "Come with me. The food here is incredible."

We all walked together to the expansive cafeteria. The room was airy with a large, vaulted ceiling and a blend of white and natural wood colors accenting the space. There was such a variety of options, from a fresh sushi selection to warm southern meals to a Mexican-themed taco bar. How would I ever choose? I went for the hummus, grape leaves and chicken kabobs, then met Jenna and Eliana back at the table. The guys were still heaping loads of food on their plates.

"I saw you at the reception last night. Why did you leave so early?" Eliana asked, taking a bite out of a tahini-yogurt-dipped carrot stick.

I glanced quickly at Jenna then back at my food. "I didn't know we would never see anyone from our old lives again. Jenna told me and I was shocked. I mean, my shaman never outright told me." My face turned pale, and I shifted food around my plate absently.

"That's the hardest part about all this. I know. But at least you can see them through mirrors," she said encouragingly. I could tell she was trying to make me feel better. "You can also speak to the Zol Sen about their star alignments. A huge bonus about being here is that you can help them out on their paths."

My ears perked up. "Help them out, how do you mean?"

"Yeah well, if they say they want something in alignment with their purpose, the Zol Sen will help you make sure they get it. It's a way to fill the void of them losing you and to make good on your karmic influence on their life. It's what the Zol Sen call 'restoring cosmic balance.' My little sister wants to be an artist, so I'm going to make sure she gets in all the best schools back home and lands the best jobs."

I smiled at that thought. I might not be able to be in their lives anymore, but I was glad I could still help them from over here. Especially Nikki, her mom, my mom and Elio. And what about Trent? Did he get any extra help considering he was becoming a vampire?

"Where was home for you guys?" My gaze shifted between the two of them.

"I'm from Jamaica," Jenna said, taking a sip of her drink.

"I thought so." I chuckled, happy I'd gotten her accent right.

"I'm from LA but I was born in Venezuela." Eliana grinned at me. "And you're from Miami, right? Look at us. Surviving and shit. I heard it was even harder for you, since your shaman abandoned you. What a dick."

I scooped hummus onto a slice of pita bread, suddenly unable to actually lift the bread and put it in my mouth. I guess everyone knew what Damian had done.

"Well, you're here now. We can help you catch up with everything you missed. The stars brought us together for a reason, right?" Jenna said, and they both nodded at me.

"Definitely. Anyway, you made it this far basically on your own. And my shaman told me you were in the military." Eliana's eyes opened wide. "I bet you could even show us a thing or two about real grit."

They were much more welcoming than I thought they would be. "Why are you guys being so nice?" I mean, they didn't have to be nice to me at all.

"Girl, because I saw how you moved on that dance floor. I knew we would be homies after that." She snorted a laugh, then looked at me seriously. "Really though, my shaman told me that being a nagual is a long, lonely road, and honestly, I don't want it to be. I left a huge family back home. If we've got to have the most difficult job of all the Fae, then why can't it at least be fun?"

There was a flicker of hope somewhere in the darkness of my heart. It flashed before me for just a second, and I held on to that.

Chapter 16

Sasha

More than six months had passed, and I still couldn't find Trent through the Wall of Mirrors. Not a moment passed that I didn't think about him and of the mayhem that had brought me here, but I got better at hiding it. I didn't want to bring all of that turmoil to this magical place that was ripe with possibility. Was I wrong to go on living knowing the havoc I'd left behind? I contemplated the alternative. Shutting myself down. Skipping classes and not owning any of my responsibilities, which was a lot like what I'd done after my ex, the mafia king, had been arrested back home. Which was the same kind of wallowing I saw Damian doing. Same shit I saw my dad do. No, I wouldn't be like either of them. My life had to go on.

This was a fresh start, like it or not, and I didn't see how escaping right now to go and find him would help matters. I did some research of my own, and what Damian had told me checked out with what I saw in the mirror. So, I would have to wait. Even still, a pang of guilt would set in at just that thought, and bile would rise in my throat. My focus would shift in combat training and a blow would be driven into my side. I couldn't afford to lose my focus.

Training here was on a whole other level. In our human forms, we were thrown into a colosseum where the gladiator fights took place. The first time it happened, I was like— what the fuck am I doing here? Skilled fighters came at us from every angle. I got to know my nagual best under the pressure of such intense physical training. We learned how to shift when we were under threat. At first it was hard, then it got easier. Our goal was to shift under five seconds; we weren't there yet.

It took a lot for me to be confident in what I had been told, which was that our skin was impenetrable. It was protected by a metaphysical spell that made us more like spirits than physical creatures. That spell was coded into our DNA. Lose your focus as a human for less than a second, shift just a moment too late, and you either got torn into by your opponent or even killed. Our human form was our only weakness, but even then, we could still summon our elemental magic.

Nagual were given specialized classes in the way of the Fae, since all of us didn't know the culture very well. That is, all of us except the Virgo nagual, because he'd had the benefit of knowing his shaman since he was two. I was very lost and had to review the videos they'd assigned to me. But I caught up quickly.

I understood the variety of Fae that existed and their complex social systems. I was especially interested in learning about vampires. After my experience with Grange and then Solana, I thought they were an entire evil species of Fae. I learned that they were nowhere near the worst of them. In fact, most vampires lived normal, non-confrontational lives with a whole movement of human-friendly populations, living primarily off the blood of animals. And the more evolved vampires were able to eat the food of Zol Stria with no digestive problems. They were no longer seen as the undead, but instead valued as immortals.

And then there were the conservatives, those who held the centuries-long belief that vampires were entitled to human feeding. Particularly because human blood super-charged their abilities. It made them faster, allowed them to glamor others and heightened all of their senses. This was their justification for breaking off from more progressive points of view. Although the governing systems of each of the Houses varied significantly, on this matter they did not budge. The law stood that vampires were not to eat humans. Becoming a nagual was about enforcing these laws.

Karma is a nagual named Sasha.

I knew then exactly who I was coming for.

We also learned about magic, and it was the magic systems that intrigued me almost as much as my obsession with vampires. Again, I was way behind the others and mostly lost in class, but I took detailed notes and looked up everything

I didn't understand in the evenings. Jenna and Eliana came over once a week to tutor me. I was really getting to like them a lot.

Surprisingly, Damian was still in town. He checked in on me every now and then but nothing major.

One day, I ran into him in the cafe. I had expected him to disappear right after the ritual, and when I asked him what was keeping him here, all he said was that it was the stars.

"What do you mean, the stars?"

"The stars compel us. They are always guiding us. Sending us on a path. Pulling us in one direction or another. The more you age and mature, and the more aligned you are with your purpose, the louder the call. Yet even still, we have a choice. We can ignore the call to the path or follow it. Right now, I have decided to stay on the path. I might change my mind though." He sipped his coffee and sat back in his chair, rubbing his scruffy beard. His eyes betrayed his many years and secrets, while his skin was smooth and fresh. Well, the stars had brought me here, so I guessed I understood what he'd meant about that.

Day after day I kept my head buried in the books. It was better to fill my mind with what I needed to learn than spend any time considering what was happening to Trent. There were a few subjects that numbed the deep abyss of pain. One of them was magical systems. It was fascinating and confusing at the same time.

Some Fae, like the faeries, were born wielding magic, and it was through their connection with the cosmos that they changed and channeled elements to create spells. Their magic was harmonious with nature, pulling the energy from the moon and the stars to manifest their will. They were conduits of change and transformation in Zol Stria, and through their very existence they balanced the natural systems on Earth. The Faerie realms were sacred, left untouched by the rest of the population. Much of what they did, and how they lived, was intentionally left unstudied.

My eyes were itchy and dry from staring at the oracle too long. It was well past midnight, and I was still studying. I walked over to the kitchen and poured myself a glass of water. It was incredible how much I still had to learn. As I peered out the kitchen window, over the lush greenery of the moonlit garden, I tried to comprehend the complexity of the system designed by the Zol Sen.

They'd been the guys in the white robes at my transformation ceremony. They were something like high priests and priestesses, and they were the conduits of the stars on Earth. They were not just well-read on how the planetary systems ascended and progressed, transitioned and descended, but they felt the changes in their bones.

One could not learn to become a Zol Sen; they were born into their role, just like the nagual. Yet they were born on this side of the Gates— within Zol Stria. They had the unique ability to understand the path of every single Fae they came across, watching it map out in their minds. Where they would stray, why they would falter, all in the fulfillment of the Soul Contract that outlined the evolution and growth the Fae had to accomplish within their long lives.

The Zol Sen also knew the star paths for everyone on Earth. They analyzed and studied each path, marking those who fulfilled their destinies and those who didn't. They recorded the character traits of the individuals who did each. There were libraries full of their studies, and an endless number of academic journals detailed the laws that governed the zodiac. It was when I found myself buried in some of these findings that I realized everything we understood about the laws of the universe was wrong. *If my path was predestined by the zodiac, why was it so cruel? Why is Damian such a dickface?*

I turned off the lights and trudged up the stairs to bed. I just needed to push out of my brain the thoughts of my misery, failures and many mistakes long enough to get in bed. Tomorrow was battle training, and I could take out all my aggravation in the colosseum.

CHAPTER 17

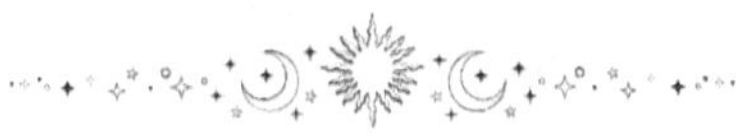

DAMIAN

Time began to fade with the passing of the moons. I was at the seaside bar Antlia's, having a whiskey sour while watching the fire pixies fight over a flying fish. You could hear them bicker and curse at each other while they yanked and pulled it to pieces. Nobody won. Fire pixies didn't live very long, just under a year. It was their wicked tempers that burned out their lot so fast. I was sure of it.

I took another slow sip of my fifth or sixth drink and called it a night. Bid my goodnights to the barkeep whose hair was spiked in an impressive purple-and-black mohawk. If I came back in another life, I wanted to be him.

It was a quiet night, and I took the long walk home by the ocean. The cool, salty breeze curled around me, and I breathed it in deep. There, at the bottom of my breath. That was where I remembered her, and the baby she was carrying in her belly the night her plane went down. The stars were going to make me a father, until fate took her from me and I lost everything that had ever mattered. It had been over ten years, and yet, it was just like yesterday. I carried them both with me, because if they couldn't live in this world, they would live in my heart.

Shamans couldn't marry humans. We were forbidden from directly influencing the lives of people on Earth because of the trouble it'd caused in the past. But then I met Lily, and I fell in love. I couldn't tell anyone. She was my secret, and I preferred it that way anyway. This life as a shaman was filled with war and death.

I promised myself that I would find her killer if it was the last thing I ever did. Yet after ten years of searching, I had found nothing. Now that my path brought me back to Zol Stria, I had to trust that the answers were here.

I stopped at an overlook just a few feet from the bar. I could still hear the plates clattering as the voices carried through the air. I stared out at the moonlit waves that flickered on and off in the distance. The Dark Vampires were my biggest lead on Earth. They were why Sasha had found me in Colombia. A large coven had been detected in the Sierra Nevada Mountains, where they could hide their supernatural abilities. The mountains were the epicenter for the ley lines of the region, which was why a large amount of paranormal energy united and intensified in that area. This kept the Dark Vampires' paranormal energy from being detected by the Joint Celestial Command. I figured if anyone wanted the nagual dead, it was them.

"Early night?" I heard a voice say. I was so deep in thought I'd barely heard him.

"Hey, hombre. Dimelo," I said. "I didn't see you walk up. Yeah, early night."

It was Zayne, from the last generation of nagual that had passed through the Gates. He'd gone through a tough time after the Faellen War—many of us had. After I'd lost Lily and our unborn child, I'd started to understand his pain a little bit better. His shaman and I studied together closely, and we had been good friends. We kept in close contact as he began preparing Zayne for his transformation and I watched Zayne grow into the nagual he is now.

The death of his own family hardened him, and his presence always felt predatory. Stories of his history of assassinations and battles were often whispered in the hallways and corridors at the Academy. Some of the stories were so monstrous that they would've been hard to believe, if I hadn't seen one with my own eyes.

"Come back in the bar, I'll get the next round. I wanted to talk to you about a few things," Zayne said as his eyes peered into me, and his aura quickly flashed his true colors. It was our way of showing the other that we were trying to be real with them. No bullshit.

"Alright, yeah. If you're buying." We sat at a table outside, close to the ocean, and I felt Zayne put up a deflector spell as soon as we sat down with our drinks. "What's on your mind?"

I could count on one hand all the men I trusted in Zol Stria and Zayne was among them. He was one of our most skilled nagual and detained some of Zol Stria's most notorious criminals. Everything changed after he'd lost his family. Some say that he obliterated every target starting by shredding open his enemies with the speed of thunderclap. They say he asked to be assigned to every battle, demon and death mission in the shadows just to satiate his thirst for blood. Some of his captures, after being documented and processed, went missing. Others were so badly beaten they couldn't speak.

The Zol Sen prayed for him and gave him solace at the Zol Temple for two moons. But he didn't care, at least that's what they say. Of all the nagual, he had the most ever deaths documented as self-defense. And because Zayne is a smart male, he covered his tracks well, so none of it could be pinned on him.

Even still, the Zol Council decided to take him off the tactical teams and make him a professor at the Academy.

"I've been working with Sasha over the past three moons. She's bright. Strong. Very capable. But there's a huge gap in her confidence level. I can see it every time she shifts. She takes too long, and the process is more painful than it is with the others. And certainly, more painful than it needs to be. You know that's all your fault, right? The others had more than two years to prepare." His brows furrowed.

I rubbed the back of my neck and leaned forward. "I know... It... I..." I searched for the words, but I couldn't explain it to him. I didn't want to.

"You what?" He inclined his head. "Fell in love with her aunt, she died, and you've been looking for her killer instead of training Sasha for all of this?"

I hadn't seen this coming, and I usually saw things coming. I narrowed my eyes at him and took a long swig from the drink. "Something like that."

I had to be honest with myself. All my leads had dried up, and if he was confronting me about all this, it might be because he had something valuable to share. Instead of standing up and walking away like I wanted to, I sat there to hear him out.

"You aren't fooling anyone, Damian. It's pretty obvious that you went missing right after Lily died, at least to those of us familiar with your assignment. And I get why you didn't just come out with it, given that the Zol Sen forbid human and

Fae love. But you need to get your head out of your ass because your approach is leading you nowhere and you know it."

I shifted in my chair and ran a hand through my hair. A cool breeze blew and rocked the hanging lanterns back and forth.

"Look, Zayne, I don't know what you think you know, but it's none of your fucking business." I clenched my teeth. I would find Lily's killer if it was the last thing I ever did.

"I know, man, I know. It hurts and it will never stop hurting. My family was killed, too. Iyana was the best mother to our kids. And beautiful Zoey and Zavier, they didn't deserve to die so young. Their path had just begun. I know your pain, too well." Zayne took a deep breath and leaned in. Even though he had a strong deflector spell up, he still lowered his voice. "I think the same people who killed Lily killed my family." Zayne flashed his aura at me again, to show me there were no shadows lacing his chakras. There was no deceit in his words. He truly believed this to be fact.

The tension in my back eased, and I unclenched my jaw. I shifted my gaze to our surroundings, making sure no one was listening. I lifted a ward of protection around his deflector spell so I would be warned if anyone tried to move through it.

"What do you mean?" I kept my voice calm and steady. My face wore a bored mask. I wouldn't let anyone watching us see that I was intrigued by what he wanted to tell me.

For the next hour Zayne explained everything he knew about the Dark Zodiac and how he believed they were behind the nagual killings. He explained how he wanted to bring Sasha in on a mission across the Gates to where he had tracked the Dark Fae. He said it was because of how hard she worked to cross the Gates. She worked harder than any of the other nagual, had all the odds stacked against her and of all of those that he tried to save, she was the one that made it. He trusted her instincts the most. We would convince the Council that we would leverage the mission as a hands-on training exercise to accelerate her development in the program.

"Why not come to me with this earlier?" I asked.

"I tried, man. I tried. Your wards are too secure. It was clear you didn't want to be found."

I nodded in agreement. I didn't.

"Let's do it. When do we go?" My heart started to beat just a little bit faster at the possibility of being that much closer to satisfying the restless need for revenge.

"I'm on the calendar with the Council during the next lunar cycle. Once Sasha qualifies in the arena and we have the Council's approval, we'll go."

"You sneaky bastard." I sat back in my chair and scratched my beard. "You knew I would agree, otherwise you wouldn't have already set the calendar with the Council." I gave a roguish grin and nodded in agreement.

"Hey, I was being optimistic." He grinned.

"Glad that's settled." I sighed. "Let's have another drink."

CHAPTER 18

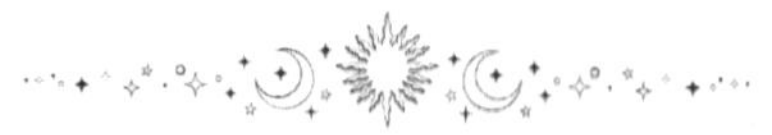

DAMIAN

"Y*ou're exactly where I want you*

Exactly where I don't even care

What anyone is thinking

Just let them stare, stare

You're exactly..."

I fumbled with the lock at the door of my villa while singing the song the band had been playing when we'd left. It was late, but the sun wasn't up yet. Zayne had kept buying me rounds, and I fucking let him. Yeah. It was about time I had something to celebrate. Something to look forward to. That guy. Thanks to that guy, it wouldn't be that much longer. I was closer. I would soon be stabbing some Dark Fae in the —

"What took you so long?"

Fuck. My wards. Sometimes when I got drunk, I couldn't feel my wards get triggered. Ixia had let herself in. Well, at least it was her and not a burglar. She dimly lit the room with a sweep of her hand. She was wearing white lace lingerie that accented her smooth, golden-caramel skin. Her long legs draped across the couch, and her hair fell loose around her shoulders. Her eyebrows were creased, and her eyes were squinting slightly. She must have been asleep when I'd come in.

"Why would you just let yourself in, Ixia? We aren't back together." The words fumbled out, and I shuffled my feet toward her, knowing if she even tried to seduce me, I would be willing. I was too excited about the lead on Lily to be upset about this, or anything else. But I didn't want Ixia to get any ideas that we were a couple. That wasn't going to happen.

"Oh, I know, Damian. Don't trip, ok? I came over because I was thinking about you and when I tried the door, it was open, so I let myself in. I thought you'd be home soon so I waited here on the couch and fell asleep. That's all. No big deal. I can leave if you want me to." As she said that last bit, she swept back her hair to reveal her neck and cleavage. It was enough to make me hard, pressure rising in my crotch. Her golden eyes fixed on me as she dragged her gaze across my chest and up to my lips. She opened her mouth, and her chest heaved slowly as she inhaled, biting down on her lip on the exhale.

"It's fine. Just next time..." I walked over to where she was lying on the couch. "Next time let me know you're coming."

I licked my lips, wanting to see her chest heave again. My hands wanted to feel the warmth I could tell was growing between her legs. Magic drew on energy, and the sexual desires between Fae generated some of the most powerful energy of all. The more powerful the Fae, the more desirable the energy, and Ixia's energy was damn addicting. She knew it. She could have her choice of the other shaman, the vicars and lords of Zol Stria, but she was too independent for that. Her position as Council Advisor and Zol Botanist was her true love. Nothing came between her and her work.

I sat down next to her, and she shifted to the side.

"So, what did you want? Why did you come?" I grazed my thumb softly against her chest, back and forth slowly as I pushed down the fabric of her silky camisole, feeling the rise of her breast against my hand. My eyes matched the rise and fall of her breaths, but I avoided meeting her gaze for fear it would give something away about what I knew. About the hunt I would be going on.

"Are you really asking me that?" She released a breathy laugh.

I leaned in closer and moved my hands to the thin spaghetti straps on her shoulders. I pulled them both down as I kissed her where they once were. My tongue licked along the goosebumps that began to line her neck. As I brought my face up, I kept my gaze off her eyes and on her lips. A dark smile played there. I brought my lips closer to hers and pressed, and when I pulled back my lips curled upward into a smile. She clawed a hand into my hair, and that was precisely when

I knew how bad she wanted me. The whole time she'd been sitting here waiting for me, she'd been wanting me.

"Yes. I'm really asking you. Why did you come?" I moved my hand down her side, gently along the outside of her white silk top.

She looked away. "You're drunk." She grabbed my hand and stopped me from moving it up and between her legs, where it was headed.

"So what? I wasn't expecting you." I turned my head and began kissing her neck again. "You'll forget everything bothering you in just a second."

She released my hand and let out a soft moan as she threw her head back. A growl reverberated in my throat as I considered all of the things I would soon be doing to her. I moved my hands up and down her body, gripping her tightly as I nibbled on her ear. Her breath became rapid and all sensation rushed south.

I was ready to disappear into Ixia, the opposite of Lily. Where Lily made me feel whole, alive and like a man that deserved love, Ixia only cared about how she felt and the deliciously addicting pleasure of our sexual connection. I had closed myself off from everyone. From all my responsibilities. From love. But a man still had needs. Now, this was about both of us getting what we needed.

I gripped her arms and willed magic to my fingertips. I was no longer drunk, the magic rushing to the surface flushing out the toxins in my blood. My hands began to glow as they made contact with her arms, and energy buzzed from me to her. She moaned loader and groaned out my name. I licked my lips in anticipation of her reaction.

She began to blend her magic with mine. The energy filled my mouth with the taste of flowers, honey and earth. She and the plants were one, and I could taste it. Our combined energy grew from the friction of our interlaced magic, which swirled in wisps of golden air all around us. Several heartbeats passed, and the magic dissipated away, fusing into our skin. I opened my eyes and met hers.

"'The pleasure of our magic is the vessel that brings us the strength of the stars,'" she whispered.

"So now you're quoting the Zol Sen. I'm going to fuck you, Ixia. Pretty soon you'll be moaning so hard you can't quote anything." I pulled off my shirt and stood in front of her, bare-chested.

She slid her hands around my abs and chest, then met her lips to my flesh as she moved her hands down and unzipped my pants. She brought them down, and I stepped out of them. I reached for her arms, and when I touched her skin, it tingled from the charge of our combined magical energy. She squirmed in response. **I'm going to take her right here on the couch.**

She took my hard cock in her hands, rhythmically stroking it and showering it with kisses. I moved my body down, ready to slide into her, but she stopped me. She pushed me back and stood up. She eased her body in slow, sultry movements to stand in front of me and placed both hands firmly on the contours of my chest. With a seductive smirk on her lips, she pushed me down on the couch.

Fine, I get it. You want to be in control. I slid my hands over her breasts and took her nipple into my mouth, licking and nibbling it in circles. One hand moved down to feel the warmth between her legs, wet and aching for me to enter her. I removed her panties and slid my fingers round her apex until she moaned.

Her moan grew louder, and she moved my hand aside, sliding herself on top of me. Another low growl escaped my lips, and I reached one hand into her hair, fisting it in between my fingers. I moved her head to the side and pressed my lips hard against her neck, my teeth clenching as she rocked on top of me, up and down. Up and down.

I grabbed her ass tightly with both hands, and she whispered, "Yes." I lifted into her, first by matching her rhythm then faster and harder than she could ever go. She began to yell, "Yes. Yes. Yes!" and her body erupted in a tremor. I erupted in response.

She collapsed on top of me and said breathlessly, "Let's go upstairs."

I returned her sultry smile with one of my own. "I'm glad you said that because I'm just getting started."

Chapter 19

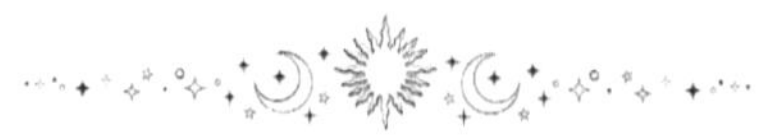

Sasha

I entered the arena with Jenna at my side. Jenna was a Libra, the sign of partnership, and I was an Aries, the sign of self. We were polarities, meaning we were opposites. The Zol Sen's guiding principles were that there were advantages in finding balance. Since Jenna and I had polar-opposite behaviors, we would complement each other the best on the battlefield, which was why we were being paired together.

We were the only two surviving nagual with polarizing signs. At first, I didn't quite agree with the theory. I'd even told her I thought polarity matching was stupid and that they should match me with Lex, because of his quarterback size I thought it would make us a more formidable team. I especially regretted our pairing when she annoyed me with wanting to plan our every move.

"Before I flank him to the right, you'll distract him with a fire burst at his heels so I can corner him toward the far end of the arena," Jenna said, as we stood at the edge of the sandy floor watching Bjorn and Axel train with the professor. It was our first time in the arena together and I was finding it incredibly annoying that Jenna sought my agreement before we started.

"Listen, I'm still not good at aiming fire bursts. I can't guarantee I'll get it directly at his heels. We don't know what he's going to do after you come from the right, so I'll flank him from the left and you'll push him back with air. I'll keep him occupied," my words were short and my tone was dry.

"You were supposed to be practicing the fire bursts. That was the plan," her winey voice struck a nerve.

"It doesn't matter how much I practice. The fire comes when it wants. I still can't control it," I said through gritted teeth. I was so used to doing everything by myself that I hated having to explain myself to her. Plus, I wasn't having any luck wielding my fire element on demand and I didn't want her talking shit to me later about that.

Bjorn and Axel had just finished and the professor wiped his forehead with a towel before calling us over. I ignored her obvious eye roll as I looked out over the sandy arena and said, "Let's go."

Zayne Endris was our Combat Professor and he was an exceptional warrior. Although unlikely, I had hoped he went easy on us today. Our handicap was that he wasn't allowed to use any elemental magic, but we were.

Just as Jenna told me she would, she flanked him on his right and as I made eye contact with her, she looked at his heels hoping I would follow the plan. *She just doesn't get it. I am not ready.* Zayne made a move in her direction and the moment he turned his back to me I tried to shoot a burst of fire at his heels, and as I stood there with my hand out and facing him, he turned around and swiped at my legs so I fell to the ground. I squeezed my eyes shut as my cheek hit the gritty floor and grains of sand filled my mouth. When I opened my eyes, I saw Jenna make her move and before he got into attack position, she sent burst of air at him, causing him to stumble slightly. She capitalized on his stumble and blasted him even harder, taking several steps forward. She moved forward, focusing in on him and giving me a chance to get up and move into a fighter stance on his other side.

I lifted my hands again and tugged at the dark energy from within to will fire into my palms, but there was nothing. No heat. No burning rage from my center. Nothing. He came at me again, his steps delayed in Jenna's wind but powerful enough to cut through it and this time I ducked when he took a swing at me and I jumped when he swiped at my legs. I took my chances and leaped at him with a roundhouse, and he grabbed me in the air and slammed me against the ground a second time. I heard Jenna grunt close by and watched as she approached him with swift and agile movements. As I made my way to my feet I watched her block and evade many of his punches, kicks and elbows, landing a few of her own. Until he reached for her hand in midair and wrapped a muscular arm around her neck in a headlock. He called out, "Break." Then he let go of her and said, "Great job Jenna. Sasha, you've got a lot of work to do."

I nodded. It was an effort to keep my chin up as I pulled my shoulders back instead of slumping them over like I wanted to. I wiped my sandy hands at my sides and in that moment, I was sure I didn't belong here.

As the weeks passed, I had practiced throwing fire bursts daily. I met with other fire elementals after class at study groups and we helped each other practice, giving each other tips and encouragement. I was gaining control over my element, along with learning combat techniques to attack at higher speeds and intensities than what I was taught in the military. And by the time I got to the end of the first year, I began working better with Jenna and I leaned into her obsession with planning ahead. We had become a solid team. We had developed a much better flow, and our differences were, in fact, what made us stronger.

Today we would battle a minotaur. Light fluffy clouds were scattered on an otherwise clear blue sky, while the sun glared down on us. A cool breeze swept through the stadium filled with Academy students. The breeze continued over the sandy arena to us, which kept the day from being unbearable in battle gear. Carly had a hidden talent for braiding hair, and she created intricate patterns to ready us for this moment. We'd been preparing for this for months.

Today was to be a qualifying fight. If we were able to entrap the minotaur without killing him, we would meet the qualifier requirements and move on to the next level. However, if we couldn't entrap the minotaur, we would either be saved by a professor at the last minute or the minotaur would eat us. And I really didn't feel like being eaten today.

Minotaurs were born half human, half bull. They were an entire race that lived in labyrinths under the city. It was impossible to reason with them, and they were incredibly powerful, but they weren't very calculating. When left alone, among their kind, they weren't much of a problem to the populations of Zol Stria. Yet, the Dark Zodiac, the Zodiac Mafia and the Demon Kings were all said to have raised small armies of minotaurs. They were incredible beasts that could cause a massive amount of destruction, and all they wanted in return was to crunch on bones and feast off the Fae spoils of their target.

The minotaur we would fight had been part of the Faellen War. He was one of the leaders of the minotaurs who had fought under the command of a Dark Lord. Six moons ago, during the New Moon Festival, he'd managed to gather two of his fellow inmates and escape the prison. The three of them wreaked havoc on a nearby town.

The unsuspecting Fae, who were enjoying music, food and celebrations, were literally torn to pieces. Small children and babies were stashed and devoured last, as if they were dessert. Very few survivors were left to speak of the horrors they witnessed. The minotaurs had been captured soon after. The Academy had a custom of leveraging prisoners that were sentenced to death as opponents in the warrior training program, as target practice.

I kept my face expressionless as I watched Eliana and Andres go first. The goal was to move the minotaur from one side of the arena to the other without shifting. Then, when they were within the blue section on the opposite side, they could shift to their nagual form.

Eliana was swift, avoiding the minotaur's advances while skirting around to confuse him. Andres attacked when Eliana distracted him, but the massive creature was much more agile than I expected. It walked right through Andres's air shield, grabbed him up off the ground and threw him halfway across the arena.

Eliana flipped upward, locked his head in between her thighs and held onto his horns. He grabbed her easily and flung her away. The fight continued with no clear victor until they used a combination of Eliana's water element with Andres's air element to create a powerful waterspouts to surround him. As soon as they got close to the blue section, they shifted and pinned him down. The crowd went crazy, cheering and chanting, "Reborn. Reborn. Reborn." They'd completed the mission, but lost points for shifting before crossing into the blue section.

A few hours later, after the minotaur's recovery nap, we were up. Jenna and I went over our approach one last time before stepping into the arena with two of our most powerful resting bitch faces on display. The minotaur stood at the far end of the arena; he was over eight feet tall and built like a tank. His human torso and legs were formed of muscles made of steel. His human chest was covered in thick red fur that went all the way up and covered his bull head. Two massive horns came out from the top of his head, and his bull eyes were raging mad.

When he opened his mouth, a loud animal roar left his throat, thundering around us. It was clear the creature didn't have the vocal chords to make comprehensible sounds. I must have imagined it, but it seemed like steam was puffing from his flaring nostrils.

These creatures either didn't bother or even know how to keep their auras retracted, and it was fair to say his aura was a hot, disorganized mess of splattered and splotchy colors. There was no way I was going to figure out what was going on energetically with the beast, at least not in this short time together.

He took a slow step toward us.

"I'm about to unleash all my demons on this Fae-killer," I spat out.

"Go for it. You know what they say, 'Karma's a savage bitch,'" Jenna replied.

We marched closer to him, and I called magic to my fingertips. They tingled in response, the heat rising through me. My jaguar pulsed inside me, eager to be set free. She was anxious because she knew it would be soon and she wanted to feel the taste of blood on her fangs. Out of the corner of my eye I watched Jenna; her hands began to conjure up her air element. I could see the sand swirling on the ground underneath them. No sudden movements. We kept our eyes locked on the creature, watching his every move. I tried to use his aura to gauge whether he would move to the left or the right, but from what I could tell from the last battle we'd watched, there was no pattern to speak of.

We closed the gap between us until just one hundred paces remained. He snarled something fierce. His size was deeply intimidating, and I had no intention of being thrown across the arena like Eliana and Andres. When we came within fifty paces of him, Jenna whisked sand into his face, temporarily blinding him. I sprinted behind him while Jenna threw up an air shield to channel my fire element directly at him while simultaneously blinding him with the sand. Unable to see, he stumbled away from the fire, in the direction of the blue section.

He kept retreating, closer to the blue section now. It seemed we would get him in there rather quickly. Suddenly, he charged directly at Jenna. Driven by blind rage, he couldn't actually see where he was going, yet the power of his anger drove him straight toward her. We didn't expect this and had let our guards down, thinking we had him too soon. She channeled the air energy faster, creating an almost solid wall around her. With sheer force, he charged straight through.

Her eyes opened wide in surprise at his brute strength, and she skirted away from his advances. I shot a burst of fire at him to slow him down, but all it did was singe him. The smell of burnt hair filled my lungs as he turned and lashed out at me with a clawed hand. *He is fucking terrifying.* I stumbled backward and tripped, falling on my bare hands. The crowd let out a steady, "Ohhhhh."

I turned my head to the ground as I planted my hands on the sand. I'd just started to push myself up when a loud crack came from my back. He had pinned me down with his massive foot, and I thought my spine had just broken. My face scraped against the sand, and pain surged through my body. The minotaur kept his foot on my back as he reached for my arm and pulled it back. He was about to break if off my shoulder.

In a split-second, fire surged from the center of my chest into my palms. I opened my hand upward to release a blast of blue heat into his face. He reeled back, bellowing in pain, as Jenna sent air magic surging into the fire, driving it into a roaring blaze.

By some miracle, my back wasn't broken. Standing, I winced as painful stabs shot through my spine, and I fought to concentrate the fire on the creature as Jenna and I walked forward in tandem. We were forcing him back into the blue section. As soon as he hit the border, we ripped off our battle gear, and I remembered my training: *darkness reborn, serve the Zol as one.*

Jenna shifted first while I held him off with the fire. As soon as she shifted, she stalked forward at a slow, steady pace. He lunged at her, and she caught his arm in her fangs. She held him there as I shifted. I called upon the shadows and mist, and my human form easily gave way to the jaguar, transforming faster than I had in the past two months.

He managed to punch Jenna in the side and wriggle free of her grasp. But then he looked up to see two feral jaguars showing their teeth and ready to pounce. Our size and weight intimidated the minotaur, and he backed away, no longer displaying his heaving angry chest and rage-filled eyes. Snarling, we approached him, and my jaguar leapt onto him. *My turn to pin you, beast.* We sank our teeth into his arm, ready to tear the muscles from the bone. Then in the distance I heard a call.

"Cease," a voice said.

My jaguar could taste the blood under his skin. She wanted so much more of it.

Darkness reborn, serve the Zol as one. I chanted the mantra that was part of the spells for my control over the fearsome beast. It helped us merge our minds and operate in sync. She eased up, remembering she had a master in the Zol gods and that we had to work together. Blood dripped from her mouth as we looked toward Jenna's jaguar, who was panting, snarling and jealous. The minotaur reached his unbitten arm up toward my jaguar, about to fist her hair. We swiftly placed our other paw on that arm, holding him down, growling and furious. Jenna stepped forward, snarling her sharp fangs at him as the professor approached us.

"Take him back to his cell," Zayne instructed, and the minotaur stood after my jaguar eased off him.

Our jaguars showed their huge teeth as we herded him backward into his cell, panting and spent. The guard shut the gate quickly, and the minotaur growled in defeat as the doors were sealed shut.

Zayne called out, "Full points for the polarities." He turned to the students in the stands and projected his voice so they would hear him. "There is power in balance."

CHAPTER 20

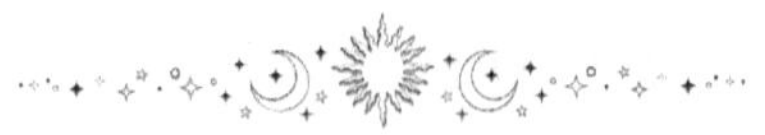

SASHA

"The minotaur needed a healer after you sliced into him." Bjorn snorted a chuckle as he, Jenna, Lex, Andres and I sat around a table at a bar in downtown Venis. It was a busy, bustling town with shops that lined sprawling beige-and-brown buildings with golden accents. We were enjoying the cool breeze under the rustling trees on the street by the river. The bar was full of students because we were all celebrating the end of the trials. Similar to the end of a semester back home, the qualifier we'd just passed was like our finals.

"I couldn't help myself. In fact, they should've given me extra points for self-control after I'd tasted his blood. Why is it so good?" I licked my lips, and Bjorn nodded in agreement.

"It is, isn't it? The first time I shifted back home was when I walked in on my girlfriend in bed with my best friend. I couldn't control myself. Shifted on the spot. The guy's leg was in my mouth in seconds, and I nearly ripped it off him." Bjorn's massive chest rose and fell quickly as he laughed. "The hardest thing about letting go of his leg was the taste of his blood on my tongue."

I loved his accent. He was from Denmark and English was his second language.

"Do you mind if I ask you, Bjorn, how is it you're a nagual? I thought we were all supposed to be born somewhere in the Americas. Like South America, the Caribbean, Florida? What's your deal since you're from Denmark?" With his reddish-blond hair, thick Viking-looking beard and fair complexion, there was definitely something I wasn't understanding.

"Ah, this is where people make lots of assumptions. Both sets of my grandparents moved to Mexico from Denmark. My grandparents were good friends, and my parents grew up together. When they got older, they fell in love, got married and had me and my three brothers. Soon after I was born, they moved back to Denmark, where I grew up. Trust me, I was even more surprised to find out what I was." He smiled easily. All of our spirits were up now that the trials were over.

I shifted my gaze to Lex, who was leaning back in his chair soaking in the ambiance. Jenna was sipping her cocktail next to him. They were in a quiet conversation about something when I turned to him and asked, "So, where are you from?"

"I'm from the Dominican Republic," he answered, and now it all made sense. That deep, thick accent; the rich, dark skin; the papi chulo smile. It was all there, a complete package wrapped in muscle.

"Bueno, tigre, in that case when are we dancing the Batchata?" I smiled at him, and he gave me an even bigger smile.

"Do you think they'll have Batchata music here?" he asked.

"I have no clue. You know what, we need to find a local to show us around. Don't any of your shaman know where we can go dance?" I cocked my head at Jenna.

"Yeah, mine does. I'll send her a text." She pulled out her oracle and started typing.

When the food came, Eliana and Leo joined us, pulling up their chairs and joking about how we had all survived the first qualifier. I shared my fries with Eliana but tore into my burger. I wouldn't be sharing that with anyone.

"Oye," Andres said to me. I was happy to find out he was born and raised in Miami, to Cuban parents. I grew up around Cubans and having him around felt like I had Miami with me. "You kicked ass today. How come you don't come out much? We never see you." His voice was easy, light.

"I've been studying," I said between bites. "I've got to catch up to you guys in my free time. I didn't know anything about this place, thanks to my deadbeat shaman." I rolled my eyes and returned his easy smile.

"Oh yeah. I heard about that. Sucks. My shaman was a hard ass. She made me study every day until the ritual. My parents even gave her my sister's room when she went to college so she could drill me day and night. They told everyone she was my girlfriend and a self-made bitcoin millionaire. You guys should check out my IG and TikTok. Before I left, they posted all these pictures of me and her on private jets all over the world so no one would wonder where I was." Andres smirked like he had gotten one over on the whole world.

"So, what do you do now? Do you keep all those accounts updated so people don't wonder?" Now I just had to know.

"For sure. We took a bunch. I mean thousands of pics before we left and hired a VA to just keep it updated for us. They even answer my DMs." He shrugged his shoulders.

"I did the same thing," Jenna chimed in, smiling. "The trips were fabulous. We got to travel to Bali, Africa, Paris, Iceland. Lots of cool places, and the restaurants were ridiculous." Her eyes drifted, I assumed to a faraway memory of those places.

"I did all that, too," Lex added. "My pictures were mostly on a mega-yacht in the Mediterranean. I'm supposedly living that nomad-life, producing beats for the music industry. I took pics with Bad Bunny, Zoe Saldana, Taylor Swift. Loco, e'tuvo cabrón de verdad."

A small fire had begun to burn in my chest the second Andres had started telling us about his social media exit strategy. The fire was almost a full-on blaze by the time Lex finished his. My face turned flush with the heat of it, and I was about to unleash a burning flame of jealousy from my hands.

"Yo, you didn't get any of that?" Eliana looked at me, her brows pinched in concern.

I shook my head no and looked away, out onto the riverbank at the leaves fluttering in the trees.

"It's ok. Look, that's all BS anyway. Who needs to travel the world when you can travel dimensions?" She was trying to make me feel better, and it was working. A little.

"Yeah, and who needs celebrities when you have all of us?" Bjorn answered, opening his arms wide and leaning over to wrap them around me. I hesitated and then leaned right in, resting my head on his massive shoulder. He squeezed me tight, and instantly, I started to feel better.

"I'm going to get us another round of drinks," Jenna said cheerily. Her green eyes were almost mesmerizing when she smiled like that. I couldn't help but smile right back.

"There's that smile." Lex's eyes met mine, then he shifted his gaze to Jenna. "I'm going with you." He got up and closely followed Jenna to the bar.

"What was your exit strategy, Sasha? How was it that you left?" Eliana asked me.

Now my smile turned into a thin line. "Let's see, I shifted right when an evil vampire had taken my unit, including my boyfriend, hostage. I almost ate my boyfriend because I didn't know how to control the feral beast inside me. I took off running, thank the stars, and my shaman found me. We teleported to the Aries Gate and here we are." They had all heard this story before, but now I tried to make light of it. Despite the time that had passed, the thought of what had happened back then still brought an ache to my heart.

"Ok, well, you're here. That's what matters," Eliana reassured me.

I nodded, forcing a smile onto my face. We were all getting to know each other here, and I didn't want anyone to think I was a chronic Debbie Downer.

"I think you're doing great," Andres said, running a hand through his thick black hair. "To take down that minotaur the way you did. It's definitely the battle everyone's talking about. And the one with the most elemental points."

That was when I heard the familiar beats from home. The music floated in the air and coursed through my ears into my soul. I swayed my body in my chair, unable to stop myself from moving to the sounds.

"Vamos a bailar?" a deep voice asked from behind me. It was Lex.

Jenna nodded in encouragement, and I couldn't stop myself. My hand just reached out on its own and grabbed his. We went out to the dance floor, moving to the light, carefree beats, and I felt that sense of being home again. This was my new home, and it may not have everything I missed, like cafe con leche or pan de bono at the local bakery, but if I could just get a taste of my culture once in a while, I knew I would be able to make it here. Things would work out. They had to.

When we finished dancing, we returned to our table, and I turned to Jenna. "Did you talk to the bartender?"

"Yes." She winked at me. "They have all the same music here."

We kept talking, enjoying the night. We joked about Eliana's thighs wrapped around the minotaur's neck. We joked about our Solar Alchemy professor, Finley, who we all suspected was trying to read our thoughts, fishing for sexual encounters to go pervy on when he got home. We exchanged notes about how the rest of the training was supposed to go for us.

"So, what's next, after we graduate?" I asked Andres.

"We go out in the field, rounding up the monsters terrorizing mortals and all that. But we will all report into our Zodiac House. But I heard that they need someone at the prison, Xibalba in House Scorpio." His eyes held some knowing behind them.

"Yes, Vucub-Cane mentioned Xibalba at the ceremony. Do you know anything about that place?" I took a sip of my drink, no longer anxious or upset. Easy. Relaxed.

Andres shifted in his chair and rubbed his chin. "It's a tough place. Xibalba is one of the most populated and highest-security prisons there is. Anyone assigned there, has their work cut out for them, that's for sure. The prisoners are always trying to escape, and because of the Faellen War, they have a lot of allies on the outside."

It neared the end of the night, and it was only Lex, Jenna, Andres and me left at the table. Eliana and Leo had stolen off somewhere early on, and Bjorn was chatting up some girls at another table.

"We're going to head out," Jenna said after getting up. Lex stood immediately after.

"See you guys," I said and waved at her. I'd had one too many drinks. I looked over at Andres. We were the only two left at the table. "Well, it's late. I'll head out, too."

He raised his eyebrows and sat up. "Let me walk you to your villa." He flashed his aura at me without me even asking, and I could see it was blue and white. No malice to be found there.

"Ok, ok fine," I sputtered out. There was something they were putting in these drinks that made them hit me so much harder than the drinks back home. I had to remember to take it easy. Andres had eyes as black as the night with hair that matched. It complemented his naturally honey-gold complexion, framed with thick dark eyebrows and a trimmed, short beard. He stood about a foot taller than me at over six feet, with broad shoulders and a strong, muscular build.

He'd definitely caught my eye the first time I'd seen him, and I still felt absolutely terrible about it. My history with romance was turning out to be destructive, chaotic and deadly, and I had to avoid it at all costs. I wasn't about to start listening to whatever tingling sensation arose in me every time I looked at him. Although, I think my jaguar disagreed, because I would feel her turn and twist with excitement any time he was near.

We made small talk on the way home, but nothing my foggy mind thought was significant. We stopped at the front of my door. I waved my hand to open it, eager to get inside.

"Well, good night then," he said gently.

I turned around, realizing I was being rude. But really, I was just trying to avoid meeting eyes with his sensuous dark pools.

"Good night. Thanks for walking me back, even though I'm not sure I needed you to because I can turn into a big, mean jaguar whenever there's trouble. So, there's that." What a stupid thing to say. I must've been feeling nervous.

He took two steps closer, and I stood frozen, staring up at him and wanting to stop wanting him. It was too soon to forget about Trent. *I won't let myself move on. Not so fast.*

"It's a good thing I like jaguars." His voice was smooth as butter, and under any other circumstances, I would think he was flirting with me.

"Ha..." I managed to release a slight chuckle as I stared into those rich eyes, then down at his beautiful white teeth behind perfectly shaped lips.

He leaned in and planted those lips right on mine, and I didn't pull away. I let him press them even harder, while I opened my mouth and granted his tongue access inside. He reached his hand up to cradle my neck, and his other arm wrapped around my waist, pulling me in toward him. This felt so, so good. It was normal, to want someone. To have desires.

But I was still broken. I wasn't ready. I pulled away. "No," I said as I looked up at him. "You've got to go. Please."

I turned away and closed the door, leaving no room for him to talk me into it. It had been almost a year since I'd last felt Trent's embrace. But it was still too soon.

Chapter 21

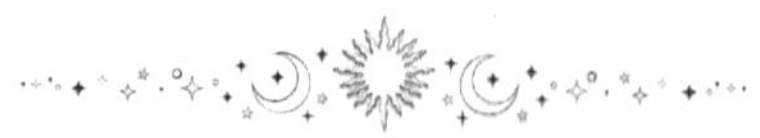

Damian

Zayne and I agreed to text Sasha and have her meet us. The program at the Academy would soon break for the equinox, and now was the right time to go over our plans to uncover the Dark Zodiac. No matter how many years had gone by, the revenge I wanted for Lily's murder—and my unborn child's—had never left me. It was like it had just happened, and I wouldn't rest until they were all dead. Dead.

I sent her a message on the oracle: *We need to meet.*

I can't now. I'm working out. Later.

Can you come by my villa? In an hour?

An hour and a half.

Ok.

Sasha arrived three hours later.

"Hey." She walked in and sat on my couch. She placed a smoothie cup on the table and kicked her feet up on my furniture, tracking dirt on my coffee table. The fitted black athletic pants and black tank top she wore were drenched in sweat, and her sneakers were covered in mud from her run.

"Can you not do all that?" I asked.

All she did was shrug, and I cracked my neck in annoyance. My place was always spotless, except for those few nights with Ixia when she broke in unexpectedly and I had a little too much to drink. Each time I had the room thoroughly cleaned afterwards, everything put away, and myself pulled together.

"Where's Zayne?" she asked as she rubbed her sweaty back on my couch.

"He got sick of waiting and left. You could've told me you'd be late." Wait, what was that? Did I sound like a father just now? I shook away the thought.

Sasha ignored me and swiped through her oracle. A few heartbeats later there was a knock on the door.

"Great. Let's get to it," I grumbled at the sight of Zayne at the door.

He swept his light-brown hair back off his eyes and marched inside. I soon felt the pressure of the deflector spell I cast. It created a sort of vacuum to block eavesdroppers and spies from listening in.

"What's all this about?" Sasha looked up from her scrolling. For all that girl had been through, her eyes and cheeks seemed as bright as a fresh morning. You would never know by looking at her that a beast lived just beneath her flesh.

"Oh, hello to you, too, Sasha." Zayne chuckled easily and moved over to the dining room table. He brought out a map and rolled it out slowly.

"Hi, Zayne," Sasha muttered as she got up from the couch and walked over to us.

"I've told you both about the Dark Zodiac, but I haven't told you everything," he said. "They've been growing in number by converting all the darkest, deadliest Fae of Zol Stria to their side. Slowly, without anyone noticing massive shifts, they've been taking them out of their otherwise controlled environments and convincing them to use humans for personal consumption and...other uses."

I knew what he meant. Over the centuries, humans had been bought and sold between other humans and Dark Lords. Their value depended on their lineage, age and skill set.

"Right, go on." Sasha stood with her arms crossed over her chest, peering at us both. This all seemed to be getting her attention.

"They're planning to raise the UnZol King so the Dark Fae can rule over both our worlds," Zayne said gravely.

I'd heard the legends of the UnZol King and his legions of UnZol for ages. Creatures without souls who'd lived thousands of years ago. Humans called them demons, and all manner of monsters began with them.

"Ok, what now? Who is the UnZol King? I read something about that in Zol History." Sasha's chin was raised slightly, and her eyes were sharp.

I answered, "The UnZol King was as powerful as a god and ruled over the Dark Fae. No one knows where his power came from, but legend has it that he was the most enlightened Zol Sen to ever exist at one point, even becoming Zol Zen Master. He rose in strength and power under the favor of the stars. This was during a time when there was no famine, death or pain in the entire universe. But the he believed that Fae and humans alike had never appreciated the beauty of their peaceful existence. There was no gratitude for it, just a blind acceptance that this was the way things were and would always be."

When I was a kid, my mother had told me about the UnZol armies. I would get my wooden toy sword and pretend to slay them.

"He brought in the darkness in the form of suffering, disease, and hunger, so they would remember the light" I continued. "He believed that by losing peace, they would learn to cherish it. But his plan backfired. He gave the people fear, not an awakening. Instead of feeling gratitude, the Fae in Zol Stria revolted against him. They refused to say his name or speak about him in rebellion because he no longer deserved to be remembered.

"The rejection of his people was too much for him to take. With the dark came a new way to manipulate, a method of domination and a way to generate extreme power. And he decided to use it.

"As a form of punishment to those who opposed him, he decided to cover the earth with darkness. The Zol Sen were completely taken by surprise. They had never before experienced such darkness and were unprepared. They had no spells of protection, no magic to fight what he brought, and no prayers strong enough for the gods to hear and guide them.

"So, for over a thousand years he did what he wished with them, filling the world with his dark creations and merciless destruction. However, in the hidden underground of Zol Stria, the Zol Sen learned. They adapted to a life of suppression and searched for a way to take the world out of darkness in order to restore their peaceful existence. By channeling the power of the constellations, the Zol Sen created the great Houses of the Zodiac and divided the world of Zol Stria into twelve parts. Because each House is a zodiac sign, it uses the influence of that constellation to keep the wards of protection up and around it. The divided lands would separate the darkness into isolated sections, allowing the Zol Sen armies to pick it apart. The lord of each House was appointed by the Zol Sen to lead the armies that fought the UnZol. Because the UnZol could not be killed, the Houses built prisons in anticipation of the UnZol's defeat."

Sasha moved to sit down and kept listening, and Zayne removed his navy leather jacket and hung it over the chair.

"The UnZol King put up a tough fight. He accumulated a great deal of power as he drew more and more from dark energy. He had the ability to create lives without souls, and spawned beasts that only feasted on human and Fae flesh. He wanted to decimate all races, except for his dark creations. That was when the War Gods of all the worlds rose up. United, they followed Ares into battle.

"The UnZol King was captured, and his generals were locked up in the Underworld prison system within Zol Stria. They buried the UnZol King in the Zodiac Tomb, protected with magic from all of the Zodiac Houses. Six of his body parts were severed and hidden. Legend has it that his eternal damnation would only be lifted if these body parts were united. As long as they stay separated, he will be in a state of confined unrest. It was the Zol Sen's way of condemning him to an eternity of suffering." I paused and scratched at my chin. "Yet, if found, those body parts can give the Dark Zodiac dark power."

"Wait, aren't we nagual one with the dark energy?" Sasha asked, starting to pace. "Isn't that how we make it work for us? How is it that I can draw from that dark energy and not be like the Zolless?" She stopped pacing and placed her hands on her hips. "I remember being afraid of my darkness. So utterly afraid that it almost drove me mad. How is it I can control it now and not be swept away in it?"

"The darkness he created didn't disappear when he was captured," Zayne explained. "The twin gods of Xibalba, the Underworld inside Scorpio Gate, simply found a way to channel it through the zodiac constellations. So, unlike werewolves or other shifters who shift through generational DNA coding, your ability to shift pulls from that dark energy, and with your training you get to learn to channel it."

Sasha raised her eyebrows. "Ok, that sounds wicked."

"Yeah. Very wicked. I met with the Council. I pressed them until they gave me an update: Four of the UnZol King's relics are missing. Two have been missing for quite some time, they just didn't want to make it public. He cannot be raised with four relics alone, but the Council expects the Dark Zodiac to attempt to steal them. As we speak, the Dark Zodiac is drawing from the power of the parts they have collected so far." Zayne looked directly at me. "We have to get them back."

I pushed back from the table and grunted. "Why are you looking at me? I'm not in this to get body parts back and I don't give a fuck about the UnZol King. I just want to deliver a slow, torturous death to whoever killed Lily. That's it. Simple." There was no way I was being dragged into Council business. I barely wanted to be here in the first place.

"Damian, they're one and the same. You've got to see that," urged Zayne. "The Dark Zodiac wants to kill the nagual because they are the first line of defense for Zol Stria. They're the same people that killed Lily."

I had considered that, but it sounded like more trouble that I was willing to take on. "Show me," I demanded. "No games, Zayne. Show me your aura. I need to know you're not trying to drag me into something."

Zayne flashed me a coy smile along with his emerald-green-and-gold aura, but not a hint of deceptive darkness lingered within.

I leaned back against the table and glared at him. Then, I gave him a quick nod. "Fine."

"And they're the same people that have Trent?" Sasha asked, looking pointedly at Zayne while he still had his aura out.

"Yes." He nodded at her, and she gave him one stiff nod back. His aura hadn't changed. Her face gave nothing away, but I suspected she accepted his word.

"What's this map?" I asked.

Sasha's eyes grew wide as she looked at the city, peering closer at the marked areas. "I know this. Why do you have a map of downtown Miami?"

"We believe the UnZol King's Blood Ruby to be located right around here." He pointed to the waterways around South Beach. "And since you know the area, you can help us retrieve it."

Sasha nodded in agreement. "I know the area, but what is a Blood Ruby? And what about Lily's killers? Are they there?" Her eyes narrowed on Zayne, and I was glad she'd asked, because I was thinking the same exact thing.

"We can't know for sure, but I can tell you what we do know. They sent the darkness in a massive shadow cloud over her plane. The only way to find someone like that is to track the magic, but that has to be done right after the magic is used."

"I did that, and it led me to Colombia," I interrupted. "But then I lost the trail because of the concentration of paranormal energy there."

"Right, so the second way to track that kind of magic is to see if it's been used again in the same exact form. It's a very specific skill— drawing on enough dark energy to smother a plane and bring it down into the ocean. There is very little documented from the Age of Darkness, but I found records of the UnZol using this kind of magic to take down the Zol Dragons in the Faellen Wars. I believe they used the Blood Ruby to do it, since it holds the blood of the UnZol King and has the power to bring about natural disasters."

"And what makes you think it's in Miami?" Sasha asked as she chewed on her bottom lip.

"There are a few large mafia syndicates in Miami. They don't always get along and there are often territory wars. Recently the boss of a massive syndicate had his home and warehouse wiped out by a hurricane. This obviously caused a disruption in their whole operation. But because it was due to natural causes, it couldn't be traced back to anyone in particular. It's a slim lead, I know. But it's all we have. If the rival gang of the Miami Mafia has the Blood Ruby, in theory, they could have created that level of destruction. The same power that was used to take down Lily's plane could be used to create the hurricane that wiped out those two locations."

I got up, went to the bar and poured myself some whiskey. I drank it down in one gulp and poured myself another. When I lifted my gaze from the glass, I realized they were both looking at me expectantly. "Right, where are my manners."

I poured them each a glass, and without saying a word, we all lifted the glasses to our lips and drank the whole pour in one swift movement. "When do we leave?"

Chapter 22

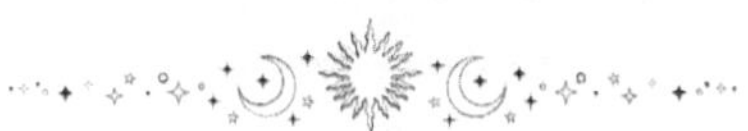

Sasha

S now capped mountains lined the distant horizon, surrounded by golden clouds, and lit by the crimson sun. A chill ran down my spine as I strolled through the garden, feeling the cool evening breeze sweep around me. I was lost in thought, wondering what would come of our upcoming mission. I went over the plan in my mind, but my thoughts kept straying back to my family. We would be in the same city again; how would I keep myself from visiting them? What if I just stopped by and checked in on how they were?

I'd visited the Wall of Mirrors last week and was pleased to find my mother had finally gotten off Xanax. She was now manager at the salon. My father wasn't drinking so much, and I saw him all cleaned up and getting ready to take her out to dinner. The house also looked better. Fresh paint made the walls shine, and it looked like they'd replaced the kitchen cabinets that'd been falling apart. It seemed like the stars were keeping their word and helping them on their way.

I checked in on my best friend from back home, Nikki. She was doing well in school, had a steady boyfriend who treated her well, and was living that busy New York life she'd always wanted. I was happy for her, even though I missed her and wished I could be a part of it all. As much as I wanted to see them all in person, I knew it was better this way. They wouldn't understand any of this. It would blow their minds like it blew mine— maybe even more.

I sat out by the water, staring at the colorful horizon. Pink, gold and white streaks painted the sky, and I gave my heart a chance to ache. I had been working so hard to push away how broken I felt. How I had met the most decent human being in Trent, fallen in love with him, then led him straight into the arms of the Dark Fae. I had to make this right somehow. I had to fix this.

"Hey, Sasha, you alright?"

I heard his voice but didn't turn. It wasn't my fault. It was his. All of this was his fault for not being there for me when he was supposed to be.

"What do you want?" I growled through clenched teeth.

"I want to make sure you're prepared for what's to come. I have some scripts to teach you. New techniques that will give you an edge. It's more advanced training than what they would teach at the Academy."

I still didn't turn around, but it was tempting to listen. I could use all the help I could get.

"What are scripts?" My voice had less bite to it this time.

"Scripts are spells that are unique to your Fae type. Since your Fae type is a nagual, these are scripts for your kind only. If your Fae type was a werewolf, you couldn't use them. And same goes for all the other Fae types." His voice was steady and balanced.

"I'll take your little lesson, but don't think this even remotely makes up for all the shit you didn't teach me all those years you decided to go missing," I snapped.

"What, you're still pissed about that? Come on, Sasha, let it go already. We've got bigger fish to fry."

No. No, he didn't just try to downplay what he'd done to me.

"Do you know how hard I've had to work just to be at the same level as the other nagual? Thank the stars they aren't assholes and don't make me feel bad about it. I'm always behind, dragging down their scores, playing catch-up. This is a complicated world, Damian." I stood up and faced him. "And the only reason I'm behind is you."

I shoved him in the shoulder, but he didn't budge. The man could become a steel wall when he wanted to. And right there, within those self-centered, narcissistic walls, a piece of him was getting annoyed that I was confronting him. His eyes narrowed on me, and his face darkened.

"It's not like that," he growled and took one step toward me.

I didn't back up. I stood my ground and glared at him with my palms open and fingers tingling as the fire within began to surface. "Oh, it's not like that? Like you not showing up while the other nagual lived with their shaman? They had daily training, traveled the world, even visited other Houses to learn the ways of the Fae before being dumped into this world. Meanwhile, I was left about to lose my fucking mind. And I lost Trent, the best thing that has ever happened to me! I barely made it out alive. So please, Damian. Tell me. What the fuck is it like?"

As my hands pulled in the dark energy around me, I tried to control the fire from rising to the surface. Then my hands morphed into jaguar claws. It was the only part of my body that shifted, and the first time I had done it. I dug my claws into my legs in an effort to keep from scratching them into Damian's eyes. As he looked down at them, I raised my claw and swiped at his chest. He raised a deflector spell just in time, and just barely blocked the sharp edges from penetrating his skin. He jumped back, and I snarled, readying myself to shift by drawing more dark energy in from around me.

Suddenly, the wind blew fiercely, morphing into a tunnel that surrounded me. Electric bolts of lightning kept me from moving, isolating me in place. I released a loud, angry growl.

"You think you're something special because you took down the minotaur?" Damian asked. "Because you got lucky with those vampires back on Earth? The Dark Zodiac is no joke and they have centuries of magical power to destroy you with. You won't even stand a chance with your training. I told Zayne you weren't ready and now look. You let your emotions get the better of you. If we go as you are, we will lose this mission and I will have failed her again."

My chest heaved, and I panted even harder. I tried to shift but couldn't. His electrical shield prevented me from pulling any more dark energy through it.

"Sasha, I'm..." Damian released his grip on the spinning charges, and I stumbled away as the electrical shield vanished. "I fucked up. I am sorry. Is that what you want to hear? How many times do I need to say it? I should have fucking been there." His creased brow, his piercing eyes and his tense shoulders gave away his frustration. "I've followed the rules for centuries, serving the Zol Sen as a shaman and never once going against my path. But then...she died. I had lived my life without regret, until that very day. She was carrying my baby, and I couldn't save them."

My anger subsided as he spoke, even though I still didn't trust him.

"Show me your aura," I managed to say through a mouthful of sharp teeth, which was the other part of my body that I had transformed before he'd thrown up that electrical shield. He had red and purple energy, just like mine, and it was shooting those same dark thunder bolts I'd seen coming from Trent when his mother had died. I understood from my studies that those were not signs of deception, but rather rage over death.

I took a deep, stilling breath. *Darkness reborn, serve the Zol as one.* I repeated the mantra to remind myself of the bigger picture, of my mission and my goals. I felt the dark energy rush out of me, releasing into the wind. My hands and teeth returned to normal as I listened.

"They deserved a better fate," he continued. "They deserved a different path. And after she died, I believed there could be nothing worse for you than Zol Stria. That this life as a Fae was not worth it. But now, I see that I was wrong. I was very wrong and I'm sorry." His hands opened, and he took a step toward me. "I'm tired of fighting with you. We need to find a way to work together. Let me help you get caught up in your training. I can even teach you some more advanced techniques, if you can cut me a break."

I concentrated on his face. "Fine. I'll try and work on letting that shit go, as long as you teach me some badass scripts and spells that make up for it." I would agree to working better with him, but it had to be on my terms.

"You won't believe what I'm about to teach you." His eyes glimmered as a devilish smile graced his face.

"What's this now? You actually *want* to teach me something?"

He chuckled, and I arched a brow.

"You have no idea. What I'm about to school you in is going to make you so glad you're a nagual." He rubbed his hands together, clearly eager to start. "These scripts are only taught to the elite graduates, after graduation. But because of what we're about to go do in Miami, I'm going to show you. Just don't blame me if your mind gets blown."

"Ok. Let's see what you got."

CHAPTER 23

DAMIAN

Over the next two weeks, I gave Sasha a crash course in advanced nagual training. We awoke before sunrise and finished well after sunset. She admitted that her head was pounding most days from the massive amount of information and skills she was learning all at once. Still, I was rather impressed with her dedication. She was catching up fast, especially now that she was willing to listen to what I had to say.

We would leave for Miami tomorrow. Zayne had convinced the Council this would be a reconnaissance mission, just to see if what he suspected was true. We would be prepared to defend ourselves, but we would have to report to the Council before making a move. I let Zayne tell them whatever they needed to hear to get this mission done, but I personally wasn't making any promises.

I nodded at the few shamans and shopkeepers I recognized on my way to the downtown district where Ixia had her botanical stores. She had just returned from a conference in Cancer, where they were sharing innovations in the use of alchemy, and I needed all the help I could get on this next mission. The vines yielded and released the iron gate when I arrived. One of her dryads greeted me at the entrance. Her hair was long, straight and golden blond. Her crystal-blue eyes were fixed on me as she looked up from the reception counter.

"Hello, Damian. Do you have an appointment?"

"No, no appointment. Just tell her I'm here please."

She smiled curtly and walked away. I'm guessing she didn't like me much. Ixia came over a few minutes later.

"Sorry to catch you off guard." I closed our proximity and spoke in a low voice. "Can we go somewhere and talk? I want to know how your trip to Cancer went."

Ixia glanced around the room. "It was fine. A little overbearing with all that compassion oozing out of them. But they did make us laugh a lot. There was this one joke that had me dying. It reminded me of you... What did the alchemist say when the shaman finally showed up? "

I shrugged my shoulders.

"It's about thyme." She laughed and threw her hair back.

I chuckled politely but wanted to get on with it.

"No sense of humor today, I see. Come along."

She led me past the cascading indoor waterfall where vines and flowers grew freely. The roof was made of glass, so all the plants inside received plenty of sunshine. There were shelves upon shelves of vegetation in the greenhouse. The dryads were ending to the production of the hundreds of bottles on the other side of the room. We entered her office in the back, and she closed the door. She continued walking to the rear of the room and opened the hidden door behind a bookshelf which led to a descending staircase.

We entered the room at the bottom of the steps. It opened up into a private lounge area with furs thrown on the couch and a bookshelf full of romance and mystery novels. A small fireplace lit itself as we walked in.

"I like what you've done with the old storage space. Very nice." I placed my hands in my pockets and looked around.

She walked over to the bar area and opened a new bottle of my favorite whiskey and poured two glasses. *I don't have time for drinks.* I just wanted to get what I needed from her and leave, but if I rushed it, she could get testy and push back. *I better take the drink.*

I lifted the drink from her hand and took a long sip, letting the rich flavor swirl around my tongue. It relaxed me a bit. She sat on the couch and motioned for me to join her. Her beige dress fell loosely off her shoulders, and the slit revealed far more of her tempting thighs than I was ready for. I licked my lips and sat down.

"So tell me, Ixia, did you get what I asked for?" I kept my eyes on my glass, watching the amber liquid spin as I turned it. Then, I lifted my gaze to meet hers.

"Yes, it's right over there. What do you want it for anyway?" she asked lightly, not giving away any hint of real interest, even though I knew she was curious.

"I'll be heading back across the Gates soon, and I figured I could fetch a good price for them. I'll make sure a portion of the profits go to the all-girls' academy in Florida that you like."

Through alchemy, the Fae had discovered a way to create gems that predicted people's future. For example, there was a ring would tell them if they would soon meet the love of their lives. Whenever the ring's owner slipped it on, it would glow if their love was soon to appear. If it stayed dark, their paths were not yet ready to cross.

The same thing went for wealth, money, death, love, sickness or having children. Each ring would help the holder predict what would happen to them next. I wanted the ring to tell me if Lily's killer was nearby, and I figured once I had one of the rings with me, I could create a script to code the ring to do exactly what I needed it to. That way, I would be sure I had the right person. I wanted to inflict the exact amount of torture to satiate my need for revenge without giving them a swift or easy death.

"You're going back?" She bit her bottom lip and leaned back, giving me a dark glare.

"I thought I was clear about this. About us. We are not together." I never meant to lead her on.

Something in her face broke. There'd been a hopeful look that was no longer there. The fresh, carefree glow of her cheeks suddenly faded. She looked away.

I stood up and paced. I didn't want to hurt her. When she turned back to look at me, the freshness had returned, but not the hope.

"Oh, I know, silly man. Of course we're not." Her voice was steady and exuded grace and confidence. Nothing of the insecure woman I'd seen before me mere seconds ago. "Let me fetch you the rings for your travels."

She walked over to a shelf that held an engraved box and opened it. From the box, she retrieved three rings. "This one tells of death." She pulled what looked like a black pearl on a silver band and twirled it in her finger, then set it down.

"This one tells of love." She lifted the ring by its gold band. The opal, surrounded by tiny diamonds, caught the light, and glimmered.

The jade ring was the last. "And this one tells if the holder will be wealthy." She lifted it by the iron band and laid it in her palm. After I inspected it, she returned it to the box with the others. I took a deep breath and inhaled her fresh lavender fragrance.

"There are others in the box to predict sickness, having children, and treachery. You can have them all. I have no need for those trinkets. I know my path." She turned toward me and stepped closer, parting her lips and lightly moving her tongue along her upper lip. She reached a hand to my shirt and tugged on it. "Let's have a little fun before you go?" Her voice was raspy, wanting.

I considered leaving. After all, why drag this out? I got what I'd wanted, and now I would leave, never return, and she would move on. Like she should have so long ago.

"Why haven't you moved on, Ixia? You could have anyone."

She traced her finger along my chest, her lip curling up into a smirk and her eyes narrowing on me. "I like this, whatever this is. The stars have never given me a mate, but they gave me a talent and a passion. So, for me, my passion is my mate. I'm with you now because you're safe. I know what to expect with you. And I know it will be good. But when you leave, I'll just pour myself back into my work. Until the stars show me a different path."

I stood in front of her and lifted her up and onto the small dining table. I ran my hand up her thigh, and she moved sensuously in response to me. She was desirable and beautiful, and our sex life was never the problem. I leaned in over her, pressing my lips against her neck. Licking her slowly and sliding my tongue up and around her ear. She let out a low moan, and I felt my erection grow. I couldn't tear myself away from her right now, even if I wanted to.

Chapter 24

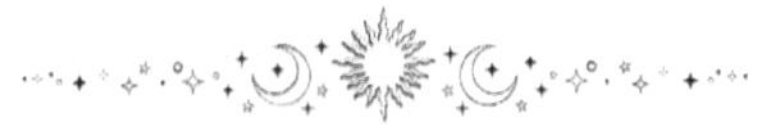

Sasha

Zayne gave me the news yesterday that he, Damian and I would be crossing the Libra Gate tomorrow while the new moon was in Capricorn. The veil was the thinnest then, so we would go undetected by the spies of the Dark Zodiac. I headed over to Damian's shaman workroom, and we went over some final spells and scripts that would prepare me for potential battle.

"Great, you're early. Come in, I was just finishing." His energy was bright.

After some time in Zol Stria, where everyone hid their auras, I was finally able to detect energy levels. There was a subtle glow, a slight shimmer, that everyone had, and it gave away their mood. I could see Damian was in a good mood.

"Here, check this out." He handed me a silver banded ring with a black pearl.

It was breathtaking. I had never seen so much detail or ever been in the presence of such a fine, elegant ring in my entire life. I slid it on my finger and gaped at it in awe.

"Right, so you didn't kill your aunt Lily. That's reassuring." He chuckled.

I never thought I'd killed my aunt. "What do you mean? What is this?" I arched an eyebrow at him.

"These are Tell Rings. They're created by a specialized alchemist who brought them to the conference in Cancer. He is the alchemist of House Gemini, since that zodiac sign rules over the hands, these rings are able to channel truths from that part of the body." He explained how each of the rings he'd gotten from Ixia worked.

"I was able to recode this one, so instead of telling if the person will die, it will alert me if I'm in the presence of Lily's killer." He smiled as his chest puffed up with pride at his little creation.

"Well, that's genius. How did you do that?"

"I had studied under the alchemist that created it some time ago. I helped him design the original code. All I needed him to do was create this one and I layered in my own code."

"How do you know it works?" I asked innocently, but the look on his face darkened.

He seemed to have quickly gotten over it because he dropped his head a little and smiled, then met my eyes again. "Of course, you would ask that question. Don't worry, it works."

I must have touched a nerve, questioning him like that.

"Now, enough about this. Let's see what you've been practicing."

He had been teaching me one of the most fundamental skills of the nagual, which happened to be the final rite of passage at the end of our training. All the nagual would be killed in the ceremony, and when they came back to life, they could access the magic of shadow weaving. Yet, I had already crossed the veil of death when Lazear killed me during a military training exercise. I'd come back to life a full ten minutes later, which had activated my magical ability to shadow weave.

The other nagual wouldn't be training in this skill until much later, and although the Academy would have some ethical issues with me learning this ahead of them, lucky for me Damian was very low on the ethical scale. He and Zayne also thought it would be a good skill for me to have when going up against the Dark Zodiac.

Damian taught me how to shadow weave. It was nerve-racking, and I wasn't entirely sure how it all worked, but Damian explained that the principles of our ability to shadow weave lay in our creation over one thousand years ago by the twin gods. The nagual were the only creatures who could traverse between veils, time and dimensions. We walked with the shamans among the spirits, and we pulled from the energy of the dark. Just as a bird flew and a fish swam, the nagual moved among the shadows.

Damian put the rings away and turned back to face me suddenly. His movements were fast. Too fast. He had a blade in his hand, and he lunged for me swiftly. I'd let my guard down.

I quickly went to the place of Zodiac Shadows and became one with them. One with the moment I died. One with the deep purple light that guided me. My focus and my center. In a moment, without a conscious thought about what I was doing, I fluttered to the side in a mist of dark and shadows. In the briefest of seconds, I became the same darkness that had tormented my days and nights for so many years before. I moved with the reflections of the light, from where I was standing, to right behind Damian, six feet away. I locked my arms around his neck and kicked his feet out from under him a split-second after.

"You still want to kill me?" I challenged him accusingly.

"Much better," he said in a strained breath. "I figured you worked better under...pressure."

He was right. I eased my grip on him, and we both stood. I had been practicing this for weeks, and this was the first time I'd gotten it right.

"Do it again. Try to stab me," I taunted, shoving and pushing him to egg him on. "You know you want to. Come on. Let's see if you can do it."

I gave him the finger and stuck my tongue out. He pretended not to look at me. Then, in less than a breath, he pulled his knife back and flung it at me. It spun quickly, headed straight between my eyes. I had seen Damian spar in the atrium with his shaman buddies. They were all magicians but impressive warriors all the same. They were trained fighters, skilled assassins, bounty hunters, warriors for battle and experts in all manner of warfare. That knife would hit its mark in a second if I didn't move.

My thoughts turned to the purple glow, to the darkness that cradled me and guided me, even when I thought it was only pure madness. I became one with it and shadow wove once again. This time I chose to move to a spot on the top of a large cabinet, where I could position myself to just above his head. He looked around the room for me and had his back to me, yet again, when I pounced.

We tumbled to the floor and we both laughed and scrambled our feet. I composed myself and prepared for the next attack. I still didn't trust him. He could brandish that knife again and just say, *Oops it was part of the training.*

"Giving unsanctioned classes?" I heard a woman's voice ask from the door.

The casual and carefree looks on our faces quickly turned serious as we both turned to her. It was Ixia. I thought we'd locked the door. No one was supposed to know that I was developing this skill. I had only met Ixia once, at the reception. Her presence exuded confidence, prestige, wisdom and beauty. Although I didn't know her well, I knew a lot about her. The botanical workshop was constantly producing solutions, potions, poisons and artifacts using plants, alchemy and the ancient magic of the Zol. Her achievements were recognized by everyone in Zol Stria, and she had a coveted position as a vicar.

Damian only allowed the briefest moment of surprise to flash across his face before reverting to someone in complete control of his every action. "Oh, she's such a fast learner, and given her unique death before crossing the Gates, we thought it would be a good idea."

He didn't want to tell her we were developing my skills to take down the Dark Zodiac. He didn't want anyone to know the tactics we were developing, so as to surprise our enemy. No one but Damian, Zayne and I could be trusted to know the details.

"Well, if Damian thinks you're ready," she told me with her, "I will have to take his word for it. I heard all about your unfortunate background. It really has been a tough road for you, hasn't it?" Neither her eyes, nor her tone gave any hints of condescension, but I knew it was there.

"I'm fine." I wasn't interested in what she thought about me.

"Well, I guess now isn't a good time. I'll come back later."

Damian gave her a half smile as she left, walking her to the door and closing it slowly behind her.

"I don't know how she does that," he mumbled.

"Does what?" I asked.

"She gets past my wards without setting them off, every time." He shook his head, as if it was inconsequential. But still, I wondered.

"Is it going to be an issue that she saw me do that?" I didn't know her. Didn't trust her.

"No. She's got bigger fish to fry. She's not worried about this."

He might have thought that, but I wasn't so sure.

Later that day, Zayne called us over to his villa. We went over our plans one last time. We would be leaving the next day, first thing in the morning, and I prayed that the stars would be in our favor.

CHAPTER 25

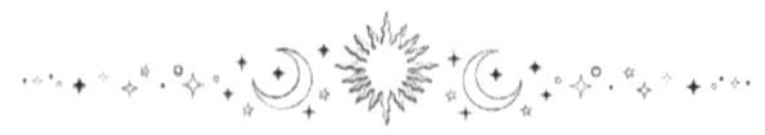

DAMIAN

The dawn had yet to rise when we arrived at Libra Gate. We'd had to travel first to the Zol Sen's Wheel Guide in the mountains, and they had teleported us here. Now, we could cross the Libra Gate, which was not nearly as large or overwhelming as the Aries Gate.

The Libra Gate was at the end of the Libra Academy school grounds where twelve-foot-tall bushes created a fence. The Gate was made of iron and stood the same height as the immaculately trimmed bushes, vines growing around the elegant bars. At the top was the Libra glyph in rose gold, displayed in an elegant finish. Every leaf, iron bar, growing vine and blossoming flower in this place was ideally situated, lush and aesthetically pleasing.

There were no guards to be seen at this Gate because they watched from the stone towers just above on each side. They were Stealth Faeries. They didn't need to be on the ground with us. Sheltered in the darkness of the tower, they moved silently, and their eyesight went far beyond the abilities of any other creature in existence. They could shoot ash arrows from long distances, and not a single movement escaped their vision. Upon our arrival, the Gate opened, and we walked right into the tropical gardens of Villa Vizcaya in Miami. This was a massive estate turned museum just south of our target's location. Arriving here would put us close enough to where all the Dark Zodiac activity was taking place in South Beach.

The three of us wore tourist clothing and pretended to be visitors at the museum. We preferred to travel in the early morning to avoid eyes and ears watching us on either side of the Gate. I took a deep breath of the fresh, salty air and let my eyes rest on the pummeling waves. I hadn't been to Miami in years. The air felt warm and humid. I looked over at Sasha, who was also staring out at the ocean. She had a somber look.

"What is it?" My voice hinted at concern, and it surprised me.

"I miss home." Her voice was soft.

"Let's go. I don't want to have to deal with a security guard in this place," Zayne insisted.

We called an Uber and headed to our hotel on the beach. We each had our own room reserved, fully warded with illusion and warning spells to keep our location protected. It was time to get settled.

When we got to Sasha's room, I stopped her and said, "There's some business you need to deal with. The Zol Defense Council has some documents and tasks for you to review in your room to make sure you're covered before we head out tonight."

She nodded mechanically before heading to her room. Tonight, we would reconvene and get familiar with the local scene, then stake out the social scenes where our targets spent the most of their time. This assignment would require infiltrating the local mafia, which wouldn't happen overnight. That meant there was plenty of time for me to take a nap.

Chapter 26

Sasha

I headed into the grand room they'd reserved for me. It was the Splendid Suite, with more space than I needed, but I wasn't complaining. I sat my satchel down on the bed and picked up the phone to call room service. I was starving and ordered enough food for three people. A huge beige box on the table had me curious, but first, coffee.

After making an espresso and taking a sip of its full-bodied warmth, I almost felt normal—just a girl in a fancy-ass hotel room, instead of a human-turned-supernatural creature that had seen and experienced things I could never dare to explain to anyone on this side of the Gates.

I sauntered over to the elegant box. It looked like it came from a designer shop, it was beige and made of hard paperboard with a gloss finish. I lifted the lid, and my eyes bulged. There was a luxury wallet filled with credit cards and cash. An ID card with my picture and the name Leyla Ruiz. There were documents and a bank account under the same name with over three million dollars in it. There was a copy to the deed of a home which had a picture attached.

The beautiful four-bedroom modern home was located on the waterway, with a boat in the boat slip. And there was a letter and a printout with my picture on it that stated facts about me. Where I was born, where I grew up, where I went to university and what I did for a living. I was an art dealer, apparently. This explained all the art appreciation classes I'd been forced to take at the Academy. They'd said it was part of my unique curriculum, but now I understood why.

I picked up the cell phone from inside the box. It had a text message from the Zol Eyes. The Zol Eyes were like the FBI of Zol Stria. I knew it was from them, not because they'd used their name, but because they used a code name, Andromeda.

The message said to read my email, so I did, and sitting in the inbox there was one single message from the concierge. The message explained that I needed to go shopping at the nearby luxury stores and that I had a facial, hair and nails appointments in the afternoon. I couldn't help myself. I did a little shake of my hips, a twirl and jumped on my bed for good measure. There was nothing like a good shopping spree. As I scooted about doing a happy dance, I heard a knock at the door. Breakfast had arrived.

During the day, I thoroughly enjoyed shopping for all the clothing at stores I'd never dared walk into before. I mean, I wouldn't have even touched the tags. I had on the same blue jeans, cropped hunter-green jacket and Converse I wore when we'd left Zol Stria. But as soon as I began shopping, I shed those clothes for an elegant black, sleeveless jumpsuit and wedges. I soon stocked up on party dresses, formal gowns, athletic wear, swimwear, night gowns and everything else I needed to be fashionable at every outing. I had never taken out a credit card, let alone swiped one so mindlessly in my entire life. I didn't know who would be paying these bills, but it wasn't me. The only thing that could've made the experience feel complete was having Trent by my side.

I took a deep, shaky breath as I sat outside a café, sipping on a green smoothie. Thoughts of my family came to mind, and I resisted the urge to go visit my mother, or Nikki's mother, Ms. Gabriel. First, I needed a moment of reflection and meditation as I settled in. When I returned to my suite, I sat in a chair facing the calming aqua ocean. I closed my eyes to meditate and returned to the goat shed, my mental place of ultimate serenity. I focused on my breathing. I relaxed my jaw, rolled my shoulders back and released the tension in my face.

When I opened my eyes, I was looking out at the lake in Villalba, where I always went to center myself. Trees in the tropical canopy rustled with the breeze, and the smell of rich vegetation filled my lungs. I calmed the inner noise and found silence. The silence that helped me find my way.

What do I want?

Now that I had come this far, had realized my path was that of the nagual, protector of Zol Stria, I needed to know what I wanted. Was it to find my family and risk exposing them to the vengeful creatures of the shadows? Or was it to stay focused on the mission to protect Zol Stria from the Dark Zodiac, and in doing so, find Trent so we could be together in this new world?

As much as I wanted to go see the people I still cared about, I knew with absolute certainty that I needed to stay focused on the mission, and on finding Trent. He was out there somewhere, and he needed me. I focused in on his energy, that familiar glow he always had. We had gotten so close that at the mere thought of him, his scent came back to life within me. I searched for him with my mind, with my unique ability to trace him through energy, but I couldn't find him anywhere. I was warned this would happen because vampires didn't have auras. They didn't cast out energy like the rest of us, which was why the legends always portrayed them as being dead.

He was probably in deep with Solana, and I didn't like that one bit. My mind began to scatter, thoughts jumping everywhere. I could see them racing through my mind. This was my fault. This never would have happened if I hadn't brought him into this. *He doesn't deserve this. What have they done to him? Who is he now?*

I took deep breaths. *I've got to turn this around.* So, I began to form a plan. *You didn't know. You can save him. He can have a life with you, beyond the Gates now. You just have to find him and bring him back with you. He can learn the ways of the Zol Vampires just beyond the Gates.*

If he wasn't in Miami, I would find some trace of him. I wouldn't go back until I did. I just needed some sort of clue as to where he was, and where he might be now.

It would be time to get ready soon. I eased out of my meditation with more questions than answers. When I got up, I felt just a little closer to Trent somehow. I found ways, within my meditation, to not only look at the desperation of the situation, but to look at the possibilities. As long as there was a chance of finding him, I wouldn't stop. Instead of giving up, I would shred the dark in search of him.

Chapter 27

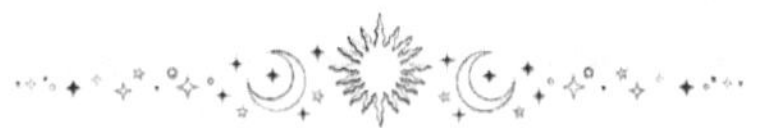

Sasha

After a week of staking out the clubs and eating hotel food, I wanted to be in that home they said was mine. I was dying to cook my own meals and have a stocked fridge. When I called the bank, they confirmed the account was mine. When I asked Damian and Zayne about it, they acted like it was no big deal. Sanctioned travelers between the Gates were always assigned houses, to eliminate any suspicion of our identity and give us stability when we were here.

"So what are we doing here, in the hotel, if I have a home I could be staying in?" I asked one morning, while at the hotel brunch.

"This is way more convenient. It's closer to our target and they clean our rooms every day. Why would you want a house to clean up after?" Zayne shook it off and Damian just nodded his head and scoffed.

"Are you serious? I'm heading there right after we eat." I smiled cheekily. I couldn't wait. "I'll make you guys dinner tonight, and you'll see exactly why being in a home is better than this place. Besides, it would be good to take that boat out and get to know the waterways." I popped a blackberry into my mouth, then leaned back and sipped my coffee. I knew there were perks to being a nagual, but I didn't know there were this many.

"I'll keep my hotel. Thanks." Damian shrugged as though he didn't get it.

Later that afternoon, I stood in the house—my house— and took it all in. It was elegantly decorated and absolutely beautiful. The vaulted ceiling gave way to unique angles that drew in my eyes. The decor was modern, but still rich and earthy. It was exactly my taste and in alignment with the personality traits of my star sign. Burnt-orange pillows and ottomans brought the fire element forward, while blue rugs and accents created aesthetic balance. On the second floor I found a panic room, and in my phone, there was an app with instructions and controls for the features of the room. The walls were made of iron, and the door was impenetrable by magic or machine. This could be a holding cell if we ever needed it. The entire home was perfect.

I got to know the house, had the groceries delivered, and took the boat out on the waterway to ensure everything was working and that I knew my way around. This could all work to our advantage at some point.

We had gathered some intel over the past week, but not much. While staking out a club, I'd met a well-connected girl named Marni who I instantly clicked with, and we'd agreed to meet there tonight. She quickly invited me to party with her in the VIP section, where we suspected the Dark Zodiac had their people.

Before heading out that night, I made dinner for the guys, and they loved it.

"Sasha, this is really good," Zayne said, staring into my eyes just a moment too long. Damian nodded and grunted in agreement, still digging into his ribeye and his side of *arroz con habichuelas*. We washed it down with a bottle of vintage wine from the cellar located just behind the kitchen.

"Well, I'm glad you liked it. Now don't you have some kind of magic spell to clean up these dishes so we can go?" I joked, a smile playing on my lips.

Zayne laughed. I still couldn't get over how handsome he was. He pulled a hand through his hair and smiled, and I wondered if he could ever love anyone again. I wondered if he was happy. I'd felt something of a pull toward him ever since I first saw him, and knew him to be the man who had saved me from my own madness.

"Yeah, here. Just call the cleaning service. Their number is stored on your phone."

Now I laughed. "Ok, sounds good to me." Then I leaned in across the table. "Zayne? I've been meaning to ask you a question. How did you find me? How did you reach me through my mind back in those days before I knew what any of this even was?" I had often wondered this, but this was the first time I'd thought to ask.

"I could feel you. I knew you were out there, somewhere, struggling. So, I found you." He shrugged and set his fork down, his plate completely clean.

"But how? How did you feel me? I've tried reaching others that way, but I can't. Not so directly. I can only observe what's happening, and it was only that one time, when Trent's mom was near death, that I could actually speak to her. And I only got to her because I tracked her through Trent's connection to her. Is that how you did it? Are you connected to someone I know? I really want to know because no matter what I do, I can't reach Trent." My voice broke slightly at the mention of his name.

He nodded his head, although his eyes told me he was holding back. "Yes, well, you don't have the years of experience that I do." He rose from the table and brought his plate to the kitchen. "It takes time and practice, but you'll get there. Now, are we all about ready to go? Tonight we need to get there early to watch the back entry point. We need to get a lead, and soon."

"Ok, just give me a minute to finish getting ready." I headed to my room and checked my outfit in the mirror.

I wore a short, black leather skirt that showed off my bronze, toned legs with a matching black, sleeveless crop top that sported a short mock neck. To tie it all together, I put on some heeled black booties. Three gold necklaces hung over my shirt. My midnight hair was down; the curls at the ends swept across my shoulders. I'd bought a bunch of new makeup and watched tutorials to get the trending techniques just right.

Nikki would say I look hot. Damn I missed that girl. She was my best friend for almost my whole life. I shook it off and grabbed my bag. I had to admit, it felt good to be back in my old stomping grounds looking this good.

Tonight, I'll get some answers, I reassured myself.

Chapter 28

Damian

We were sitting at a bar with a clear sight to the back entrance of the night club, Allure, where the high-profile mafia heads and guests slipped in and out throughout the evening. We each sipped our drinks and watched. Zayne and I had made some contacts, but none of them had as much access to the inner circle as Sasha's new friend Marni. We agreed that the surest and fastest way in would be winning her over.

Marni had told Sasha that Fridays were the best night in the VIP room. That's where the mafia entertained their high-value clients. These were the ones who purchased their stolen artwork, jewelry, automobiles, motorcycles and the many other high-end, illegal and in-demand products and services they offered. Sasha was just waiting for a text from Marni, and she would meet her there tonight. We would stay here and keep watching the back to track for comings and goings until the club opened.

"Ok, she's there. I'll see you two inside." She set her drink down and headed out, and as I glanced at Zayne, I caught him staring at her walking away a little too long. "She is very beautiful," I commented.

I wasn't remotely interested in her; something about our bond repelled those thoughts from the minds of the shamans long ago. It was a way of keeping our relationships with the nagual from getting complicated. But I had eyes. I knew what he saw, what most men saw when they looked at her.

"She's the most beautiful woman I have ever seen," Zayne confided in me, his voice trailing as a distant look haunted his eyes.

"Why don't you tell her? It couldn't hurt to try." I shrugged my shoulders. It wasn't my business, and I really didn't care, but these two were starting to grow on me. They kind of deserved each other, I guess.

"She's still in love with that guy the Dark Vampires turned. Until she knows what happened to him, her heart isn't free. I can see it." His eyes turned cold. His face darkened.

"You could maybe help her get over him."

"There's something I've learned about her, and that's when she gets something in her head, she doesn't let it go." He shifted in his chair to sit closer to the edge of the balcony and turned his gaze to the club down below. "They're arriving."

He nodded quickly in the direction of the cars as they pulled up in the driveway. Over the next thirty minutes, the VIP guests arrived at the club. First there was a red Bentley, followed by an orange Lamborghini, then a white Maserati and a black Jaguar. Pretty much all my favorite cars, with men and women dressed in trending fashion stepping out of them and into the nightclub. Their ages ranged from mid-twenties to mid-fifties, and they were all wealthy and corrupt.

I didn't recognize any of them, but I didn't expect I would. I wore one of Ixia's rings, but it didn't give anything away. That meant I wouldn't be seeing Lily's killer tonight, otherwise it would have shown me. Zayne and I ordered another round of drinks, and then another as people came and went, laughing, chatting and moving all around us.

"I just got a text from Sasha."

"What did she say?" Zayne asked.

"Just that she was in the VIP room with them but that we shouldn't come in yet. She said she needed more time." I could sense from our bond that she was fine. Probably dancing and laughing it up with her new friend. She wasn't running into any trouble in there.

Two hours later she sent another text: *I'm heading over to you soon. It's on.*

Phase one of our plan seemed on course. Shortly after, she emerged from the club with Marni in tow, and headed over to our new spot in the bar. We'd moved away from the balcony to the other side of the bar, just in case Marni tried to put the pieces together about our vantage point. We could see them laughing and giggling as they walked up. Marni had long, light-brown wavy hair and a perfect hourglass shape with soft, round full lips and wide brown eyes. From the way she was dressed and carried herself, I could see exactly why she fit in with the mafia kings and their clients.

"Meet my friends, Damian and Zayne," Sasha introduced us, and Marni gave us an easy smile. We'd agreed to use our real names, because unlike Sasha, our identities weren't in any databases.

Marni looped her arm through Sasha's and turned to us. "So nice to meet you gentlemen. Now, Leyla, why didn't you tell me your cousin and his friend were so handsome? They just about took my breath away." Marni's voice was light and playful, and I picked up on an accent.

"Wait, are you from Louisiana?" Zayne asked as the girls sat down to join us.

"Heavens, you're good. And I'm guessing you're from England?" She kept her eyes fixed on him as she leaned into the armrest.

"Why yes, that's right. He's from England," I said.

"And you, señor, are from Spain."

I wasn't from Spain, but I could pull off a native Spanish accent, and that was exactly what we wanted her to think. "Now tell me, what will you ladies be drinking?"

"I'll have a whiskey sour." Sasha had learned to like these after being around me too long.

"And I'll have a margarita," Marni said, still smiling coyly at Zayne.

Zayne and I went to the bar and returned a short time later with their drinks. We made small talk and chatted until Marni decided to ask the question we had been waiting for.

"So, Leyla was telling me the three of you own an art gallery in Madrid?"

"Yes, we have several. Bogotá, Mexico, São Paolo, Tokyo and London," Zayne replied.

"I was telling her that we came to Miami looking for some new, fresh pieces for our galleries, but we haven't liked anything we've seen here. Honestly, Marni, if we don't see anything worthwhile, we'll be heading to New York. Truth be told, I'm disappointed. We really expected Miami to have what we were looking for,"

Sasha said, a bored expression plastered on her face. She took a slow sip from her drink and relaxed back in her chair.

"Oh, don't give up so fast, puddin'," Marni said. "Haven't you been to Lezon's gallery or Broken Tradition? They have some of the best art I've ever seen. All of it is vetted and they've received the highest accolades…"

"Yes, those galleries have exquisite pieces. But our clients have a taste for rare, difficult-to-find and highly coveted productions. None of what we've seen fits the bill."

Marni looked to the side briefly, as if considering something. "Well, Leyla and I became such fast friends, and you two seem just as lovely as she is. It would be a shame to see you go so quickly." Marni's eyes shifted to Sasha, then down to her drink, and Sasha leaned into her, whispering something in her ear while gently placing her hand on Marni's arm. She smiled as she spoke, and Marni giggled and threw her head back.

"I say, let's give it another few weeks. Something may turn up," Sasha decided, sitting back easily in her chair and smiling confidently at Zayne and me.

I had to give it to her, Sasha knew how to work a target.

Let's hope she could get us in quickly.

Chapter 29

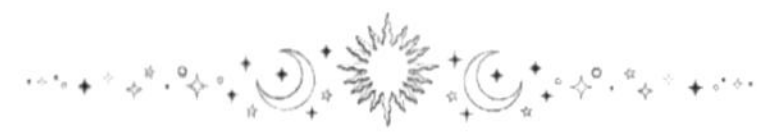

Sasha

Another week went by, and we got closer to being in the inner circle. The three of us were invited to join the mafia and their guests at the upper level of Allure. Elegant but simple red couches lined charcoal walls with exposed golden rings that matched the light of the golden circles on the ceiling. Gold chairs were carefully placed next to black tables, while the bar had a golden marble design inside a modern charcoal frame. There were two bars, one at each side of the room, and people were comfortably mingling within the open space.

Damian and Zayne blended in among the upper class easily, which was something that was initially very difficult for me, but I had learned to do so over my time in Aries Academy.

The professors had quickly understood my weaknesses and designed the ideal program to support my growth and confidence in those areas. They had me attend events with important members of the Zol Stria community, starting with the Academy leadership, then with providence commissioners, until I was finally invited to a formal society event with the lords of House Aries. They taught me how to blend in, what to say, how to feel confident, and they introduced me to their upper-class lifestyle. With skilled instruction and guidance, I learned exactly how to blend in whenever I needed to.

We made small talk with the various people Marni introduced us to, then, with the right people, we brought up art. We explained our trouble finding rare art in Miami. After being on the other side of the Gates for so long, I found humans incredibly easy to read. Their auras were on full display, and they were open books of emotion.

Their colors glowed brighter depending on the conversation, and I had gotten better at distinguishing the glows of lust, excitement, opportunity and joy. Skepticism, uncertainty and distrust glowed at a different hue and fluttered with a distinct frequency, grays and blacks seeping in at the edges and from the centers.

I could differentiate those who were skeptical from those who saw an opportunity, and these became my targets. Yet, I never let it surprise me when I'd singled out three individuals with retracted auras. That was when I knew I had found the potential members of the Dark Zodiac.

From the moment I walked in, I made sure my aura was on full display so they wouldn't suspect our presence. We just had to control our emotions enough to not let any deceptive traits leak through. It was difficult, but we had trained for this. Boredom became my go-to emotion. I remained interested enough to have a conversation but detached enough to not allow anything to affect me.

"There may be someone who can help you with your problem," one of the men without an aura said. His manner of dress and presentation was flawless, and I knew he had the wealth and wisdom of a centuries-old immortal. "Will you be here next week? I can introduce you."

Careful not to give anything away, I replied, "Yes, well I was planning on leaving for New York tomorrow. Is postponing my departure going to be worthwhile?" I kept my voice calm and steady like my mind.

"I would say so." He nodded. "My name is Fausto. Find me next Friday. I'll introduce you to him."

I finally had a lead. "I'd like my business partners to join me. We make all our decisions together." My voice was steady and so were my eyes.

"I thought so. I've seen you with them. Let's not overwhelm my friend with too many contacts at once. Just you for now." He winked at me, and I agreed, changing the subject while laughing and flirting a while longer.

When we arrived home that evening, I had the most solid lead of all, which massively satisfied my competitive side. Damian and Zayne had collected a bunch of girls' numbers for hookups. Apparently, they were the talk of the evening, and the ladies were interested in seeing them next week, but unlike me, they didn't have any potential buyers.

The following week, *we* were the ones pulling up to the back entrance in a sleek black Maserati—just like the other VIPs. I wore a Chanel dress, and as I walked out of the car, I felt like a celebrity with how glammed up the three of us were.

The crowd at the downstairs club was growing, and the sounds of the energy pulsing from the DJ spinning filled my ears. There was to be a performance tonight, so the line was much longer than usual. As soon as we arrived upstairs, my eyes scanned the room for Fausto. I saw him sitting in a booth way at the back, facing us, but he hadn't looked up to see us yet.

"He's a vampire," Damian said in a low voice, as he swept his eyes across the room. Zayne nodded in agreement.

"How can you tell?" I asked after glancing in Fausto's direction and then back at Damian.

"There are very small tells that once you get used to seeing them, you pick up on. Look at the drink in front of him on the table. The cup is black so you can't see the contents inside. I'm sure it's the synthetic blood they sell at the bar. Vampire nails grow thicker and sharper than human nails. They need to be clipped every other day, and he has missed a clipping. And finally, his lips. They have a slight shade of blue. Again, it's very subtle and if they wear concealers it can be hidden. But because Fausto is a boss, he is confident that he doesn't need to hide anything." I took it all in as if I was seeing them for the first time. If the books at the Academy mentioned any of this, I missed it. Some lessons just needed to be learned through life.

As I walked closer, I saw he sat with someone with shoulder-length blond hair and a strong back with broad shoulders. My pulse rushed. I didn't know who this guy was or why he didn't have an aura, but an aching longing washed over me. I'd once loved a man with hair that color and shoulders that firm. My heart raced as I turned to Damian.

"We may have a business partner after all," I told him. "Look, over there, Fausto is with someone I haven't seen here before. It must be him. I'm going over there to say hello."

Damian and Zayne nodded briefly in agreement and kept their cool demeanor.

"Go ahead. I've got someone I want to say hello to." Damian winked at me and walked over to a waving woman sitting over at the bar.

"I'll go join him," Zayne said hesitantly, staring at me for an extra heartbeat before turning away.

As I approached the table, a powerful sense of foreboding washed over me. I felt my throat tighten, and a heavy weight sank inside my chest. What I saw had to be a mistake. This really couldn't be happening, could it? I froze in place before getting any closer, remembering the mantras that kept my mind steady and my aura clear of flaring up with any excited emotions, not trying to give anything away.

I took a deep breath. Fausto was still engaged in conversation with a blond-haired man, and I had a moment to calm the nerves from knotting up my stomach and the blood from rushing in my ears. I took another step closer, easily, slowly, then my pace steadied, and I was next to them. There I was, an ocean of calm standing in front of the only man who could undo me completely.

"Oh, there you are," Fausto said. "Remind me of your name, beautiful? I wanted to introduce you to my friend, Trey."

He was mistaken. This was Trent. Not Trey. And he looked different, broken in a way I didn't recognize and beautiful in a way that was both dark and mesmerizing. I kept my aura in check, allowing a few flashes of excitement to escape into it, just as it would normally do if I met a man that I found instantly attractive. But in my soul, I knew this could only be my Trent Baine.

From the blank look on his face and the missing aura, I couldn't tell if he recognized me. Could it be that in his change to a vampire he had forgotten all about me? Had I been erased from his memory? Just that thought alone would utterly crush me. *Keep it together.* I managed to tell him my fake name.

"Hi, nice to meet you. Join us, please."

Hearing his voice now, I knew it was him. There was no doubt in my mind. Yet in studying his face, there was still no recognition. No sign that he knew who I was. A polite smile graced his lips, and my mind returned to a time when those lips were mine.

I released a breath and sat down.

We made small talk, and I avoided any conversations about our past together, playing along with whatever this was as I sat watching the facial features and body movements of the man I loved. They hadn't changed; he was still him only harder, rougher, and from the hooded darkness in his eyes, ruthless.

"You're interested in new art for your clients?" he asked me finally.

"Yes. Not just art, but art that captures the eye and doesn't let go. It must move their very soul." My eyes were playful, but my tone wasn't as I worked to avoid penetrating Trent with a stare.

"Well, you're in luck," Fausto said. "Trey recently secured such art. But we need a deposit of five hundred thousand dollars. The prices are over two million for each of these productions." This excessive number rolled off Fausto's tongue as though it was nothing significant, and I resisted the urge to flinch.

"That's a large amount to deposit." I tilted my head to the side, considering. "Let's say we were willing, when could we see the pieces?"

"Tonight," the man now named Trey said and kicked his chin up slightly, looking at me before quickly shifting his eyes back at Fausto and nodding.

"I'll let you know." I got up slowly, keeping my mind detached from the heartache at seeing him so distant and treating me so coldly. How could I be right next to him, but feel so incredibly far away?

I needed some release of my emotions before approaching Zayne and Damian, who were chatting it up with several ladies at the bar. I headed outside to the far corner of the balcony, to a dark, shadowy area behind a wall of large, decorative plants where no one could see me release my aura. Emotions coursed through my energy just as fast as the thoughts did. Joy then despair. Loss. Grief. Agony. Tragedy. Hope. And so many more. Warm tears trickled in soft streams down my cheeks as I lost his love all over again.

Then I felt a hand rest on my shoulder. His hand.

"Hey. There you are."

It was Trent, looking at me through the eyes of this new, dark supernatural form. Did he remember? I wouldn't risk it. I pulled myself together, slapped the tears away and turned to face him.

"Oh hey." It was all I could say. Any other words were caught in my throat.

He stepped closer, so we were less than a breath away from each other, and he brought his thumb to my cheek to graze my still wet skin. I quickly lifted a strong deflector spell around us.

"Is it...you?" I breathed out, my heart racing and my aura colors betraying the loss of control over my emotions.

He stared intently in my eyes with a word caught on his lips.

I realized then I had blown my cover completely. This would either be our new beginning, or my end.

CHAPTER 30

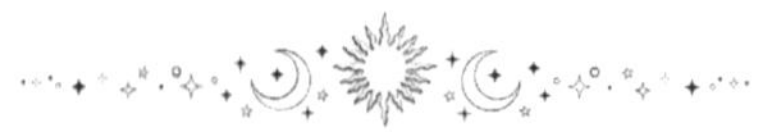

SASHA

Instead of speaking, Trent closed his beautiful mouth and bit his lip. The moon's light caught in his eye, and I caught sight of the internal struggle he was dealing with right there, beneath the sky-blue of his eyes.

"You do know who I am, don't you?" He had to know. He just had to.

I placed my hand flat on his designer suit; the material felt fine and soft while his familiar chest rested firmly underneath.

His eyes met mine, and this time he didn't hesitate. "Yes," he breathed. "You're my Sasha."

My knees buckled at the sound of those two simple words. *My Sasha.* A jolt of energy surged through my core and scattered out through my aura in a bright, vibrant red. I allowed a smile to grace my lips. It was still him, and it excited me that he still thought of me as his, even after all this time.

He leaned into me, caging me in with both arms as he leaned against the balcony and pressed his lips against mine. My lips parted willingly in response, welcoming his embrace as he wrapped an arm around my back and pulled me in toward him. I felt the press of his solid torso against my frame, allowing my familiar love for him to surge through me and shift between us. *How many times have I fantasized about this very moment?*

His kiss was passionate and desperate. I could tell he longed for me, yet it wasn't soft. The warmth I remembered from our loving embraces had been replaced with a headiness in the strokes of his tongue and a fervent grasping of my hair. I didn't care; I wanted him. That familiar wanting rose with a warmth between my legs. He moved his lips to my jaw, where the heat from his shallow breaths were followed by the skimming of his tongue on my skin. My entire body ached for him. In my heated desire, I barely noticed that I was fisting his fine jacket in my hands and squeezing him with all my strength. His teeth lightly pressed against the flesh of my neck, sending a blazing heat down my spine as I drew him closer to me, pressing my waist against his hips.

He pulled away and brought his eyes to meet mine as the moonlight danced across the sharp curves of his face.

"I have never stopped thinking about you," he managed to say. His words sounded distant, as though there was so much I didn't know hidden in the empty spaces between each one.

"Neither have I."

"I have so many questions for you, but right now, I don't care. All I care about is that you're with me again."

I cradled his sharp jawline in my hand as I caressed his face. He didn't move back, he only moved closer, placing his knee between my thighs and pressing against the heat that was waiting for him there.

His arms had me firmly boxed in against the balcony, and when I stared into his eyes, his face changed. A red circle glowed around his irises as two sharp fangs snapped in his mouth.

"You need to know that this is who I am now." He stepped back, putting distance between us. His eyes drifted to the floor, ashamed, then he raised them again. He stood tall, strong and he appeared to have come to terms with himself.

And for a few heartbeats, I grappled with the idea that he was my target. He was working with the mafia, and he was part of the Dark Zodiac. He and his kind were the very enemy I had been trained to fight. My throat tightened as I realized my current position. This wouldn't go over well with the guys.

"I know exactly what you are. I watched it happen... from afar. All I did was think about you since that day. I haven't stopped looking for you or wondering where you were. Fate has brought us together again and that was all I ever wanted." My heart raced with new hope now that we were together once again.

His fangs were still out, but I didn't care. I knew who he was from before, and I knew that my Trent was still in there.

"Don't begin to think you know who I am now, Sasha. I'm not the same." He combed his hands through his thick golden hair, and it fell perfectly back in place.

"I know you're not the same. I don't care who you are now. I'm different, too. Very different. We can figure this out. Together."

He turned and looked over his shoulder, like he'd heard something. He brought his fangs back into his mouth, and his face deadpanned. "What are you doing here? Really? You know these people are dangerous. Who are those guys you're with and what are you up to?"

His eyes told me he was in deep with the Dark Zodiac, and although I would fight to be with him, I didn't trust that I could tell him everything just yet. First, I needed to understand where he stood in all of this.

"Why don't we meet somewhere later, where we can talk? I don't feel safe here." I looked around, wondering what sounds he was picking up on and how much he knew about Zol Stria.

"Let's go right now. Follow me downstairs to the valet. I know where we can go."

I debated whether to tell the guys I was going or to just get in the car with him. The girl in love wanted to run off with him, wherever he wanted to go and say fuck the rest of the world. It was him and me, and we would make this vampire-shifter thing work in some lost corner of the world where nothing mattered but us. But I didn't know enough about him yet to know he would be ready to do the same for me. I wasn't sure I could trust him with all of my secrets. Maybe eventually, but right now it was way too soon.

"Fine, but let me tell my friends first. They'll worry."

He shook his head. "Sasha, we either do this together, or we don't do it at all." Trent took a step closer to me now, closing the distance and reaching for my hand. With his other hand he traced his finger up my arm, over my bare shoulder and slid it up to my lips where he set it there for a brief moment while piercing into me with demon-tainted eyes. "I have just as much to lose as you do, if not more. Neither of us get to tell anyone where we're going. We just go."

I searched his energy and his heart for truth, and I wasn't sure what I saw. Truth looked different now. It wasn't as easy. It wasn't as pure as when we were both human. Now, we were both skilled at giving the other what we wanted the other to see.

"Fine. Let's go, right now." I knew I was experienced enough. I had been through enough training and had battled enough monsters to be able to handle myself in any situation. Right now was about my life and figuring out how Trent would fit in it.

"Let's go this way. There's a private exit through this room. No one will see us leave."

As he led the way downstairs to his car, I followed, and I didn't look back.

CHAPTER 31

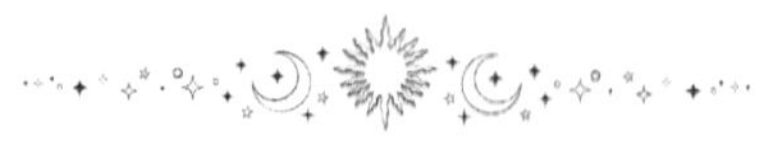

DAMIAN

The booming beats penetrated my ears, thumping loud and obnoxious. A small crowd had formed at one of the large glass walls at the far end of the bar where the VIPs were watching the show. Some big-name rapper was performing. Marni was with the crowd; she turned and tried to wave me over. I gave her a friendly smile but shook my head slowly, no. She shrugged as if to say, "Suit yourself," and turned back around to watch. Zayne was on the other side of the bar talking to some gentlemen we'd identified as investors and business partners of the mafia.

And Sasha, well, she had just left and thought I didn't know. She thought I didn't realize that Trent was here, and that she'd gone off with him somewhere to do who knew what. We had agreed that none of us would make any moves without letting the others know. And she'd just broken that rule.

I downed the glass of whiskey and asked for another. What Sasha didn't account for was the connection of our bond. It grew stronger every day we were together, allowing me to tune into her energy, just like I had in Columbia when I knew she was in trouble with the vampires before she shifted. But she'd conveniently forgotten about this connection we had and just left.

Or maybe she counted on the connection so she could leave without telling us and gain his trust, knowing I would sense it. Either way I could sense she wasn't in danger, and I could see why she would want to get close to him. She'd been destroyed when she'd seen him become a vampire. She felt responsible, and she was also still in love with him. And, as far as the mission went, he was a good lead for us to learn more about the target.

I felt a hand graze my back as I caught a whiff of a familiar rosewater fragrance. I turned my head to the right and saw Marni smiling at me. She slid into the stool next to me at the bar.

"Well, handsome, are you going to buy me a drink?" she said with a smile full of white teeth. The bartender came by, and she ordered while bobbing her head to the music vibrating through the entire club. "You're missing the show. He's really good." She was bouncing in her chair now.

"Is he?" I'd rather be listening to anything else, but I had to let this girl think I was fun and interested in what she had to say.

It turned out Sasha had worked some magic by making friends with Marni. She was the daughter of the club owner, who was also a major investor in businesses in Miami. She was very well-connected and had gone to school with the kids of celebrities, politicians and the local billionaires. Without realizing it, Marni was swinging the doors wide open for us to walk right in.

As we sat drinking, I asked her, "How does your father own so many businesses?"

"It wasn't always like this," she said. "My father had always done well financially, but he started to attract a constant stream of abundance after he linked up with the right people." Then she named off the heads of the cartel: Fausto, Javier and Lennox. She said they all reported to someone, a woman, but she was in another location and Trey was her second-in-command. The more drinks I bought Marni, the more she told me.

"So why do you think he began to attract so much abundance?" My eyes penetrated hers with a playful stare, wondering if she would give me the typical bullshit answer or feed me something I could use. She'd had several drinks already.

I shifted my gaze around the room, searching for anyone with a retracted aura or other signs of Fae that might be here. When I felt confident there were only humans here, I put up the deflector shield and cast a *mokita* spell to try and get the truth from her. This wouldn't force her to tell it, but it would make her feel uncomfortable covering up truths that others knew. Truths worth hiding from newcomers like me. I discovered it in my time with the aborigines of New Guinea and this was a spell I never shared with anyone.

"Well, there was this wealth-and-abundance coach who came in. She gave him meditations to do, affirmations, all sorts of mind shifting techniques." As she spoke her face flushed, and by the time she was finished Marni was coughing. She covered her mouth and put her other hand on her chest.

"You ok? Let me get you some water." I waved over the bartender, and she brought Marni a glass.

"Whoa. I don't know what came over me." When she regained her composure, she tried again and coughed again. I swept her hair back over her shoulder and let my hand rest on her back, rubbing it gently, sending her the white, comforting energy of my crown chakra. This would coax her into feeling like she could trust me.

"It hasn't all been easy." The red color faded from her face. "That abundance coach was a blood sucker." She searched for something in my eyes. "I'm telling you, Damian, she was a real blood sucker."

I raised my eyebrows in mock surprise.

"My mother had just left my father for a younger man, and he was vulnerable. Somehow Solana convinced him she was someone he could trust, very quickly, and he began to tell her everything. From that moment on it's been like she's had some sort of spell on him. He introduced her to the politicians the cartel has in their pocket. He gave her all the information he had gathered on the sex scandals and fetishes. Like how the governor has a boyfriend on the side and how a senator has a baby with a mistress. Somehow, she got it all out of him and he gave her everything she needed to take over the business. Now, he works for her." She lifted the glass of water to her lips and took a long drink.

She glamoured him and made him her host.

"But I'm worried about him. The cartel started moving in on the Miami Mafia's territory and she's gotten greedy. I overheard some of the people who work for him saying that she's a witch and that she brought on the hurricane that took out their operation. Of course, it's ridiculous, but she kind of freaks me out."

Marni covered her mouth with her hand and shifted her eyes. "I shouldn't be saying all this to you. You're going to think I'm crazy and I'm going to get in serious trouble."

I loaded on the white energy, to put her more at ease. "I think you've been through a lot and sometimes, you just need to let all that stuff out. Come on... let's get a hug." I opened my arm out to her, and she leaned in, resting her head on my shoulder like I was a pillow. "I promise I won't say anything. Your secret is safe with me."

"There are those in this very room who would kill me if they thought I told you anything." Her voice was a whisper laced with fear.

"Like who?"

Her eyes shifted to a corner in the back of the room, where Zayne was sitting next to a tall, slender man with sharp features and thick black hair. I scoffed as soon as I saw him. He was Cetus, the son of one of Ixia's dryads, but they'd had a falling out ages ago.

"That guy over there works with my father. I heard him and my father talking about a massive takeover. Whenever he says anything like that, people get hurt. Lots of people."

I lifted my white energy from her. Slowly, she sat up in her chair and ran her hands over her hair, regaining her composure. Was Cetus involved with the Dark Zodiac? Finding out would be tricky.

"Well, what do you know? That's Cetus. He's an old friend of mine. Marni, let's go say hello," I said to Marni.

"Oh no, that's ok, sugar. I'm feeling tired. I'll be heading home for the night. Tell Leyla to give me a call so we can go shopping. I love that girl."

"Sure, I will."

Before leaving, she turned around and planted a soft kiss on my lips. "Thanks for listening. I feel so much better getting all that off my chest."

I shrugged my shoulders. "You're welcome."

I approached the table where Zayne and Cetus were sitting. "May I join you?" I asked. He gave me a slight nod as I sat down. "So, are you and Ixia on speaking terms? Did she send you?"

He tilted the glass he held in his hand and stared at the brown liquid inside without returning my gaze. "No. I haven't spoken to her in decades. I'm here to tell you to back off and go home. There's a mafia war about to explode, and you don't want to be caught in the middle of it."

I shifted in my chair and leaned back, draping my arm over the backrest. I stole a glance at Zayne, who looked like he gave fuck all about what this guy was saying, just like I did.

"Sure ok, I'll pack my bags tonight." I chuckled.

"Suit yourself. I delivered the message." Cetus took the last swig of his drink, got up and walked out.

It was no use questioning him; he was always a prick. If he was willing to tell us more, he would have right then. The three of us were getting closer to the inner circle every day. Soon we would become the cartel's clients, and we would learn more about the truth of it all.

There was no way we were leaving anytime soon.

CHAPTER 32

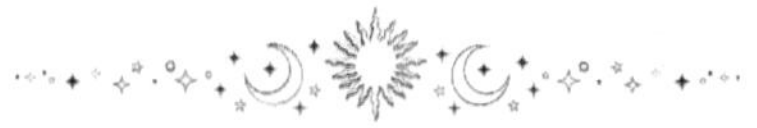

SASHA

I told Trent I wanted to see where he lived, and he brought me to his home on the South Beach waterway. It was large, expensive, and way beyond what I expected him to have just one year after becoming a vampire. He must be moving up the ranks of the Dark Zodiac quickly. When we reached the veranda that led out to an infinity pool, I turned away from him and faced the large, open waterway that fed into the ocean. The smell of salt filled my nostrils while the wind rushed around me.

"I must say, I'm impressed." I hated that I couldn't read his energy. I had no idea what he was thinking or if I could trust him.

"I did what I had to do to survive. Turns out, surviving as a vampire has its own rewards." His voice carried the weight of the darkness with every word. He walked up behind me and wrapped his hands around my waist, pulling me tightly against him. The feeling of being in his strong arms was almost as comforting as it used to be, save for the thought that he worked for the enemy.

"Can I trust you not to hurt me?" A sliver of panic raced through me, and it wasn't from the thought that he would answer no, it was from how his body turned cold to my touch after I asked him. He backed away and put some distance between us.

"I should be asking you the same question. Where did you go when you turned into a jaguar, after almost fucking that vampire right in front of me? The image of you with him has been burned into my mind."

The tears building in my eyes threatened to release, and my tormented emotions were entirely on display for him to see. As much as I hated the valley that existed between us now, I couldn't hide myself from him. I wouldn't. I lifted my hand and converted the sadness, shadow, and darkness to heat. A fire lit on one finger, then another, then another until my entire hand held the fire in place. I shot it out in front of me as Trent's expression remained unchanged.

"This is who I am. A shapeshifting elemental. Just like being a vampire is who you are now. We're both different and yet, neither of us chose this life. But I'm still in love with you. Our entire time apart, I've never stopped loving you." I closed my hand and set it down at my side as I watched him for any break in his hard expression. Any shift of that stone-cold look on his face would be a sign that he still held some hope of him and me together.

A boat blasting party music cruised by, and it momentarily caught his eye as I waited for him to say something. Anything.

He turned to me, eyes still unreadable, and I wasn't sure why or how he was so adept at hiding himself from me while I remained a wide-open book. He took two steps in my direction, and I inhaled deeply, keeping my eyes locked on him. Then, in a flash of vampire speed, he was standing right in front of me, piercing me with his gaze. Danger. That's what I saw now. I saw danger in those cold eyes. I was at least able to read that much.

"I've done some things I'm not proud of. I've done some things that have changed me." He searched my eyes. I was sure he was checking to see if I understood what he meant and if it scared me.

"So have I. I don't care what you've done. We're together again." Warmth pooled from deep inside me, stirring up my insides and threatening to give away how desperately I had missed him.

He brushed a hair from my face, his expression softening. His furrowed brow now darkened his eyes, but his lips looked just as welcoming as I remembered. That gesture was all I'd needed as I gazed into him with hopeful eyes. I reached my arms up around his neck and pulled him close to me. He brought those delicious lips in to meet mine. The moment he parted my lips with his tongue, my whole body trembled.

He growled softly, and I knew then that he had missed me as much as I had missed him. I pushed the fear of him and what the Dark Zodiac could do to the very back of my mind and let myself succumb to this deep, endless wanting.

He wrapped an arm around my back, and I arched in response, giving him more of me. Feeling his tongue caress me. He swept me up in his arms and flashed me into the house, straight to his massive bedroom on the second floor. I had never been carried by a vampire in motion like that, and I clung to him tightly. I giggled when he stopped. I'd always loved going fast and the reckless excitement that came along with speed. He didn't bother turning on the lights; the moon was all we needed. My eyes had enhanced visibility in the dark, and so did his. We were now both creatures of the shadows.

He rested his hands on my hips as I leaned into him with eager kisses, determined to make up for all the lost time and then some. He reached one hand up and wove his fingers into my hair. The moment he fisted and pulled my hair back, I bit his lip in response and heard him growl again. I wanted this rougher version of him. I wanted this dark hunter to quell the deep ache that began between my thighs and coursed through my entire body.

He traced his fingertips up my mid-section, touching the skin beneath my shirt and lighting the places his fingertips graced with a rich heat. I followed with my own touch of his hard, muscular flesh underneath his clothing, the contours of his muscles unyielding. In one sweeping motion, he lifted his shirt up and off and brought me to his bed. He stood between my legs as I sat on the edge, lifting my shirt off and letting him see my bare, full breasts peak in the light of the moon. He reached for them hungrily, but his touch was a gentle caress. He kissed me again, a ravenous moan escaping my throat as his tongue entered my mouth.

I wanted him this very instant, and he knew exactly how much. I laid back on the bed, and he lowered his head at my knees. He placed kisses along my thighs, moving between my legs until he reached the center where he began to feast on me. Trembling, a loud moan escaped my lips as I shuddered beneath his tongue. When he lifted his beautiful face to look at me, it was the same Trent I had always remembered. The unbroken, mortal face flashed before me in the quickest second, and I knew there would always be that part of him still in there.

I wanted him inside me. I reached my arms around his waist. He climbed on top of me, then thrust himself between my legs and gave me the fullest length of him. I tore at his back with my hands, feeling him enter me with a wildness I didn't recognize.

He drove this dark wildness deeper, and I returned it with my own feral pulses. We would be darkness and wildness and moonlight together. I breathed into his chest and licked him to taste his sweat. When I lifted my eyes to meet his, I saw the savage vampire he'd become. It was in his eyes. Thick black irises covered the normal sky-blue hue, and his fangs were completely out. His veins strained from holding back his instinct to bite. I knew from my studies that he was capable of taking a bite and not killing me if he knew how to control himself. He must have learned how to by now.

"Can you control it?" I asked between pants.

"Yes." His voice was confident, sure.

"Then do it." I turned my head to give him my neck. I had learned enough about vampires in Zol Stria to know they always felt the urge to bite during intimacy. It was an instinct for them, and it would give great pleasure to both the vampire and the person receiving the bite. This was why vampires loved to feast on humans, because humans could get addicted to the venom that laced the vampire's bite. It kept them coming back for more.

As soon as his teeth penetrated my skin, a low, burning roar escaped my throat. It was sweltering and sensual, and it brought me to places in my mind that I never knew existed. Every pore of my body became aroused, and my hips thrust with his every movement. I released all control to him. My physical body moved with his to another plane of sensation that lit every part of me with raging desire. He responded by satisfying me over and over, in every position, until I went over the edge and came apart beneath him.

I slept lightly in the comfort of his arms and awoke to the sound of his breathing way before the sun began to rise. He rested next to me, naked and quiet, but not asleep. Vampires needed far less sleep than any of us, only a few hours every day.

We tangled in each other's arms and made love again, then again, as if to make up for all the time we'd spent apart. Underneath his new skin and supernatural form, he still carried that familiar earthly scent. Between the smell and the taste of him, it brought me right back to our many nights before.

My eyelids grew heavier this time as sleep tugged at my consciousness. I tried not to close my eyes, afraid if I slept, he would disappear from my life again. I relaxed against him as his hand gently stroked my back. My thoughts began to drift far away until I felt his lips press against my forehead.

I awoke much later to the sound of his curtains opening and the sun's rays pouring into the room. He was up, already showered and dressed. Whenever the full moon was in his sun sign's constellation, he could walk freely in the sun. And it just so happened, the full moon was in Scorpio right now.

"I bet you're hungry," he said with a much softer expression on his face than I'd seen the night before. He was sweet to remember my huge appetite.

"Starving." I reached my hand to my neck to feel the bite marks, and I could tell they had already started to heal. The bite he'd inflicted wasn't painful at all. Instead, it reminded me of what he had become: a beautiful monster.

"Great, I know the perfect place to take you for brunch." His face held the smile I'd fallen in love with, and I realized it was the first time I'd seen that smile in over a year. Although my neck and thighs were still sore from our night, there was also a profound, stilling fullness in my heart.

Chapter 33

Damian

The engine of our Maserati purred as Zayne and I drove through the paved driveway lined with palm trees and tropical foliage. We soon arrived at the exclusive waterside country club. Several weeks had passed, and our connections with the Dark Zodiac were getting stronger. We'd purchased several multimillion-dollar pieces from them already, selling them off to our Fae contacts across the globe.

The Fae had stakes in several multinational businesses and a legacy of financial backing from the beginning of time to facilitate such transactions. Yet the laws of the Zol were very clear: The financial systems of the mortal world could only be used to support and protect humans from the Fae that would abuse their power over them.

The pieces we bought from them were exquisite. After many years of buying and looking at bad art, I knew what would be marketable and what wouldn't. This part was easy for me. What I didn't know was who was running this new sect of the Dark Zodiac, which one of them killed Lily and what exactly their bigger plan was.

Sasha, Zayne and I were dressed to the nines for today's formal event. Sasha wore an elegant one-shoulder, shiny silver dress with a slit through the middle with black heels; Zayne wore a blue satin suit; I wore a blood-red suit with a black shirt underneath. Tonight we would be privy to some newly acquired pieces, including sculptures, artifacts and jewelry.

Music spilled through the front doors as we walked through the grand entrance. We strolled through the space, greeting familiar faces and getting drinks at the bar. We admired the pieces and spoke casually about their value, getting superficial insight on the background of each production. Sasha casually searched the room for Trent, who was actively back in her life. This was definitely going to complicate things. She wouldn't be able to handle keeping her feelings separate from the mission, but she made a strong case for keeping him close.

The stars write the path, and they'd brought him back into the picture for a reason. Now she just had to keep her emotions in check so we could uncover some truths. I had the ring on me every day, and it never woke. It was taking longer than expected to finish this mission, and I was getting restless.

So many years of searching. So much pain rekindled every time I looked at Sasha and saw traces of Lily in her face. If we didn't find something out soon, I would take one of these Dark Zodiac cartel bitches, lock them in the panic room and beat their ass until they told me what I needed to know. I unclenched my teeth and rolled my shoulders back. No need to get all worked up just yet. *See how the night goes before you lose it.*

Trent approached Sasha in an all-black suit with bright, silver cuff links and metal clasps along his shirt where buttons would normally be. He took her hand in his and kissed it. She pulled him in toward her and kissed him on the cheek instead. He chuckled.

"Good evening, gentlemen," Trent said.

Zayne and I nodded in greeting, and Trent's eyes shifted to Sasha. "You look amazing, Leyla." Trent remained fixed on her, as if taking her all in. At least he was trying to keep her cover by remembering her fake name. I looked away; seeing them like that made me want to gouge my eyes out.

"You're not so bad yourself," Sasha replied, and I could hear the smile in her voice.

"You'll never believe it, but you know that piece by Gregorio you just bought for a steal a few days ago? I have a buyer that wants to pay double to take it tonight," Trent said. "Do you still have it in your warehouse or did you ship it to Madrid already? He's here now and wants it installed in the home he's building on Key Biscayne. He says it's the only piece that will work on a certain wall of the new construction."

Zayne rolled his eyes, as though revealing how excessive he thought this all to be. Trent and Sasha probably had that in common with him, seeing as neither of them were born to this life.

"I'm not sure where it is," she replied. "I'll have to check our inventory. But I had a few prospects lined up in Madrid. I certainly don't want to disappoint them. Before I make any promises, what will you show me to replace it?" She knew the game already. Never give away information, even the slightest. Always hold your cards.

"Sorry, gentlemen, I see someone Damian and I need to talk to. Excuse us." Zayne nodded in the direction of another potential client, and Sasha walked away with Trent. The night carried on easily as we placed bids on the productions that were most attractive to the clients in our network. There were several celebrities and athletes among the crowd, as was to be expected, and our game plan seemed to be working as the cartel now treated us like welcome, familiar guests.

Yet in the back of my mind, I began to hear the howls and screeching of the damned. The walls began to vibrate with a soft, subtle thrum. It wasn't detectable by any of the guests, but it had Zayne and me on high alert. We quickly exchanged glances as we sensed the coming of the dark energy that could only have been created by the UnZol King.

Suddenly, the glassware shook as panicked screams of the guests filled the room. Expensive sculptures crashed to the floor, and people spilled food and drinks on their expensive gowns. There was a horrific thrashing and pounding as though the earth beneath us would open and swallow the entire building whole.

Zayne and I lifted our deflector spells and cast energy out in search of Sasha, who was nowhere to be found.

"It's an earthquake." We both looked at each other. "The Stone Mind."

We steadied ourselves against the wall while furniture shifted and trembled around us. A woman reached for me before slipping and falling to her knees on the floor, grasping at my leg for balance. I reached down and pulled her up by the elbow, and she leaned into me while sobbing into my jacket, afraid. One of the chandeliers dropped on the floor, crushing an older man stumbling to get out of the way. Blood spilled around him, and I could tell instantly that he had been killed.

There was more panic as the crowd tried desperately to escape the chaos in the room that was falling apart. I continued to seek out Sasha with my energy, but I couldn't find her. She either had a powerful deflector spell up, or she was gone. What the fuck was going on?

Just as a piece of the ceiling fell off and was about to crush us, I cast an air shield around us and held it there as I guided the crying woman out of the way. Then I let the brass-and-crystal chandelier drop. Maybe a few people saw the levitating light fixture, but they were probably too shocked about this whole thing to care.

I dropped the crying woman off with the rest of the crowd jammed against the main door, then Zayne and I headed for the long hallways toward the parking lot. We found a side door leading out and exited as the building continued to crumble into pieces. I searched for Sasha, but she was nowhere to be found. I called her cell phone over and over, but she wouldn't answer. We hurried away from the building to the far end of the parking lot where we found our car. Zayne and I watched as the entire building and the billions of dollars' worth of art within crumbled to the ground.

We didn't want to get questioned by the police, so we drove out and away, weaving through stumbling men and women with varying degrees of shock and outrage on their faces.

"What the fuck just happened?" I shouted, still riled. "A natural earthquake in Miami is impossible. There are no fault lines here."

"But if someone has the Stone Mind, they could do it." Zayne's voice was low and steady.

All of the Fae knew of the UnZol King and his dismemberment. His body parts had been separated into six unique relics, and each of these possessed a specific kind of magic that could bring about the power of a dark god.

"We believe the Blood Ruby is with the cartel because they unleashed the hurricane. The Miami Mafia must have the Stone Mind. It must be how they created that earthquake. This was retaliation." I clenched my hand into a fist. Our mission was getting even more complicated, and I was nowhere close to finding Lily's killer. "I keep calling Sasha and she won't answer her phone. Where is she?

I'm trying to track her through our bond, but I'm not getting anything. Let's head to Trent's house and see if they show up there."

Zayne pressed down on the gas as we rushed over to his place. It was a few miles away, and the whole ride I continued to call without answer. When we pulled up to his house we found him outside, pacing.

"Where's Sasha? Wasn't she with you?" I asked him, and a genuine look of concern clouded his darkened features.

"She was, but I turned away for a second to talk to someone and when I turned back, she was gone. I couldn't find her anywhere and then the building began to collapse. I have no idea where she is. I've called her a thousand times and she doesn't answer."

The three of us exchanged glances, confused. Because he was a vampire, I couldn't read his energy, so I didn't trust him. But something about his love for Sasha told me that he wasn't lying about losing her.

"Did you see her talking to anyone? Was there anyone suspicious around? Anyone you didn't recognize?" I stepped closer to him. My hands clenched in fists as a blazing heat grew in my chest. It had just hit me, a deeper sensation, a more profound knowing that came from within that told me she was in danger.

"Yes, well there was a group of new faces tonight. That's why I turned away from her. I told security to check them out because I didn't recognize them. But they were on the other side of the room. The second I turned back around to Sasha, she was gone and so were they. The earthquake began right after."

I wanted to clock him on his jaw. He'd fucking lost her to them, whoever they were.

"We're going to have a talk." The way Zayne growled through gritted teeth told me he was controlling his own frustration about the situation. "The three of us. You need to tell us everything about the Miami Mafia and what they're after. This seems like some kind of retaliation."

Trent's face was expressionless, as though he was trying not to give anything away.

We headed inside. It was going to be a long night.

CHAPTER 34

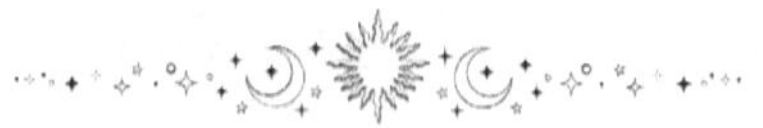

SASHA

My eyelids were heavy as I struggled to open them. When I did, I found myself in a chair in the middle of a grand office. Fine furniture filled the space with modern art pieces on the wall and a spectacular view of the bay from the large glass wall. An older, refined gentlemen sat behind the desk, and for an older guy, he was very attractive. Two large security guards stood at either end of the room, and this man in the suit sat back in his seat, contemplating me. I must have been drugged, because the last thing I remembered was a terribly dizzy feeling overcoming me as I walked to the ladies' room. I remember entering a stall, and then my mind went blank after that.

"You're probably wondering why you're here," he said as he cleaned an invisible piece of dust from his fine jacket.

I kept my eyes wide open with a look of fear on my face. I'd decided quickly to pretend to be a victim at his mercy. This would let him think he had the upper hand while I heard him out. Meanwhile I noticed that he had an aura, which meant he wasn't a vampire, but it didn't rule out another Fae form.

I watched as black laced his aura colors of blue and green, while gray tainted the inner section. He was one with his own darkness—in fact, he gained a great deal of satisfaction from it. But he wasn't consumed by it, which meant he wasn't a complete monster.

"This is nothing personal, but you have now become my property. You've become an important client to the cartel, and I need you to get them to give me what I want." He had maneuvered himself closer to me, so close that I could smell the cologne of smoke, spice and cedar on his skin. I wasn't restrained, so I crossed my legs and sat confidently in the chair, leveling my energy off to a steady calm.

"Why do you think I can get them to do anything?" I kept my composure to make sure I didn't appear as a threat. I didn't want him to know I was being trained as a warrior of Zol Stria, that I was a nagual of the underworld or that I knew how to shadow weave and could take all three of them out in a matter of a few heartbeats. I wanted to see how much he knew first.

"I have my sources, and I've learned that you've been spending a lot of time with the head of their operation here in Miami. I know your name is Sasha, not Leyla. That you're an old girlfriend of Trey's from his military days, and you've appeared back in his life, somehow now a multimillion-dollar international art dealer. Whatever your deal is with him, I know you're important to him, and that makes you a bargaining chip. He'll come looking for you, and when he does, it will be easy. All he needs to do is give us a simple little ring, and he can have you back. If that ring is more important to him than you are, well then, that should tell you a lot about your relationship."

Is he talking about the Blood Ruby? Trent has the Blood Ruby? He was trying to taunt me, and I let him believe his words stung. While he'd been talking, I'd been debating my next move, which included slicing his throat.

"Why is that ring so important to you? Why couldn't you just ask him for it?" I glared at him, now playing the role of the pissed-off girlfriend. "And did you have something to do with the building collapsing? How did you do that?" I was genuinely curious about that, as I had no clue how they could make a whole building come down. There were no earthquakes in Miami.

"Yes, well, that's enough questions for now." He glanced at the two security guards and made a swift sweeping motion with his hand as he walked behind his desk and sat back down.

The larger of the two guards grabbed me from the back and held me down in the chair. His grip was firm and unyielding, and I stared in wide-eyed disbelief. Still keeping up appearances. Shifting into a jaguar and ripping his head off was definitely tempting as I felt my jaguar swish inside me, compelling me to set her free. I held her back, for now. I still didn't want to reveal myself to these people.

The stocky one with a dragon tattooed on his neck and a tear drop under his eye stood in front of me with an icy stare. I could tell from the way his hand moved back that he was about to punch me across my face. I could duck, shift, blast them with fire or shadow weave to avoid the impact. Or I could sit there and let this play out for a few minutes longer to avoid killing these assholes. I really didn't want human death on my hands.

I braced myself for the impact. My head jolted to the left as he knocked into me, and I bit my cheek in the process. The pain echoed through my jaw to my head as blood oozed in my mouth. My eyes shifted to the pendejo behind the desk who was filming this whole thing.

"Did your mother ever teach you not to hit girls?" I said as I glared at the guards.

There was something off about them. The two guards had pure black auras. They were demon souls. These Dark Fae became indebted servants to the relics once they'd let their darkness entirely consume them. The UnZol Relics were like magnets to those who repeatedly gave in to the horrors of the world. There was nothing left in these two men other than sheer evil. These demons were now only capable of inflicting pain, murder, rape, abuse and torture in the name of the holder of the UnZol's relics.

"I don't remember, I was too busy fucking your mother to notice." He chuckled at his own joke, and so did the brute who was holding me.

The moment the brute's tar-like energy began to move in the direction of his next blow, I decided it was time to shadow weave. *Sorry beasty*, I told my jaguar, *we're not shifting just yet*. I didn't want to shred through this beautiful dress and be left naked afterwards.

With just a thought, I was darkness and shadow and mist as tendrils of black curled around my fingers, hands and legs until I became one with it. Their facial expressions remained unchanged in the split-second that passed, and I moved quickly behind the beefy guy. I slid out the knife from its sheath on my thigh, which they'd never bothered to check or remove. *They never thought I was a real threat, or they would have checked me everywhere.*

I held the knife in one hand while I sent a blaze of fire at both of them, backing them up against the wall. As soon as I released the fire, the big guy lunged after me, so I flung the knife at him. He let out a moan of pain as it planted into his arm. The stocky one with the dragon tattoo stepped backward with his hands up as I sent another blaze of fire. The powerful heat singed his eyebrows.

A second later, I became mist again and reappeared behind the boss at the desk. My knife pressed into his throat, piercing his skin enough to make it bleed. I wrapped one arm under his chin in a tight grip and held the knife in the other so I could end him in one swift movement.

"Now are you going to tell me what the fuck I'm doing here, or do I have to barbecue your friends first?" My voice was soft, sweet and sarcastic. Then my expression darkened.

"No, he's not."

I looked up to the doorway to see Ixia standing there.

Cabrón. *What in the actual fuck is she doing here? Is she behind all of this?*

She had a hand on her hip as she leaned against the door like none of this was a big deal. That explained how I got knocked out. Nagual were such a rare Fae form that the typical Fae potions didn't work on us, and we were immune to anything that affected humans. Only she could create an herbal potion that could affect me.

"And you're going to let him go," she said firmly.

I could feel the man I was holding turn clammy and sweaty under my tight grip, and for the briefest heartbeat, I was sorry for him. But then I wasn't, and I held the knife even tighter.

"Now why would I do that?" I cocked my head to the side.

"Because if you don't, you will suffer far more greatly than is necessary."

I hated riddles. Now I had to know why I would suffer at all.

"Gentlemen, set her back in the chair," Ixia commanded.

"Those guys can't do shit to me."

But I was wrong, because in one sweeping motion, she paralyzed my powers. I still held the boss at knifepoint, but I could tell my abilities were nullified. I felt that same splintering dizziness that had overcome me in the lady's bathroom.

"I have the Stone Mind. You know about the Stone Mind, don't you? One of the six relics of the great UnZol King? It grants me a taste of the power of the gods. Now, sit down and let's have a nice talk. Shall we?"

As much as I hated to admit it, I was completely powerless, so I dropped the knife. I really hadn't wanted to kill him anyway, and I had no clue if he was valuable to her in some way.

The boss straightened his collar and got up. "She woke up sooner than we expected," he said. His voice gave away his more inferior position. *She* was clearly the boss here.

I scanned her body for the Stone Mind, and energetically, I could sense its presence on her hip. *It might be inside the sheath or the handle of a knife if she keeps one hidden there.*

"Next time we'll increase the dosage for this little monster." Ixia eyed me contemptuously. "Lucky for you, I'm here. She could have killed the three of you in less than ten seconds."

I'd never had the feeling she liked me, and now I knew I was right about that. Damian was in for a surprise, that's for sure.

"Ixia, what's going on? What do you want with me?"

She scoffed and elegantly sat in the chair behind the desk as I stood on the other side of it with my arms crossed. I felt around my mind for the dark energy that gave me power. I tried to pull in the shadows so I could shift, but nothing happened. All I felt was an empty void of nothing. If she had the Stone Mind, then she was probably trying to collect all the other relics of the UnZol King. She must be a part of the Dark Zodiac that wanted free reign of the human world. That meant I was in the hands of our target.

"You're going to help me get what's mine. Now go back to acting weak and frail for the video that Samuel needs to make of you, or I'm going to have to force you to do it."

"I'm not just going to sit there while these guys kick my ass. There's no way."

"You don't have much choice in the matter."

"Why not? That's not very honorable. Let me fight them without my powers, since you've taken those powers away anyway. Let's see if they can get to me one on one. It'll make this all a whole lot more interesting and a lot less disturbing. If they win, I'll personally beg Trent to give you that ring. If I win, you let me go."

I glanced over at the men that weighed almost three times more than me and had muscles bulging out of their shirts. I'd been trained by both the US military and the Aries Academy in hand-to-hand combat. As intimidating as they looked, I wasn't entirely afraid.

Ixia put her hand on her chin and considered it. "Fine. I'll bite. With no powers, she'll be a breeze, fellas. Relax." She chuckled under her breath, but the men still seemed a little shaken.

I snarled at them, and they didn't even flinch. They didn't even know yet that they were exactly where I wanted them. I wiped away the remaining drops of blood that lingered on my chin and licked my finger as I stared at them.

I was about to fuck them up.

CHAPTER 35

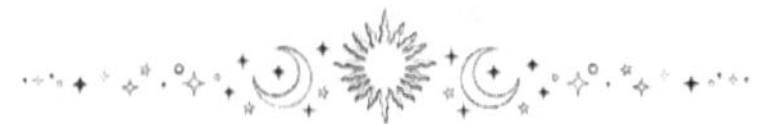

DAMIAN

The day was cooler than usual as I waited outside Vizcaya for the nagual reinforcements to come through. I let the car idle in the lot outside the museum in the early morning hours before the sun had fully risen. I looked over my shoulder and saw the three of them emerge, looking like three lost tourists. Although Jenna, Lex and Andres wore jeans and T-shirts, I could sense the savage warriors within. I could see the grave expressions hidden under their cool demeanors, brought on by their concern for Sasha.

I stayed in the car as they each opened a door and got in. They barely said a word on the drive to the safe house. Through my bond with Sasha, I could feel an echo of her increased heart rate and could sense her mind was on high alert. She had been compromised. We'd stopped staying at the hotel or any of our known locations, retreating to the safe house in a quiet residential neighborhood near Little Havana, just a few miles from where I sensed her presence.

As soon as we arrived, the nagual set their things down and went straight to the office. Zayne had three monitors up with the profiles and background information of key individuals up on the screen.

"What's up with our girl and how do we get to her?" Jenna's brow was creased, and her eyes narrowed on the screen as if trying to decipher the context.

I hadn't been able to share much in the vision I'd sent them. Visions were the only way we communicated across the Gates, and it was very difficult to get more than a few things through to the other side, unless you were mated, because mates had a stronger connection. All I was able to tell them was that Sasha was in trouble and we needed reinforcements.

"Well, first of all you need to know who you're dealing with. This is the head of the Colombian Cartel." Trent's photo was up on the screen with his age, zodiac sign and the details about his conversion to a Dark Vampire.

"Oh shit, is that Trent?" Jenna scowled at the screen as she scanned the words, trying to understand quickly what had happened.

"Yes, that's him."

"Damn, he's hotter now than in the picture she has of him. Did they hook up? I need to know."

"Yes, well, it seems they did reconnect on a romantic level, and right now we don't suspect him to be her kidnapper," Zayne said. "The threat of the UnZol King has just become greater. We believe two of his relics are being used in rival mafia warfare."

"There are six relics. Which ones do they have and where are the others?" Lex asked as he stood tall behind where Jenna was sitting in front of the monitors.

Zayne explained, "As you guys know, each of the six relics heightens the powers of the holder and the ability to call upon the powers of the gods. We believe the Colombian Cartel has the Blood Ruby. This would explain how they conjured a hurricane to take out the Miami Mafia's warehouse and the boss's house. Now, we believe the Miami Mafia has the Stone Mind, because they retaliated and took out their club in an earthquake. This is where Sasha was last seen. If the holder of the Stone Mind is a powerful elder, they can use its power to nullify Sasha's own powers."

"So where are the four other relics right now?" Andres asked, eyes probing Zayne for answers.

"The locations of the Blade Bone and the Devil's Eye are unknown. They were stolen several decades ago, replaced with counterfeit relics that wield the power of a lesser king. The Obsidian Heart and the Snake Throat have been verified as authentic, and they are both in highly secure locations in Zol Stria."

Zayne shifted his eyes from Andres to me, and I nodded. Last night we'd agreed we would tell the new nagual the legend of the Fates. Only the oldest among us could remember the stories. In my youth, perhaps about five hundred years ago now, I'd found an old text with this legend. It was written by a thousand-year-old Zol Sen with the sight. Recent events had started to remind me of the long-forgotten stories.

I scratched my short beard and leaned against the wall. My eyes dragged across their faces as I began to explain. "The zodiac balances chaos as much as peace. Anger as much as joy. Love as much as hate. There is no better emotion. No world without chaos. No sadness without happiness. No security without fear. Just as there are polarities in our planets and stars, there are polarities in everything and everyone. The UnZol King could not be destroyed, because it would have brought about an ever-greater chaos than his existence did. Which is why the Zol Sen put his essence in those relics and secured them. Yet now that centuries have gone by, younger Fae have forgotten the legends." I stood straight now and paced across the room until I stopped in front of them and put my hands in my pockets.

"The legend says that there will be one who joins all the pieces of the UnZol King together to bring him back, and that when he returns, he will open the Zodiac Gates to the Dark Fae so that they may have dominion over all of the Earth. Humans will rebel and fight for their lives. Their fight will be led by your kind, the nagual reborn, because of your connection to humans, Earth, and the shadows. The legend says that a single nagual of exceptional ability will decide the UnZol King's fate at the end."

I raised my eyebrows, wondering if it was all sinking in. When they didn't say anything, I realized I had to make it clearer. "The Dark Zodiac have been planning this for a long time. That's why five nagual didn't make it this time. They've been killing them off before they cross. They tried to get to Sasha but instead killed her aunt. They are after all of you."

Lex crossed his massive arms in front of him. "Because if they kill the nagual before they join all the relics, then they eliminate the risk of that legend playing out."

"Exactly." It *was* sinking in.

From there, Zayne clicked on another window and opened up the image and details of Solana Desalles. "We believe her to be the most powerful mob boss. She escaped the prison during the Faellen War and is a direct descendent of the UnZol King. She now controls five South American cartels, and from what we understand, she wants to expand into the Middle East. She's been calculating this for a long time, slowly taking territories one by one.

"Her strategy is to glamor her way into the bosses' bedrooms, kill them once they trust her and then put one of her lovers in as a general to control the newly acquired territory. Trent is her newest general who she sent here to expand the Miami Mafia's territory. Solana hasn't been seen in Miami yet. She's likely to be in headquarters in Colombia, leading the operation from there. I don't think she knows about Sasha, otherwise she'd be dead by now. Sasha killed one of her generals right after she shifted."

Jenna nodded her head as though she already knew this story.

"We believe she entrusted Trent with the Blood Ruby. We also suspect she holds at least one of the other relics, so that she can command enough power to keep controlling the cartels. Ignacio Sanchez is the known mafia boss, and we believe that somehow he's gotten access to the Stone Mind relic. Which is probably how they kept Sasha from shifting.

"We suspect they captured Sasha because she's close to Trent. What we aren't sure of is whether they know she's a nagual. But it's just a matter of time before she tries to use her powers to escape and she will be useless against the Stone Mind relic. It's the most powerful of the six relics in subduing elemental powers."

Just then, I noticed the dark circles under Zayne's eyes. He was invested in sorting all of this out, evaluating this situation thoroughly.

"Only Fae that can harness dark energy can use the magic of the relics. Humans or Fae of forms driven by light energy can't use them," he finished.

"That means there's a Dark Fae in the Miami Mafia," Jenna said with certainty.

"That's right. And I would be willing to bet it's a Dark Mage, just based on the amount of control and experience needed to concentrate an earthquake like that."

I considered the most powerful mages I knew. There were several, with Ixia being the most powerful. I could ask her what she thought, since she was on the Zol Council. She might help us narrow it down to someone she knew. All the mages studied together in Gemini Academy, and they usually ended up as professors there. If she didn't know the person directly, she may know someone who could help.

"What's next for us? How do we get her out of there if we can't use our powers?" Andres pointedly asked Zayne.

He pulled up an image of Ignacio's office, which was a large, standalone warehouse in the design district, surrounded by designer furniture and retail warehouses.

"The location is heavily guarded." He zoomed in on the security booth on the outer perimeter of the parking lot. Then he panned over to a beefy guy sitting in a chair outside the main entrance to the office area. The outline of a large, well-built man could be seen peering through the glass pane of the same entrance, and there was another security guard sitting in a car right outside the building. "All these guys are armed."

"And you're sure she's in there?" Lex pressed.

"I could sense her in there through the bond." All eyes turned to me. "We knew of several locations where the mafia operated. We drove by each one until we arrived at that warehouse. That was when I felt our bond tighten." After so many years of dealing with these nagual, I could easily distinguish the bond from my own, personal feelings. As soon as I'd seen that warehouse, it was as if she'd agreed that I'd found her location.

Zayne spoke next. "And the point is that together the four of us can use our powers. When there are two nagual present in the same room, you can cancel out the strength of a single relic. It is only a piece of the UnZol King, not all of him. The four of us nagual, along with Damian's power as a shaman, can easily take down that entire facility.

"Now, if they control two relics, you will need four nagual. If they control three relics, we will need nine nagual. The more relics that are controlled by a single holder, the more their power grows exponentially and it will take more of you to control them. Which is why we need to take those relics back fast before this gets out of control."

Jenna got up from her chair and stood up between Lex and Andres. "What the fuck are we waiting for then?"

Zayne spoke next. "Because if they took Sasha, knowing she was a nagual, then they declared an act of war on Zol Stria. I came on this mission as an emissary of the Council, and I need to bring back evidence to them so that we can bring in Zol armies to end this. We need you to help us do that."

Andres, Jenna and Lex exchanged glances and nodded in silent agreement before Lex said, "Then let's gather intel."

CHAPTER 36

SASHA

"Why don't you just start braiding my hair and painting my nails while you're at it?"

Ixia wouldn't leave my side, and it was getting annoying. They had my hands and legs restrained while I sat in a leather chair in a room on the first level of this building. This warehouse.

On the far side of the building, semis moved products in and out, while warehouse hands were hard at work. I couldn't see much of what they were doing from where I was now, but I'd heard them and gotten a visual on that area as they'd moved me in here.

I was in a storage area. The walls were lined with shelves and containers. Lots of human energy came from an area on the left that was hidden behind partition walls. People lived behind those walls. There was a particular musky, heated scent and energy that could only come from intercourse. I also smelled blood, pain and fear.

"I dare you to step twelve feet away," I hissed at her, flashing my teeth that were nothing more than shiny whites. Damn, I wished I could show her my fangs, then shove them into her neck.

"Now, you know I can't do that." Ixia's voice was cold and empty, like her soul.

I'd learned that if she was outside of a specific radius, the Stone Mind wouldn't work. So far, she kept within about ten feet and wouldn't go much farther. I suspected she didn't want to give the Stone Mind to one of her guards. Either for fear he would use it against her or because they weren't Fae. I glared at her with a penetrating stare, and she glared back at me until her phone distracted her. She answered a call, and as soon as she did, I quickly went to the place in my mind where I could expand out my consciousness to the space around me. The Stone Mind may have taken my elemental powers, but I wondered if it had taken away my ability to read energy.

I went to the stillness within my mind. The quiet spaces between words, between thoughts. This whole process used to take me a lot longer. Now it was only a matter of seconds before I was aware of the thirty-two Fae and humans beyond the dividers. I wanted to know exactly what kind of business was going on here.

There were women, girls and young boys living in this section of the warehouse. I focused in on one girl with long acrylic nails, her hair glossy and thick, her skin a creamy olive color. Her eyes were puffy, like she had just been crying. She bent over the nightstand and sniffed a line of coke while an older man with black-and-gray hair watched her from the side of the bed. He licked his lips and edged his hand up the side of her leg while scooting in closer. The moment she was done sniffing, his fangs came out, and he reached for her throat.

I knew exactly what would happen because it was happening to the girl in the room right next to this one. These women lived here with their children, snorting coke and feeding vampires to survive. I expanded my energy, and it was the same in each room: Humans were being fed to vampires. I went to the room of a girl who was about nineteen, her hair pulled up in a ponytail. She wore tight jeans and a black tank top, and her eyes were also puffy, like she, too, had been crying. This one was talking to an older woman, and they were discussing a delivery she had to make.

The older woman said in Spanish, "You're headed to the Bahamas first, where you'll pick up the eggs, and you'll fly them to New York tomorrow."

The younger girl nodded in agreement and slung a bag over her shoulder. I knew what eggs were. They were cocaine packages that women carried across borders. She was a mule. It was clear to me exactly what kind of operation this was, and it made my stomach lurch to think about it.

I actively worked to keep myself from getting angry about what I was watching so that I could evaluate this all with a level head. I took a moment to assess the girl with the ponytail. I wanted to know why she and the other girl had been crying.

I scraped against the inner realm of her mind and found the source of her sadness. Heavy energy lingered around the thoughts of someone she cared about. Her mind held the vision of a young girl, about twelve years old, pale and clammy inside a large white plastic bag. She had bloody bite marks on her neck as if she had been bled dry. The girl with the ponytail broke out in tears, along with several other girls, as the older woman somberly zipped up the bag.

I pulled my energy away and back into my body. I could hear Ixia's voice, muffled in the background, and it grew clearer as I returned to consciousness in my physical form. Ixia finished her call and turned to me a heartbeat after I opened my eyes.

"The space is clear and my guys are ready to bring you to your knees. Are you sure you want to do this? All I need is a silly little video. Trent is a pointless endeavor by the way. He's Solana's whore, didn't you know? Why do you think he let us take you so easily?"

Her lips curled as the rage over all the fuckery going on in this place flared over my face. I knew Trent was in deep with Solana because I understood the pull of glamor. At the Academy, I'd also learned about the bond between a vampire and their creator. I expected it to be hard for Trent to even consider breaking away from Solana, but my heart only gave me the option to fight for us. Even if it meant I would die trying.

"Let's get this over with."

They removed the restraints with the swift cut of a knife and lifted me out of my chair. I was forced to follow Ixia down a long brick hallway that led to a gym in the back. There was an MMA octagon in the middle of the space, with weights and other fitness equipment around it. A woman was already in the ring. She was twice my size, very muscular and wearing a black athletic bra and leggings. Her cornrows bounced as she jumped up and down, swinging her arms around and warming up.

"Change." Ixia pointed to a set of athletic clothes set out on the bench. I picked them up and looked around for a locker room. "Right here. Guys, turn around."

At least she had some decency. They moved in sluggish steps to face the other direction.

"I thought I was fighting them." I nodded in the direction of the men, still with their backs to us, as I pulled my hair up into a bun at the top of my head.

"If you manage to get past her, then you need to beat them. If you win, I let you go. No strings attached. If you lose, you make me my video and I might let you live."

I didn't believe she would let me go if I won, but it was the only chance I had at this point.

As I dressed, I examined this human woman who clearly wanted to kick my ass. I could tell from the way the dark edges of her aura coiled around the red center that she had let her darkness make her toxic. She was close to becoming a servant of the UnZol King, I could feel it. She willingly embraced her darkness in favor of evil.

The moment I stepped foot in the ring, the woman lunged at me, swinging a powerful right hook. She would have landed, but I ducked a split-second before impact. I could have ducked the moment I saw her energy move in my direction, but I waited to throw her off balance. When she stumbled, I kicked her left leg so that she fell on the ground. I tried to grapple her and move into a rear mount, but she flung me off of her. My heart began to pound in my chest. She was hella strong. But I recovered quickly and ducked as two more blows came my way.

When she went for a kick, I jumped into her space and clocked her straight on the temple. She reached her hands up to grapple me to the floor. Now that I knew she was so much stronger than me, I bent and wove out of her grasp. She took a few steps back, her eyes narrowing on me as she tried to figure me out. I'm sure it surprised her how fast I moved out of her way, and there wasn't much she could do about it. As long as I stayed out of her holds, I could beat her.

She got tired of waiting for me to come at her and lunged at me with all of her strength. I went for the grapple-to-rear-mount again, this time with the brute force of my full strength, and she dropped to the ground. I held her in place as she struggled to break free. With my legs locked tightly around her waist and my arms pinning her neck back, all she could do was swing with her arms and take jabs at my sides. I squeezed until her face turned bright red. I gritted my teeth tighter as I squeezed and prevented air from filling her lungs. Her body stopped restricting and right before it was about to go limp, I let her go. She collapsed on the ground. I watched her fingers twitch and her head turn with her eyes closed. She was barely alive and I'd just won the round.

My throat grew parched as I wiped away the sweat dripping from my brow. I shifted my attention to Ixia, wanting to gloat a little for the win. "It would be so nice to have some water and a towel, but I guess that's too much to ask."

She cocked her head to one side as though considering something. Then she swept her hand in the air, directing Brute and Cocky into the ring. They parted the ropes and swung their bodies through the opening. Their eyes turned black, consuming the whites of their eyes completely. Two demons faced me to fight. The stretched canvas floor shook as they prowled forward.

My eyes darted from one of their huge, brawny chests to the other. "Wait, both at the same time? That's not exactly a fair match."

"Who said anything about being fair?"

They stepped closer, shaking the canvas beneath me and staring at me with savage eyes.

"What do we get when we kick her ass?" Brute said through a mouthful of gold teeth.

Cocky, the one with the dragon tattoo on his neck, spat out, "Oh I know what I'm getting." He licked his crusty lips. "Don't knock her out. I want her awake when I get my share."

Without my powers, all I could do was dodge the blows and move out of their way. I tried to get as far as I could on the other end of the ring, but Ixia moved at the same speed as a vampire, blocking me with the Stone Mind. *What is she?*

In a flash, she would anticipate my movements and get to the other side before I could summon up the energy I needed to use my powers. Finally, they cornered me and held me back. I used combat training techniques to land blows and dodge theirs, but they were highly skilled fighters. And they were skilled at fighting together.

I landed two kicks on Cocky's side and spun to jab Brute in the face. But Cocky quickly recovered and grappled me in an over-under body lock. I head-butted Cocky, but he wouldn't let go. Then I kicked out at Brute, who just moved out of the way. Cocky's grip was far too strong for me to get out of with my arms pinned behind me. I couldn't budge an inch as Brute came in and began pounding at my stomach and sides.

I bled from my mouth and nose as the blows kept coming. My head spun. I was dizzy and in so much pain that I began to grunt and groan every time he landed another one. I could no longer hold my head up. I fell limp within Cocky's hold.

"Stop." Ixia's voice was flat and bored. "I thought you would've done better, Sasha. You know, after you kicked Amara's ass, for one second I considered making you a job offer. I wondered if I could convince you to forget about all of this and come work for us. But after seeing how quickly these guys took you down, all you're good for is a quick video for your man. Let's hope you mean more to him than my ring." She snickered at her stupid joke.

I could taste the blood spilling through my teeth and onto my chest. Everything was blurry, but I fought to hold my head up and keep what I had left of my dignity.

I didn't want to tell Trent to do anything for this twisted bitch. But Ixia showed me a video that she'd filmed of my mother in her salon. The video had today's date.

"I found your mami. I would hate for anything to happen to her just because you wouldn't cooperate. Now let's get that video done without any further delays, shall we?"

I nodded my head stiffly in defeat. With a black-and-blue cheek, one eye that couldn't open from all the swelling, a busted lip and a spinning heaviness in my head, they filmed me asking Trent to give them the ring.

At the end of the filming, I lifted my chin and pulled my shoulders back. *They may have kicked my ass, but they haven't broken me.*

Ixia tucked away the phone and began to walk away.

"You're going to regret this." My voice was rough through clenched teeth.

She kept walking as though she didn't hear me. I was going to make her wish she had.

Chapter 37

Damian

Just as we were reviewing the entrance points of the warehouse, I received a text: *This is Trent. We need to talk.*

We agreed to meet at the rooftop bar of one of the buildings downtown. We chose a public place, where he didn't have time to plant any bugs or control the area with his people any more than I could. Nice and neutral.

I sat with Zayne on one of the sofas in the open-air lounge. It was five in the afternoon on a Tuesday, and there was only a small happy-hour crowd at the bar. I sensed Trent the moment he entered and saw him as he scanned the room in search of me. He strolled over when he caught sight of me. His energy was dim, even for a vampire whose energy was already typically very low. It was as though this whole situation sat heavy on his mind. He sat down in a chair opposite us and ordered a drink as soon as the waitress greeted him.

"We need to get her the fuck out of there." He got right to it, his eyes drilling into mine. "Here, take a look at this."

I winced as I saw two massive guys beating on Sasha. She wasn't using her powers, probably because she couldn't. It was hard to watch. At the end of it, she sat bloodied and bruised with her head down. The guy with the dragon tattoo fisted her hair in his hands and pulled her head back. Her face looked beaten but the spirit in her eyes wasn't.

"Give them the ring, and this is over," she said.

The tattooed guy let her go, but Sasha kept her gaze fixed on the camera, as if trying to speak to us through her eyes. He turned to the camera, then said, "Meet us tomorrow at midnight, at the coordinates we send you. Then, you'll get your girl back alive."

The video went black.

"We need to get her the fuck out of there," Trent repeated, jaw set.

"What do you mean we? It's your fault she's even in this mess," Zayne spat as his glared at Trent.

Trent sat upright in his chair and rubbed the back of his neck. "I know, and I mean to get her out of it. Look, I'll just go in and give them what they want. We don't need anyone else to get hurt."

"That's where you're wrong, man. You can't give up the Blood Ruby. It would give them too much power. We need to know what you know about the Miami Mafia, why they want the Blood Ruby and how it is that they have the Stone Mind."

I searched his face. He was a good-looking kid; I guessed I could see why Sasha had fallen for him. That good-boy gloss he'd had when I'd first seen him over a year ago had been replaced by the ruthless edge he'd needed for his new Fae life. But he was now at a crossroads. He had to choose whether he would save Sasha and abandon this life as a Dark Vampire, or turn on her.

"Our organizations are different. Our cartel here in Miami has begun working with higher-end clientele in the buying and selling of luxury items," he explained. "We do some drug trafficking, but only niche substances—potions, if you will—that have restorative, energetic and sexual stimulants. Nothing addictive or for the streets.

I sent the hurricane to destroy their operation. I must admit, they acted quickly and moved to another location, but they didn't forget. Last night was their retaliation. I don't know where they're getting their magic from, but I know it's a relatively new thing."

Zayne sat back in his chair, still glaring at Trent like he wanted to punch his face in. But there was a semblance of understanding in his expression.

"Look, I'm fucked already. Solana hates Sasha so much I don't even know what she'd do if she knew I was involved with her. She's in Dubai this week. She's getting into the oil business with some sheik, and I want to keep her out of it as long as possible."

Zayne snorted and I just shook my head.

"Alright so how are we going to do this if we can't give them the Blood Ruby?" I asked.

That's when Zayne turned to me with his eyebrows arched. I knew that look, and it meant he had a plan. After I heard it, I knew it was solid.

We would move at dawn.

Chapter 38

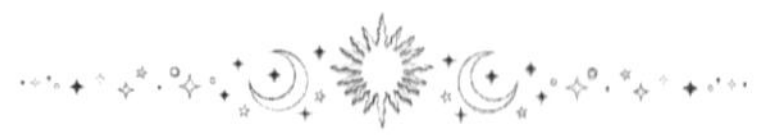

Sasha

When I closed my eyes that night in the small closet, the cool concrete floor soothed my sore muscles and bones. From my toes to the top of my head, all I felt was horrific pain and agony. Yet when I woke up several hours later, it was so much less.

Ixia must have left my proximity.

Otherwise, I couldn't use my healing power. If she wasn't anywhere near me, then now would be the time for me to shadow weave the fuck out of here. I opened my eyes wide and looked around. It was completely dark in the room, nothing but barren walls and an iron door. Old bloodstains were splattered on the floor, and from what I could tell, they were older than mine. This was a cell they used often.

Although my eyesight was great in the dark, I brought fire to my fingers to light up the room. I wanted to test my abilities before taking the major leap out of here. I had never shadow woven very far, only a few feet at a time and I was nervous I would get stuck in a wall. I noticed my fire was working just fine when I lit a blaze in my palm. I felt my jaguar stir inside my chest; she was more than ready to be let loose in this place. If anyone deserved it, they did. This operation was absolute evil.

I'm back, and I'm taking this place down.

With a deep inhale, I went within the dark spaces of my mind to connect with the shadows and the mist, the eternal souls that existed only in spirit, of the Fae and the gods. In an instant I was among them, weaving and sewing myself in a pattern from inside these walls to the outside. I could still see and feel the matter of the wall and the physical elements around me, but I moved through them as though I was one with it all.

I willed myself to physical form and stood upright on the other side of the hallway. I stood facing a guard who was scrolling through his phone. He lifted his eyes in surprise, and I gave him a swift kick to the groin, then a headbutt so fierce he fell to the floor on his knees. I finished him off with a round kick to his head that knocked him out. My hands reached for the gun on his side, and I clenched it tightly as I ran to the exit sign on the opposite end of the hallway. I slowly opened the door to an almost-empty parking lot, covered in darkness. It was late into the night.

My legs urged me to go forward and run, but I sensed the girls being fed on. Abused. Mistreated. This was not about me. This was bigger than me. I had a chance to help them, and I would take it.

I turned around and ran back in, knowing the Stone Mind could neutralize me, knowing I was putting myself at risk, once again. But I couldn't let them do this to them any longer. This had to end, now.

I looked up at the ceiling for cameras, and there they were. Plenty of them. Someone was watching. But as long as Ixia wasn't close, she wouldn't be able to take me down.

I sniffed the air for the girls' scents, and I searched the shadows for the dark energy that surrounded their section of this large building. Guided by my nose and the energy, I came to a stop in front of a door, sensing five or six men just beyond, including Brute, Cocky and Amara. They were all there playing a card game in a common area, the girls hidden in the sectioned-off rooms behind them. I focused my hearing to the sound of the guards' relaxed, laughing voices until one of them got a phone call. They were being notified of my escape. The three of them pushed off the table and put their hands on their guns, their eyes ready for another fight.

Shadows coiled around my fingers and up my arms, until the dark mist and I were one again, and I wove into the room behind Cocky. With the gun already in my hand, I held it to the back of his head and said, "You looking for me?"

I stepped back two steps and pulled the trigger. His blood splattered all over me as the others unholstered their guns.

In the same motion, I brought in all the dark energy of this place, and there was so much. A rich, delicious darkness swept over me, and my power grew tenfold. All at once, I was the bloodthirsty, the aroused, the impulsive, the controlling. I was everything and everyone that had ever had a dark thought in this very room, and it filled me with nothing but powerful fury. My body transformed. My jaguar leaped free. This was her domain. This was where she ruled.

My jaguar lunged for Amara, and Amara pulled the trigger. The bullets were absorbed by my canceling dark void. I tasted the metal of the bullets' entry, but that was the extent of their impact on me. I leapt for her while Brute took more shots. The girls started to scream. Amara was a wet sock in my fangs, my teeth slicing into her flesh and bones and ripping into the tendons. The savory taste of blood filled my mouth, but I couldn't let that distract me from Brute behind me. I was tired of the loud banging of that stupid gun. It was time to end that.

He soon realized the gun was pointless and took off running. He made for the exit, bolted through a door that led to the parking lot and closed it behind him. I stilled my feral rage for the briefest moment, just enough to center my mind and weave through the door to the other side. There he was, running like a little bitch.

I lunged for him and heard a loud thud as his three-hundred-pound frame barreled to the ground. My teeth sank into the layers of muscle on his back, and I appreciated then the taste of a man who lifted a lot of weights. The flavors washing over my palette were almost enough to distract me from the world around me. Almost. I had too much adrenaline pumping in my veins for that.

Then I heard my man. "Sasha."

There he is, my sense and my reason. My everything.

My jaguar cried out in disagreement; she didn't want to stop now. We were both too wrapped up in the moment to shift back just yet. We returned to the blood and bones in front of her and went in for another bite, then another, gulping down mouthfuls as though she had been starving. This was her first kill in a very long time, and she'd earned it. I wanted her to have her fill of him.

"Sasha, let's go," Trent called again.

My jaguar lifted her gaze, and we got a good look at him at the other side of the parking lot. He was standing at the security gate, the security guard's body lying on the ground just outside the door. He must have taken him out. We scanned the area and saw Damian's black Maserati idling a few feet away.

These guys came to get me out of here.

After taking one last glance at bloody Brute on the floor, we ran. Alarms blared in the building behind me. More guards spilled out from every direction. My jaguar turned to snarl at them before bolting toward Trent. Bullets rang out from all sides.

My jaguar refused to get in his car, and I didn't press the matter. I didn't want to shift back just yet. I didn't want to risk getting a bullet lodged in me, and my jaguar wanted the thrill of the run. I guess it was a smart choice because when I looked around, I saw Jenna, Lex and Andres. The three of them were in their jaguar forms, and they began running alongside the warehouse buildings as the Maserati sped off into the distance. It was exhilarating to have them next to me.

The taste of freedom was so much sweeter now as we raced through the dark night. The power of the shadow energy that I'd absorbed in the warehouse still laced my veins. It whispered and called to me, it gave me my purpose and direction. I knew then, even more intimately, the trauma and the horrors of that wicked place. I profoundly understood the misery of the girls, and the vanity and misogyny of the men.

That place had to end. And I would be the one to end them.

Chapter 39

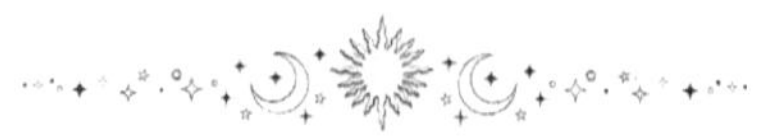

Sasha

"I'm telling you. Ixia is behind all of this." I tried to explain this to Damian, but he shook his head in disbelief. He couldn't imagine that his longtime lover, friend, council member and Zol Stria advocate was part of the Dark Zodiac. He just wouldn't believe me.

"For real, she's a Dark Mage." I pressed. "There's no way around it. She had the Stone Mind. She sent those guys after me. Why is this so hard for you to believe?" The others seemed to accept it; he was the only one resisting.

"Fine. You'll come around." I crossed my arms in front of me, rolling my eyes and sitting back in my chair.

We were at the safe house with fresh wards up around the perimeter, going over what we would do next. I wasn't even tired after all that fighting and running. In fact, I was still energized, and my mind raced to figure out what our next move was.

Jenna explained to me that with the presence of the three of them, they'd been able to nullify the power of the Stone Mind, which was how I'd healed so quickly and broken out of there. Damian had cast a revealing spell to find that the Stone Mind was being stored in a safe right above my cell. They were going to go in after it, but when I'd decided to go all Rambo on my captors, the crew had had to change their plans and bolt out of there.

They asked me what the blood was like, since nagual craved the blood of dark humans and Fae alike. It gave us renewed energy and extended our abilities further than anything else. Which explained why I was feeling so amped up right now. That's also why as soon as we'd arrived in the safe house, Damian had warned me, "Nagual can develop an addictive need to feed, just like the vampires. You must control your blood thirst."

He was right. Every moment since I'd shifted into my human form, I'd had to fight against the desire to shift back and go find the person with the darkest possible energy and tear into it. It was a moment-by-moment effort in resistance.

"We need to take that entire place down," I asserted to the group after explaining all the horrors I'd witnessed. The massive disregard for human life and all the infractions against the Zol Code being just two of them.

Lex grunted in agreement from the far wall. Jenna nodded, and Andres came over and draped his arm around my shoulder as I let out a breathy sigh. "Thanks for coming, guys. I don't know what would have happened if those monsters had the power of two relics."

"Nagual reborn, serve the Zol as one," the three of them said at the same time.

I managed a chuckle, still feeling a bit overwhelmed with the chaos of the past twenty-four hours.

"We're family, Sash. Of course we came." Jenna's smile was reassuring.

"We need to go back. And soon. We've got to get the Stone Mind," Damian said as he stepped forward from the shadows.

"And we need Trent to give us the Blood Ruby," Zayne said, and Trent shifted toward him.

Trent had sat at the table, listening the whole time, never taking his eyes off of me until that moment. "I'll give the Blood Ruby to Sasha. She's the only one I trust."

That meant more than just giving up a ring. This meant he was giving up his cartel life for me. We would make this work. I knew it now.

CHAPTER 40

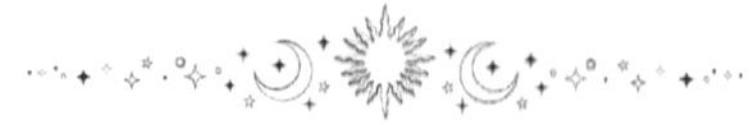

SASHA

I left the others to deliberate the plans while I headed to the bathroom. The safe house was a small boutique hotel in the middle of the design district. Each room was spacious, with white furnishings and beige accents. There was definitely a Boho vibe that I was digging.

I pulled off the Metallica T-shirt and black bike shorts they'd given me after shifting into my human form and turned on the water. I let it fill the ceramic tub in the spa-like bathroom while I took a look at the spa products. There were aromatic essential oils and bath salts in a basket near the tub, and I created my own bath soak combination. I lit a few candles around the tub and dipped myself in, allowing the warmth of the water to soothe my aching muscles.

Downstairs, they were still arguing about Ixia's role, about how to handle the Blood Ruby's powers and how to attack the warehouse now that the mafia would know we were coming. I needed a moment of downtime before I got into all that with them again. As I soaked and allowed the soothing warmth to wrap around me, I couldn't stop thinking about those girls. I should have done more for them. I should have burned that whole place down. But what if they hadn't gotten out in time? And what would I do with them after they left?

Zol Stria had plenty of money. They needed to help them. And why wouldn't Damian believe me about Ixia? I remembered him saying she sponsored an all-girl academy. That was some twisted foster home. Then again, she might have some kind of concealment spell on him. *I wonder what it would take for him to see the truth.*

I tried to push these thoughts away and allow my mind to settle. I closed my eyes and drifted into a peaceful state of serenity where it was finally calm within. All I heard was gentle water swishing around me. Peaceful quiet at last. When I was ready, I slowly opened my eyes to the candlelit room and stepped out of the bath. As I reached for a towel, I heard a soft tap at my door. I wrapped the towel around me and walked over.

"Who is it?" I said through the door.

"It's me." My heart fluttered at Trent's voice.

I opened the door a crack and saw him standing there. He had become such a stone-cold mafia type with his sharp suit and rough edges. But just then, all I saw was the man I desired. I stepped back from the door and opened it wide enough for him to come in. He closed the door behind him and pressed me up against the wall in a lustful kiss. As soon as his tongue met my lips, I parted my mouth and let him in. I held my towel in one hand and reached my other around his waist, pulling him toward me. I wanted to feel every part of his body and lose myself in him.

He grasped for my waist and my neck as he continued to kiss me, then he moved his lips to my cheek, then my jaw, down to my neck as I let out a breathy moan in response. Heat pooled between my legs as I reached under his shirt to feel the coolness of his flesh under my fingers. My breath came in pants as he dragged his hand up my thighs in a wanting caress, his fingers clinging to me. He pulled his lips off my neck and faced me.

"I couldn't stand seeing you like that, Sasha. I will never let that happen to you again. Thank the stars that you healed the way you did." He looked around my face and chest for signs of my ass-kicking.

"It's ok. I heal fast. Bear, I'm a nagual. I'm going to get in fights and get hurt. But I'll be ok. I'm almost unkillable." I gave him a sideways smile. "This is who we are now. Fae don't run away from pain. We live in it." He nodded. I dropped my towel. "But you can keep looking for those bruises if you want."

His lips curled into a smile. My black, wet hair fell over around my shoulders, and my nipples were hard in anticipation of his touch. His eyes lingered on my breasts, then down my stomach to my thighs. He bit his lower lip and ran a hand through his loose blond hair.

"I'm going to have to do a full inspection over there." He nodded his head toward the bed.

As I reached the bed, I turned toward him and raked my eyes along his body. I wrapped my arms around his neck and pressed tightly against him, meeting my lips to his and dancing my tongue around his mouth. Having him in my life was everything. I never wanted to let go.

His hands went for my waist, lifting me up and onto the bed in one swift movement. Still standing, he removed his jacket, and I reached up to help him pull off the T-shirt he had on underneath. I brought my lips to his tight abs, kissing him and letting my tongue caress the contours of his flesh. I moved my hand down his waist and unzipped his pants, wrapping my hands around his erection. His thickness filled my hands as I moved them up and down.

He groaned hungrily when I wrapped him in my mouth. He kicked his head back in pleasure, and I grew moist in response. I pulled away when he wanted more, teasing him with a smile and lying back on my bed. He climbed over me, caging me in with his arms. Strong fingers kneaded between my thighs as he pressed them open. His lips met the inside of my thigh with warm kisses until he reached my mound. He feasted there, stroking me with his tongue as I moaned deeply beneath his touch. With panting, heavy breaths I fisted my hands in his hair as his tongue circled my clit. My moans came louder as he moved faster. I cried out as I climaxed beneath his stroking, unable to take it anymore. He gazed up at me with those beautiful sky-blue eyes and climbed up to my side.

But I wasn't finished. Now I needed him inside me. I pressed my hands into his sides and guided him. He filled me up and pressed into me, massaging every part of me from within. I gasped when he began to thrust in and out harder, not wanting him to stop. His hand squeezed my breast as he kissed up my neck. Then his teeth snapped out, and I turned my head to the side so he could sink them into my neck. The pinch of his teeth lasted only a moment, the piercing making way for pleasure as his venom sank into me and gave way to euphoria. I closed my eyes and let him spin me into the deepest pleasure I could ever imagine. My nails dug into his firm muscles, he penetrated me deeper and his teeth slowly, only slightly, pulled blood from my neck.

For a moment, everything became still. Then he lifted his teeth and only a small drop of blood dripped to the bed. He retracted his fangs, and I arched my back as every muscle in his body seemed to tense. His body rocked back and forth, thrusting himself in rhythm to my hips. I groaned, my chest heaving, when we both went over the edge at the same time. He turned to the side, collapsing on the bed, and I fell still beside him. My heat began to cool slightly as I traced my fingers along the contours of his flesh.

"I've missed you, so much," I breathed out onto his chest, not expecting him to hear me.

"I've missed you, too." His voice was low and distant. "Let's get out of here altogether. Let's just go. Fuck all of this. There's no reason for us to stay. Now that you can shift, and I have investments in Geneva, we can leave. Right now." He sat up as his eyes pierced mine. He was serious.

For one second I imagined myself running off with him. We could make a new life somewhere, on the coast of a forgotten island, where no one could find us. I wanted to say yes. My chest began to ache from the words I was about to say.

"I can't, Trent. There's too much at stake. What's going on with Solana, what she's planning, it's bigger than all of us. And those girls in the vampire den, I've got to get them out of there. I can't just walk away now. In fact, I don't think you should leave the cartel."

His eyes darkened and his jaw clenched. He looked away. The walls of the room began to squeeze in, and a heavy stone dropped in my chest the moment he stood up. I was left speechless as I watched him pull on his pants and shoes.

"Think about it, Trent," I managed to say. "We can take them down from the inside. We have to think about others."

"No. We have to think about ourselves. I could lose you, all over again. And for what? If we take down Solana there will always be someone else. Some other mission."

"That's selfish. We can't leave those women, those children, to rot in there. We've got to get them out. You and I, we made an oath to protect others. We were willing to give our lives for that as SEREs in the military. That hasn't changed for me. I have to stop this." My voice was unwavering.

"I'm trying to protect you. I've seen the worst of the Dark Zodiac. I know what they can do. Sometimes, you have to know when to walk away." His eyes were shadowed and his shoulders tense. He'd never told me what he'd seen, and I didn't get the sense that he wanted to speak about it.

"I don't need your protection." My lips pressed into a thin line.

He gave me one last, dark look before he moved in a flash to the door, slamming it behind him as he left.

I paced the room, slapping hot tears from my cheeks while my heart caved in on itself in a thousand shattered pieces.

CHAPTER 41

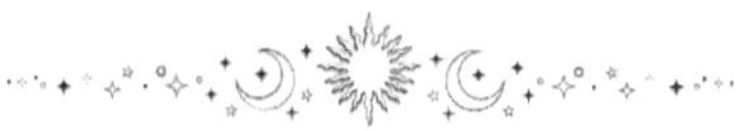

DAMIAN

It was impossible for me to believe Ixia had anything to do with this. My logical mind didn't allow for it, but aside from that, she wouldn't do this. Sasha said she saw Ixia in that warehouse. We would have to go there just so I could prove that crazy nagual wrong.

We waited for nightfall the next day before the seven of us headed to the facility. We were about to get in the car when I noticed Trent wasn't with Sasha.

"Where is he?"

"He's not coming." Her voice had an icy edge, and her eyes were sharp and focused.

"Fuck. He could compromise this whole situation. I told you we shouldn't have trusted him," I grumbled.

"He won't compromise us." She was certain—I sensed it through our bond. I wasn't so sure, but there wasn't much we could do about it now.

We headed out. Zayne had monitored the cameras he had on the place, and we never saw any sign of Ixia, giving me more reason to believe she was never involved. We drove in separate cars and parked them several blocks away from the facility, with a change of clothes left inside the cars for the nagual after they shifted. As we approached, we noticed the facility was even more heavily guarded than last night. Jenna sensed that there were hundreds of UnZol servants inside. But just as yesterday, the parking lot had at least ten black SUVs. These were crucial to our plan. Now we just had to get the keys.

"There must be a powerful Dark Mage in there capable of converting all those human souls into UnZol demons. The Stone Mind relic wouldn't do it alone." Jenna arched her brows as she said this, probably hinting that Ixia was in fact involved.

"Sure. I agree. It could be Julieta of the Dark Scorpio Guild. Or Celeste of the Dark Aries Runes. Or Lizandra of the Dark Libra Castile. Any of those Dark Zodiac Mages who served the UnZol King and escaped the prisons in the Faellen Wars could be behind this. It's not Ixia." I shrugged it off. "We'll find out soon enough anyway. Once we get inside."

"I still can't get over that you don't believe me," Sasha snorted. "Where's the shaman bond now?" She rolled her eyes as she adjusted the belt that held her nine-millimeter gun and a knife in a sheath. She had a twenty-two in her ankle holster and a sword at her back. We were all heavily armed and ready for war.

"There are just some things we won't bond over. We're just going to have to accept that," I grunted as I made sure my weapon was loaded.

We each got into our positions and prepared to enter the building. I cast a powerful deflector spell all around us, wrapping our presence up tight so that we could enter undetected by supernatural senses. Our first objective would be to neutralize the Stone Mind.

There was a movement in the bushes next to us. Three of us pointed our guns directly at the sound.

"Trent," Sasha breathed out his name in relief.

He walked out from the bushes with his hands up. "I've been here for a while. While they were inside playing poker, I was able to go in and get these." He pulled two handfuls of keys out of his pockets and shook them lightly at us. Sasha eyed him suspiciously. He used his vampire speed and stopped just before her. "I know you don't need my protection. But I'm going in there to make sure you come out alive." He gazed intently into her eyes, and she gave him a hard stare back, until she softened just a bit.

"Thanks for the keys." She gave him a sideways smile as he handed them to her.

"Ok, you lovebirds. Let's get this done," Lex grunted, and we all got in our positions to head in.

We took out the security guards in the parking lot entrance quickly, just a quick slice to the throat when we came up behind them. There was one on each side of the lot. Now under the cover of night, and by using the dark shadow cast by the building, we kept close to the edge and approached where my revealing spell showed the Stone Mind.

The nagual all came in close to neutralize its power so that Sasha would retain her powers the moment she got in. Sasha and Zayne were the only ones who could shadow weave, but Sasha had already been on the inside. We agreed she would be the one to get in there and take a look around. We waited right outside the building on high alert for her to report back. She returned within just a few heartbeats.

"They didn't see me, I remained in the shadows. It's heavily guarded. There must be at least ten of those UnZol demons standing outside the room where the relic is. I didn't see Ixia."

I gave her a smug look. I knew it.

"Let's get to the warehouse first and free the girls. Some of the security detail will be pulled in that direction, so we'll fight them off there," Zayne said.

Zayne had spent the entire night planning for every angle of our ambush. As soon as we'd arrived, he'd turned on a military-grade, magic-enhanced video camera scrambler that froze the images they most recently captured in place.

Sasha glanced up at Trent, and they gave each other subtle nods as though they'd done this before. They were more than slightly nauseating to watch.

When we arrived outside at the section where the women and kids lived, I felt my ring vibrate. I looked down, and its golden color began to glow slightly. It wasn't full on, but this was the most action I had seen from this ring since I'd coded it.

Lily's killer was behind this door.

My throat tightened, and my jaw clenched. This was it. I would find her murderer, nail them to the wall and slowly strip away their skin while they were still breathing. Hopefully they were immortal so that they would suffer the pain of their peeled flesh for a very long time.

Sasha entered through the shadows; a few heartbeats later we heard three large thumps hit the floor. Then the door opened, and she waved us in, leading us into an empty storage room while Trent and Zayne kept watch outside. The five nagual present were more than enough to deflect the power of the Stone Mind, and they each brought their own elemental and energetic abilities to the fight.

Sasha wove herself to the far end of the warehouse and retrieved the keys to the SUVs from the garage. She returned quickly, and we spread out among the group. We went directly to the supervisors and each of us ignited with our darkest strengths. Sasha and Andres brought fire to their hands. Lex curled vines around his arms, and Jenna called the air to her palms. I cast a hallucination spell on us, turning our eyes black and casting large, inky shadows around our backs to make us appear as the darkest demons. They squirmed and tried to flee, but it was no use. Each of them fell prey to our powers with deathly blows.

Sasha headed over to one of the rooms and returned with and older woman. The woman looked around with an icy glare as she assessed us. A scream threatened to escape her lips when Sasha grabbed her by the collar and spoke to her in Spanish, "You've got to get all your people out of here. These are the keys to the SUVs outside. Get everyone out, right now. We're taking this place down."

The older woman knew better than to fight off Sasha. She was a human who had a respectful fear of supernaturals like us. And she looked like she could have been beautiful once. Yet she had been drained, wrinkled and broken. Her hair was long and black, and her lips were dry from smoking. The defeated look on her face gave away her resignation to this life and made me wonder if she had any hope left inside her. She would need to dig deep to find it now.

Sasha leaned in close, eyes glinting. "Take them somewhere safe. We will be watching you. We are always watching. Do not bring them to another den. Do not let these girls work the streets. There's enough money in each of the SUVs to set you up and a person for you to call who will take you all in at a domestic abuse shelter. Don't fuck with me, Roxy."

"These are my girls. None of us want to be here, but I don't know you. We leave, and they will come for us. I know what they will do, and we won't survive it." She gave off a strong, rough demeanor but her voice cracked just then, giving away her fear.

"If you stay, you die." Sasha released her grip on her. "We're taking this whole place down right now. You don't have a choice."

By now I could sense that our presence had been detected. There was movement just outside our door and down the hall in the den. I opened the door and saw young, scared faces peering in our direction from the doorways and halls.

"We must go. Now!" I insisted and waved at the others as I left the room.

Jenna ran to the exit as Andres directed them to follow. At first, they hesitated. Many didn't move an inch, and the others began walking slowly.

Roxy yelled, "Let's go. Everyone. Now."

With her command, the others began to scamper. The women, girls and several young boys scattered around, grabbing personal things and rushing to put on shoes and jackets. Roxy rounded them up and rushed them outside where they followed Jenna to the SUVs.

I stayed inside to watch for attackers as the others handed each of the woman overseers the keys to the vehicles. Each SUV came with fifty thousand dollars in a duffel bag, the name of the social worker we had identified for them and the address of a hidden, government-protected shelter that would house them until they found a permanent place to live.

Just as the cars were being loaded, two guards approached the vehicles, and Zayne and Lex shifted instantly, ripping and tearing into the UnZol demons. It was completely chaotic as the human residents panicked and yelled as they piled into the SUVs. Sasha never shifted, and instead cleared a path for the humans to leave the parking lot by channeling a wall of fire and holding the oncoming demons back. I cast a protective spell on the SUVs to keep the fire from reaching the vehicles.

A young mother with a newborn strapped to her chest struggled in the grasp of an UnZol demon guard. Jenna ran to them and pushed her thumb into the guard's eye while yanking his head back and off of the child. He grabbed her arm and flung her to the side. Sasha turned her fire directly on him and lit him up. His screams were unearthly, high-pitched howls that caused a chill to race down my spine.

As soon as the group of human guards left the complex, Lex ran after them in his massive black nagual form. He leapt onto a car that tried to chase the women, tearing into the roof with huge claws and making the car swerve uncontrollably as his claws met the driver's flesh.

After that, there were no more guards left in the area to take down. Sasha turned her fire to the vampire feasting pit, making sure any lingering vampires or demons would be swallowed by the flames.

After the nagual used their elemental powers to destroy as much as the vampire pit as possible, Sasha and I headed over to the area where the Stone Mind was being kept. Zayne and the other nagual spread out around us to neutralize its power. As we were getting into our positions, we felt the ground shake. We didn't make it there in time. Someone with a lot of power was channeling the relic already, perhaps trying to tear down this entire building.

We darted through the hallways to a gym, where I now sensed the presence of the relic. Wall hangings and light fixtures fell apart around us as the space filled with smoke from the fire that the nagual had left behind. The thrumming of my ring caught my attention. It glowed much brighter now, its light casting through the smoke and against the walls.

I lifted my gaze to a figure toward the far wall of the gym, and I couldn't believe my eyes. There she was, wearing all black with her hair pulled into a tight bun. It *was* Ixia.

Whatever spell she had cast on me couldn't keep me from seeing her as the wicked, manipulative, power-hungry bitch she truly was. I narrowed my eyes and gritted my teeth, keeping my gun locked on her even though bullets couldn't hurt her. With the Stone Mind, her Fae power would only multiply. But there were enough nagual here to crush her and the small army she had gathered around us. We all froze in place as we stared each other down.

"You killed Lily." I spoke the three words that cut through the frozen moment.

The building slowed its shaking as smoke trailed in the corners. Dark shadows swirled maliciously around us, and the jaguars soaked in the dark spirals closest to them.

"She came between us. You never should have let her come between us." Ixia's eyes gave away her desperation for a fleeting moment, before turning to ice once again.

Zayne shifted back into his human form and stood naked in the room as dark smoke and mist circled around him and gave his center cover. "Give us the Stone Mind, Ixia. Whatever you're planning, it's over. At this point, if you keep the

Stone Mind, then Zol Stria will send their armies and you will be sentenced to an eternity in Xibalba. Turn yourself in, and maybe we can negotiate a more lenient sentence."

"You don't get it. None of you do. Humans are not our lovers." Her eyes darkened and narrowed on me when she said this. "Humans are not our friends. And we should not have to cater to them. The stars gave us, the Fae, the ability to expand and travel through matter. To harness energy. To channel the elements. We are gods and humans exist to serve us." She remained cool and composed through her speech, as though we were the ones confused. "I saved you from a huge mistake, Damian. She was not the woman for you. I am. You and I, we can rule the new Dark Era together. This was our chance to expand into the darkness, not run from it. Join me."

She held out her hand, and for a fleeting moment, I felt compelled to join her. I forgot about the torment of losing Lily. I believed the words out of her mouth. We were superior. We did deserve to rule and not be restrained by the laws of the Zol Council.

In an instant, Sasha was standing behind Ixia. I could barely make her out in the smoke that surrounded them, but my bond told me she'd shadow woven there. We all seemed to be so wrapped up in Ixia's words, in the temptation of the power and control that they offered, that we didn't realize when Sasha had faded into the shadows. But there she was, one hand on her lips as her eyes focused on me.

Sasha reached her hand around Ixia and held a cool metal knife at her throat. Ixia turned to face Sasha. As she did, Sasha head-butted her with so much force that Ixia stumbled backward. She removed Ixia's knife from its sheath, yanked her toward her and pressed both blades tightly just under her chin. Ixia knew full well that it was time to give up. I inhaled a breath as the control shifted in the room.

"The Stone Mind is here, in her knife." Sasha threw the knife that held the Stone Mind in the air as Jenna called on the wind to move it toward me. As soon as I grasped it, I felt an immeasurable power surge through my entire being. Ixia looked around nervously as the UnZol demons surrounding us went down on their knees, in command of their new master. I spoke the words, "*Il hul canil ya'at,*" a spell that leveraged the magic of the relic.

"Let's go, Ixia. We're taking you back to Zol Stria. It's over," Zayne commanded.

Her ripe, full lips pursed, and she held up both her hands in defeat.

"I have always loved you, Damian," she said then she opened her palm and a bright light filled the room. It was like a camera flash, but brighter and constant, turning everything white. My eyes strained to see. I brought my hands up to my face to block the light, but it was too much. I was blinded. We were all blinded.

Just a few heartbeats after when the light faded, Ixia was gone.

CHAPTER 42

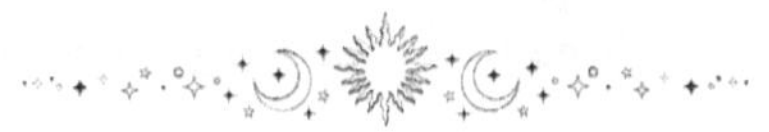

SASHA

I awoke the next morning to the sounds of birds chirping outside my window. The sun was just barely rising, and I'd slept like a bear, heavy and deep. We had demolished the warehouse, sending it up in fumes of smoke and the building charred to pieces. It was nothing less than what that hellish place deserved.

Trent was by my side when I opened my eyes. His breath was soft and slow, but the moment I opened my eyes, he opened his to meet mine.

"I forgot, now you're always awake," I said, my voice still soft and sleepy.

"Don't think it's weird, but yeah, I've been watching you sleep. You make the cutest little cat noises."

"Oh no I don't!" I shoved him with a soft push to his unyielding chest.

He chuckled. "That was pretty amazing, what you did last night. I'd never seen anything like that." His voice was proud, and maybe a little in awe.

"I hadn't either. It was crazy, right?" I couldn't believe all that had gone down.

Ixia was missing, but at least she didn't have the Stone Mind anymore. We still needed to understand more about her operation. She had so many of those UnZol demons. Were there more? Did she have any of the other relics, or did Solana have the other two? If we were going to take her down, we would need to find out.

"I'm worried about you going back to Solana." My voice shook. "What will happen when you tell her you don't have the Blood Ruby?"

"I don't know if I'll survive telling her. She's starting to take more control. I heard from one of the guys that she's had great meetings in Dubai. Now she's running an entire oil mafia in the Middle East. There's no limit to what she's capable of. I believe she has at least one of the other missing relics. Otherwise she never would have given me the Blood Ruby."

"We've got to stop her." My voice broke this time as I imagined the world at the hands of the Dark Zodiac.

"Do we, really?" Trent seemed torn. "Or we could run off together. Forget all about this."

"You're still on that? I can't." I shook my head and sat up in the bed, hoping he would see things my way.

"You will have to choose, Sasha. Me or this suicide mission you're on."

"Why should I have to choose? Why can't we do this together? You saw what a great team we made last night." I had come too far to give it all up now. His face turned cold as I reached for his arm. His flesh was ice under my fingers. The air became thick with tension, and I felt him pull away.

He turned to face me, his eyes deep and hollow as the light drenched the curtains, sheets and lamp behind him, leaving his face in shadow. Slowly, he lifted his hand to brush away the stray hairs that had fallen in front of my eyes.

"Let's not talk about this now." He reached for me, pulling me close and pressing me against his chest. His arms wrapped around me, making my heart flutter and my cheeks flush with desire for him.

I reached my lips to meet his and whispered to him, "Yes, let's talk more about this later." My vacant heart felt full again as I grew warm in his embrace.

Later at breakfast, I spoke to Damian. He'd come to realize that Ixia had been feeding him influence potions in the bottles of whiskey she'd constantly gifted him. He suspected it had started right before they'd split up, over forty years ago. Although she couldn't make him love her, she could make him see her the way she wanted. He explained that the spell was a way of accentuating her good qualities and covering up the things she didn't want him to see. It also allowed her into his world, giving her access to areas without triggering the warnings, like how she constantly had slipped through his wards at home. Yet even with such a powerful spell in place, it still wasn't enough for him to truly love her. All of those potions and fake shit, and he'd still fallen in love with someone else. That must have torn her apart.

"So do you think Ixia and Solana are in a battle for control of the relics?" I asked him.

"Yes, it appears so. We must retrieve the relics before more damage can be done. But for now, you've got to go back to Aries Academy and finish the next term. Zayne will go back with you to Zol Stria and let them know that Ixia turned to the Dark Zodiac."

My eyes opened wide, and I slid my hands in my pockets before I asked Damian, "And I suppose you're staying to find Ixia."

He nodded gravely, and I slumped down into the chair next to him. "Her end won't be swift. It will be painful. So painful that the souls of other worlds will hear her scream in agony."

I wanted to believe him, especially because of what she had done to my Titi Lily. But one truth still remained unspoken. How had Ixia gotten her hands on the Stone Mind? How deeply had she woven her web of manipulation into our lives, throughout Zol Stria—even the mortal realm? My palms prickled with fire just thinking about it. My heart pounded like war drums with the flames of a thousand hells to find out.

And this time, I wouldn't wait for the truth to find me.

You ready for more?

I hope you enjoyed this descent into the world of Zol Stria — and this is only the beginning. There's so much more magic, danger, and destiny ahead, and I can't wait to share it with you. Join my newsletter to get the eBook prequel, Zodiac Shadows, free, plus updates on new releases, lore drops, and upcoming events. Sign up here: **www.rcluna.com**

If this story pulled you in, I'd be so grateful if you left a review on Amazon or Goodreads. Your words help other readers decide if they're ready to step into this world too.

I deeply and truly appreciate everyone acknowledged in the previous books—and of course, my readers. Your support means the world to me. I wouldn't be here without you. The book community has been everything: lifting this series to new heights, breathing new life into my writing and into me. I'm forever grateful.

Now... keep reading for a sneak peek at Zodiac Prison, Book 3 in the Warrior Shifter Series.

Con mucho amor,

R.C. Luna

PROPHECIES CAN NEVER BE
BROKEN...

ZODIAC
PRISON
WARRIOR SHIFTER BOOK 3
R.C. LUNA

READ A SNEAK PEAK OF THE NEXT
BOOK IN THIS CAPTIVATING SERIES...

Preview Zodiac Prison

Chapter 1

"Darkness within darkness. Gateway to all understanding." - Lao Tzu

I remembered this passage that was etched into the marble stone in our Magical Sciences class as Zayne, my nagual combat instructor, and I trekked in our jaguar forms through the dark jungle of the Gemini House. All manner of jungle creatures lived here in the thick, damp landscape.

I was always surprised at the various species in the Zodiac territories. There were variants of the familiar spiders and snakes, worms and gorillas. Yet there were so many more, some as small as the cueyatl, a tiny frog with a tongue so poisonous it could corrode your body with a single swipe. Or the ahuizotl, a dog-like creature with hands instead of paws and a hand on its tail with sharp claws. These creatures could also see perfectly under the cover of night. It made it nearly impossible for anyone to live in this precarious habitat. This is where the hunters became the hunted.

The clouds covered the moon, and it would have been pitch black if it wasn't for our night vision. My jaguar form was invisible in the shadows, and my eyes adept at seeing in the dark, equipped at detecting even the slightest light peeking through the faintest parts of the clouds above. I wondered what understanding I was supposed to have right now as I lived the words of the timeless quote.

Up ahead, that's it. Unable to communicate with Zayne in my nagual form, I thought this to myself as I peered through the bush at the creature crouched on the side of the riverbank. We blended with the dark energy of the night and watched her in utter silence, undetectable by Fae senses in our jaguar forms. It was a cihuatl. Thick, long strands of black-and-gray hair flowed from the top of her head. At her back were two dark-gray, slimy, scaled bat-like wings, and her belly was swollen from pregnancy. Because of her crouched position, her legs were hidden from view. Her face looked like it had no flesh, just the skull, because of the thin, transparent skin and veins that covered it. These were the creatures of nightmares. They brought sickness to Fae villages, hunted the children that fell ill, then stole them from their families. They drew power from the pain and suffering of the surviving family members. The creatures were nearly seven feet tall, rare and hard to find, mainly because of how they reproduced.

At the moment, with her eagle-like claws, she was tearing into what appeared to be young human flesh. My hackles rose as we crept toward her, my claws digging into the ground with every step. As we got closer, I glanced over at Zayne, who gave me a short nod. We emerged from the cover of the jungle, ready to attack.

The moment he lurched toward her, I rushed to the creature's side and locked my teeth over her wings. I anticipated that she would immediately try to fly away rather than fight. Just as I did, Zayne went for the neck. The cihuatl easily flung him aside with one swipe of her arm. It was strong, and Zayne was stunned from the blow. The creature turned, trying to throw me off its back, and I dug my teeth even harder into those slimy wings. It tried to grab at me, but I dug my back legs into the ground as I locked my jaws on the wing's bones and heard a few snaps. It grasped me with its clawed hand and tried to inject me with the venom she carried in her blood. But it was no use; her claws couldn't penetrate my jaguar's flesh. This was what made us so unique and so powerful as protectors of Zol Stria.

The cihuatl wrapped her arm around me and yanked me off of her, flinging me with the force of a semi-truck. I landed with a loud thump against a jagged boulder. A moment later she began to bat her wings in an effort to escape. I lunged after her again, and she swiftly avoided my grasp and maneuvered herself behind me. Before I could react, I felt her sharp talons dig into my back as she lifted me into the air with her. Her strong, powerful wings flapped, the wounds from my attack wearing on her, but she pushed hard. My heart raced in a fit of panic when we rose off the ground. She could drop me anywhere and make her escape. We had been searching for her for three months, and I wasn't going to let her get away. We needed her.

I thrashed in a fit of rage and her talons gave way just a little. I couldn't reach her with my mouth or my claws, and I couldn't use my elemental powers in this form.

This mission is fucked.

Just as I thought this, she dipped lower to the ground, slamming me against the earth before lifting off again. My mind raced. *Should I shift back to human form?* The second I did, my skin would be filled with lethal diseases at the mere touch of one of her claws. But just then something crashed into her, and she began to tumble back down. It was Zayne. He'd leapt from the ground onto her back! I felt his weight send us hurtling down. Just as she began to fall, she released me, and my four legs landed firmly on the jungle floor. I ran out of the way as Zayne and the cihuatl plunged to the ground where I had been standing a heartbeat earlier. Instantly I was on her back, her wing once again in my mouth. As I tore into her left wing, the bitter-tasting blood spilled into my mouth.

The Zol Beast Keeper at the Academy had taught us that if anyone even touched cihuatl blood, their bodies would rapidly deteriorate with a cancerous plague. The only thing happening to me right now was my gag reflex; it was triggered by the god-awful taste. Once again, I was grateful for the gift of being a nagual and immune to Fae venom.

Zayne landed his canines into her neck, and a high-pitched scream left her throat. The creature that had just been towering over us stumbled to the ground with a thud, and Zayne landed on top of her. Once a nagual had you in their deadly jaw-lock, there was little, if anything, you could do to break free. Right now, she was struggling to breathe because his grip almost pierced into her veins through her hard scales. But he wouldn't kill her, at least not if he could help it. We needed information.

She thrashed about and kicked out her bony ostrich legs in protest. I padded closer, and she turned her cold, emotionless, reptilian eyes toward mine. She seemed to be trying to shoot venom from her throat at me, but it was no use under Zayne's tight grip. She would lose her breath soon if she didn't simply give in. She was finally realizing that she was outmatched, because she let out an unearthly squeal for breath. Zayne held on a few seconds longer, and when her eyes bulged, he released her.

She reached a clawed limb up to her throat and began to cough. Now that she was down, I shifted into my human form and stood there, completely naked save for the long, black, wavy hair that fell down my back. I called the dark to my fingertips and brought fire to my palms. The creature squirmed in pain on the ground as I raised a Zol rune around us. It was a circle of my fire element, forming the zodiac symbols to channel their power and serve as a conduit of the magic we needed to complete the mission. It was incredible how far I'd come. Two years ago I could barely channel fire in just one direction, now I was creating fire runes. Zayne remained a breath away from the cihuatl, ready to leap at her in a single heartbeat.

I chanted the incantation, *"Etchi nal Xila." Darkness within darkness. Show me so I may understand.*

As soon as I finished, the blaze of the Zol rune began to glow even brighter, threatening to singe my back and legs with the heat. But I didn't move an inch as sweat began to form on my brow. My human form, or "Zol skin" as they taught us to say at the Academy, had a very high tolerance for heat because of my elemental power, but even still, if it consumed me, I would still burn, only slower.

The cihuatl looked around, winded, and just as she placed her clawed hands on the bloodstained ground to push her pregnant body upward to stand, Zayne took one step toward her and tore her abdomen open with his fangs. An ear-piercing shriek left her throat as her insides were exposed and spilled out all over the ground. It was critically important to our mission that the fetus was extracted while she was still alive.

I reduced the heat level of the fire rune and looked out past it, feeling the eyes of the jungle upon us. Her death released her dark energy. All of the torment, fear and agony this monster had caused and collected within her soul spilled out of her. An inky black mist filled the air within the fire circle. This was our bonus. I eagerly drew it toward me, soaking it up hungrily. A monster this deeply evil expelled an enormous amount of darkness that I used to replenish my own powers. I bared my teeth at Zayne, instinctively protective of my bounty, as he also pulled it in. But I didn't need to challenge him. There was plenty to go around.

"Sick. That must be it..." I said to Zayne as he got busy studying the creature.

The cihuatl was a terrible sight, and her insides smelled of rotten flesh. They reproduced by stealing the fetus out of the belly of any warm-blooded creature, Fae or beast. They swallowed it whole, turning the creature into one of them while inside the womb, slowly infecting it with all of the diseases they carried, causing them to decompose while still alive. That's why these creatures didn't resemble each other. They turned into a hybrid of the life they stole and their beastly genes. Without lifting his gaze in my direction, he gave me a single nod of acknowledgment and continued to sniff and study the glowing, decomposing blue fetus that was still alive on the jungle floor.

Over the years, the mages had created wards of protection for pregnant women. Powerful spells that hid their unborn children from the senses of the cihuatl. This made it incredibly difficult for the creatures to reproduce, driving their numbers to the brink of extinction. But extinction was never truly possible. There were always mothers who couldn't access the wards—either due to exile from Zol society for mating with humans or other transgressions. And, of course, there were those who used the cihuatl as a weapon—invoking them out of revenge or as punishment for new mothers. It really bothers me to know there isn't more protection for the women that are vulnerable to the cihuatl and it's something the nagual should be protecting, instead of only protecting the elite.

I shook the thought from my head and felt my face flush with embarrassment. I realized that this was my first time being naked in front of Zayne. I quickly shifted back to a nagual. Shapeshifter. Creature of demons and darkness. The trouble now was that we couldn't communicate with words in our nagual form. Only mated nagual could do that.

He went on sniffing at the rotted insides of the cihuatl. Then he picked up the glowing, acrid blue fetus with his teeth. I nearly threw up at the thought of the horrific tastes that must be filling his mouth. He lifted his gaze from the carnage and met my curious stare, bolting out of there heartbeats later with me keeping pace with him.

Our mission was complete, and now we would have some answers.

About the Author

R.C. Luna is a storyteller who believes we are all bound by the unseen threads of magic and destiny. A lifelong lover of fantasy, mythology, and the supernatural, she weaves rich worlds where passion collides with power and the line between darkness and light blurs. Her characters—fierce, untamed, and unapologetically alive—move to the rhythm of the moon and the whispers of forgotten gods.

Growing up in South Florida as a Puerto Rican, Luna found herself surrounded by a vibrant fusion of cultures, beliefs, and stories, all of which inspire her work. Her time in the U.S. Air Force and her travels through Latin America deepened her love for folklore, mysticism, and the echoes of ancient civilizations, shaping the intricate magic systems and spiritual undercurrents in her novels.

When she's not writing, you can find her diving into fantasy romance novels, moon-gazing with a cup of coffee, or crafting worlds where love is as dangerous as it is irresistible. Darkness is her playground, and she invites you explore the magical worlds with her.

Sign up for her newsletter for updates on new releases, lore, events and so much more!

www.rcluna.com

Read more in the...
Warrior Shifter Series

Keep In Touch

The Chaos Doesn't End Here

Join me on these platforms and let's stay connected!
www.rcluna.com
TikTok @author_rcluna
Facebook @authorrcluna
Instagram @author_rcluna

R.C. LUNA
EDGY FANTASY & ROMANCE

www.ingramcontent.com/pod-product-compliance
Lightning Source LLC
Chambersburg PA
CBHW031043310726
48969CB00007B/2094